KEEP TELLING YOURSELF:
IT'S ONLY A MOVIE,
IT'S ONLY A MOVIE . . .

In the cyber-tech world of tomorrow, the rich get their kicks from watching films with emotional implants—where the viewer feels whatever the actor feels. To achieve absolute realism, the players don't know the script—they simply react to whatever happens to them. For all they know, this is real life and the film hasn't started yet. It's a dangerous job. But the money is irresistible. . . .

When Cass, Moke and Dosh sign a movie contract, they figure they have it made. Work a few weeks, run a few risks, and they can finally get off the planet. They're tough, they can handle it.

But the script is a real killer. And their co-star is a mass murderess. . . .

CRASHCOURSE

The brilliant debut of Wilhelmina Baird

CRASHCOURSE

WILHELMINA BAIRD

ACE BOOKS, NEW YORK

This Ace Book contains the complete text of the original edition.

CRASHCOURSE

An Ace Book / published by arrangement with
the author

PRINTING HISTORY
Ace special advance reading edition / May 1993
Ace edition / September 1993

ISBN: 0-441-12163-2

ACE®
Ace Books are published by The Berkley Publishing Group,
200 Madison Avenue, New York, NY 10016.
ACE and the "A" design
are trademarks belonging to Charter Communications, Inc.

PRINTED IN THE UNITED STATES OF AMERICA

10 9 8 7 6 5 4 3 2 1

Acknowledgments

Thanks to my editor, Laura Anne Gilman, without whom this wouldn't be around at all, for a lot of skilled help and kind encouragement; to Lee Matthias for good advice (not all of which I took, but I should have) and his reader, who has to be a Nice Guy; to Jean-Pierre Chaigne for advice on computers, and Serge Montigny for spending time explaining to the ignorant how to present manuscripts.

To William Gibson and Pat Cadigan, who took time out of their busy lives to read this; I know it costs.

To Dennis Dodridge and Helen, who kept lending me their printer when mine died, thus preventing me from joining it.

And to James, who reads all of it and likes it even when he doesn't have to.

Thanks, guys.

CRASHCOURSE

The opaline ceiling reflected a soft gleam on the terminal in front of my face. Over the scrolling figures I could see a ghost picture of wall-wide drapes, the frozen spider of the domestic servant with a chilled flute poised in its claw, a miniature sketch of posed flowers and the random stripes of my own mask, swollen to a Halloween horror by the distorting curves.

I was taking it easy and slow. Mrs. Waller-Gurney was slated to be out until midnight, which for her probably meant four A.M. and back feet-first with a couple of good friends to carry her. And stuff. Depending, natch, on how drunk she was. Or whatever. My sources had been vague about just what she was on this month. Always supposing the lady didn't throw a headache, fling a tantrum or get herself slung down the stairs by her hostess. All of which things had happened before.

It's the damnation of my line. You can depend on just about everything except humans. I was taking it easy and slow anyway. When you've got as much on the table as I had you can't take the risk of blowing it. I'd got down past her routine domestics and was getting into the good stuff.

I switched my caftan out of the way and fished a chip out of my thigh-pouch. A caftan's a pest to work in, it can trip you flat and you're always having to hike it up and pull it down, but it's one fair way to confuse internal security. Messes your outlines. Like the mask. Like the hood. Like my inflatable high platforms. Of course the law knows nobody's the way they look, but just so long as they can't figure what way you really look it stays cool.

I slotted the chip and keyed for copy. I never understand these rich dolls. If I had shares in half the major industry of the planet and was always too careless and too damned stoned to remember what I had where, I sure as hell wouldn't store it in a common domestic, even with sneak safeties. They know enough to keep it out of the public nets, which are infectious and raidable, but not enough not to disc it at all. If that garbage was mine, you know what I'd do? I'd write the whole lot down on a common piece of paper with a common graphite pencil and I'd put the fucker in my bank vault. Bank vaults aren't totally proof against people like me but they're a lot harder to break into than luxury apartments, and the penalties for trying are fixed to deter even the pros. Better still, I'd memorize the damn thing and swallow it. But then I've a good memory—modestly drug-enhanced around the edges. I need it.

It took two chips to get the whole list of Mrs. W-G's holdings along with her memos for tomorrow's orders to her broker, which brought the whole deal to nearly half an hour. Risky. My safeties were guaranteed for forty-five minutes with fifteen minutes' margin but only a fool sticks around towards the limits. I still had to change and get out.

"Would Madame like her drink freshened?" the spider cooed from the piano. The flute had lost its fresh condensation but it was still full. Spiders aren't very smart. But you can certainly program in your priorities.

"Thank you, Jeeves. You may dispose of the glass and fetch a new bottle. Cold. Which you may put on the table by the cabinet."

"Yes, Madame."

Of course as soon as Mrs. Whatsis came home—or as soon as she or her escorts got their legs and heads back together, whichever came first—she was liable to notice the little disorder in her living room. Actually they don't always. If you spend the major part of your life legless I guess you don't always remember what you ordered in the drinks line before you left. But it wasn't going to matter. In another hour I'd have fenced my takings and the information would be long gone.

It's like any sort of thieving. Somebody's got to make a lot of money, and I mean a lot. His name's a trade secret. My contact who's equally publicity-shy is going to make a couple of sous likewise. I'm the end of the chain. The little guy who does the work, risks its neck, takes the falls if there are any and gets what's left when the big guys have done feeding. One of Nature's jackals. Woof, woof.

I waited until Jeeves was busy at the bar, then moved to the hall door and keyed my pad to freeze off the jinx I put on him while I left. He'd stay paralyzed for as long as it took me to shut it and then he'd forget he'd ever thought I was Missy. The inside cameras either were or weren't blind. I trusted Hallway but not completely. In my job you don't trust anyone completely, not even if you like them. It shouldn't matter. All they'd get was the caftan.

I checked the snaps on my thigh-pouch, grabbed a handful of zebra gauze in the interests of not breaking my neck and hauled myself into the service-duct. I bolted the grill back before I let down the platforms and did my contortionist act with the caftan. It's lucky I'm skinny. But it's better to tie your shoulders in knots than tear the damned fabric and leave fibers with genotype contamination for some smartass cop to trace back. My last convictions were in Juve court for small possession when I was fourteen but those bastards never forget.

I folded the whole messing big-top, squodged it into a

handful and rammed it in the kangaroo-pocket of my coolsuit. The mask followed and then the soles, deflated to the thickness of paper. I did a last touch on the thigh-pouch—it's automatic, like the nervous way some guys can't quit checking their flies when they come out of the bathroom—and slid a couple of yards up the duct before I keyed for cameras. The jinx was off now. What ought to show was just some kind of flicker. When Mrs. Thing found her shares on their way into the Marianas Trench and the cops came around with the real equipment they were going to notice the discrepancies, sure, but with luck it would be too late. And now all I had to do was get outside before Hall's gadget melted off and turned loose the sensors.

Wedding-cake. Provided crawling three hundred yards on your belly through a duct eighteen inches across with only five right-angled turns, then suckering your way down sixty-three storeys of wall in the hope nobody in the neighborhood's using an advanced life-detector is your idea of icing. Coolsuits are great, if a bit hot. They blend with any known background, disappear in shadow and bollix the infra-reds. But you know that cutting edge of science. You never cut so close someone else isn't cutting closer, and the local flicaille's started to borrow equipment from the Navy.

I hoped the wavy techs weren't around tonight. The guys were expecting me home. I breathed out and started crawling.

I shucked the coolsuit and peeled my throat resonator in the outside john behind Lavery's Chinese Pizza three streets off the Strip and got my sports-bag down from the false ceiling over the third cubicle where with luck the junkos leave it be for fear it's heavy. I rolled the awkward stuff into a bundle around my tools with a damp towel and a pair of nose-filters outside to make it look real and stuffed them into the bag. Then I slung it on my shoulder and wandered

innocently out through Lavery's, where the entire clientele's on enough garbage to start a recycling plant and if you
came through on stilts wearing a clown suit and accompanied by elephants nobody would flip a lid. I typed in an
order for spring roll, ribs and pineapple fritters in passing—
working makes me hungry—and made for the corner phone
to pass a code.

A couple of giggly brats with green-gold raccoon eyes
were crammed into the booth, shoving each other with their
elbows and exchanging witticisms with a male of the
species who looked even dimmer than they did. A bad-
tempered redneck waited outside stamping his boots and
occasionally giving the door a kick to encourage them. That
sort of act can go on all night and it gives you tics in your
neck-hair. I didn't have all night. But not more than four
hours later the gigglers started to wind down and the
redneck lost patience and leaned in and threatened to fillet
them. I thought for a minute they might take him up on it,
but he had eyes like a pair of brake-lights and breath you
could have used to strip paint so they decided not. Luckily.
Street brawls are discounseled when you're dropping. The
ideal's invisibility.

I was afraid turpentine-breath maybe had a long date, but
he looked too razzed to be loving. I was right. He called
some fellow-ape, snarled some disobligeances about the
space-wrestling results, threatened to fillet him—his line of
repartee seemed limited—and crashed off making with his
forearms like Popeye. Maybe he'd been eating spinach. I
skipped back just before I got trod on and made it into the
box a hair ahead of two hookers who'd wandered up behind
and were poised on their starting blocks. We glared at each
other in passing but it was a fair win.

I rang my code, let it go three times and re-keyed. Then
I called back the same number. On the fourth ring somebody
lifted the bar just long enough to show a blank screen and

quietly put it back. Contact made. I said, "Oh, shit," loudly to impress passers-by I'd hit a wrong number twice and had some horse's ass make me lose my token, and walked back to Lavery's. On the way I did a thing of jerking around in my sleeve-pocket and managed to accidentally drop a sachet of good blue exactly two feet from the recyc slot in the wall of the Half-Moon Massage Parlor and Video Divan. By that time the chips were inside, natch. I walked on without looking behind. The outfits that employ me are efficient. Enough that it isn't a good idea to watch them.

Then I went and picked up my food.

The warehouse was dark when I got to the end of the alley. That meant nobody was working. You can't see the light of our skylight from below—the smudgy glow of bad neon rots the sky over the city all night—but I hoped somebody was home. I was feeling like company. Drinking company.

There was a scuffle from under the steps as I went up to the side door. The main one's been rusted shut for a generation. I leaned down and looked under. The hepatic wino with half a face raised a twisted lip from his pile of rags and held out what was left of his hand. The story is he was a spacer before he got on the wrong side of an engine-explosion but I don't know I believe it. The Guild looks after its people. But it's a story.

I dropped him two ribs and a fritter. It didn't leave much, but we have a relationship. So long as one of us has an eye out for him he whistles when the copts come over. And when the junkos come under. Nobody touches him. I mean, would you?

There was a leggier scuffle further up the alley and I looked at him. He shook his head. Mutes, or lovers. Not my dream-place but it's their business. Ole Yeller may not have a nose but he smells trouble faster than anyone. If he thinks it's straight it is. I nodded back and went in.

Somebody'd pissed in the elevator again and somebody, the same or different, had added "Gurments Is Shrank" in dried-blood spray paint across the back wall. Which is political, philosophical, illiterate or psychotic, check one or more. Spraying our elevator's a local pastime and by now there are so many layers you can't see the metal. Mokey rates that a plus. It stops the pee from rusting it completely.

There was a line of light under the loft door. Hopeful. I used my key—the place looks like the last minutes of the *Titanic* but we have a good lock; Moke's stuff's valuable, at least to him—and slid through. We not only have a lock on our door, we oil our hinges. Unique. For the neighborhood, anyhow.

Dosh was sprawled on his pad in a corner, the blanket rumpled under him and a pillow wedged behind his slumped yellow head. He was still in makeup, which drives Moke crazy. He had a program crystal socketed behind his left ear and his cornflower eyes were fixed on infinity with as much expression as a Barbie doll. I walked up and took a closer look. As I'd expected, he had three different derms plastered across the side of his throat, one old enough to have lost its color. Wherever he was, Planet Earth wasn't on his itinerary. That made three nights in a row. I love Dosh better than myself but it was getting pointed.

A steady ear-shredding whine was coming from behind the partition, which means either the Martians have landed or Moke's having inspiration. I dumped what was left of my supper on the draft-table in the middle and went to shove my head around.

I had to wait until he'd got through with the saw before it was worth speaking. The work was smallish for him. It didn't quite go through the ceiling, though when he'd finished adding bits it probably would. At a glance you'd say the Martians really had landed. It was a tripod of sorts with spiky bits that he was currently sawing to size. It filled the whole of the big freight elevator, which had to have been a nuisance. He usually builds the big stuff in the warehouse down below where there's room. I guessed he was looking after Dosh in his own way.

"How," I grunted as the noise died. "You guys eaten today?"

He lowered the saw, raised his face-plate and gave me a tired smile. His old jeans hung on the edges of his skinny hip bones like nothing but hope was holding them up and his bare chest was starred with minute burn-pits and glittering flecks of metal. His hair's blond, the lank dirty kind that looks greasy five minutes after you wash it. He has the face of an amiable horse and sharp green eyes. Right now they were veined with complementary red and underlined in bruise-color.

"You got away," he said.

"Nah, it's my astral body. The rest's holding up the lid of the toilet in the downtown cop-farm."

"Don't even think it."

He was serious. Moke's got this superstition there's things you shouldn't invoke ever, even—especially—in joke, in case they happen. It really worries him.

"Right," I said. "You tried to hit Dosh out of it?"

"Done my best. The newest of those is mine but I'm scared to do anything violent. Don't know what kind of shit he's got in there. Seen a guy go into shock hooked on the wrong mixture. Guess he's got to come out the other side."

"One day he's not going to."

"You're telling me?"

He dumped the saw and shucked his helmet. His hair was slicked with sweat under the band and crimped into a wave at the back of his neck. He ran a dirty hand over his forehead, shook salt off his nose and reached for a T-shirt.

"Give me a hand stripping him, Cass? Hate to see him lying around in work gear but he's too heavy for me myself. Been waiting for you."

"Poor Moke. Worry the hell out of you, don't we? You're a natural nanny."

I thought he might laugh. Wrong. He turned me red-veined eyes and said, "Yes."

Against the shot blood his irises glared like floodlights. He sounded terminally tired.

I followed him through into the loft. Dosh hadn't moved. I wasn't sure he'd even blinked since I last saw him.

"You sure we can't peel at least one?"

"Yep. Trust me. Unbutton his shirt and I'll try and get it over his arms. It's the first elbow that's hard."

I knew. We'd done it before. I worked on the blown crystal flowers that blossomed down the lamé overjacket. Dosh was inert, only the slightest rise and fall of his chest showing he was alive. Mokey and I might as well have been invisible. For him I guess we were. The damned flowers stuck and I had to twist them around. Dosh's work gear costs too much to spoil.

"Okay, that's got these. Let me at the one below. Can you move his arm?"

"Holy sweet Jesus," Mokey breathed.

I didn't say anything. I'd dumped my leather jacket on the table alongside my Lavery's insupacks when I came in. I picked it up and started putting it back on. The insupacks sat congealing. Dinner was postponed indefinitely.

Mokey had his arms around Dosh's shoulders and was cradling his head, the bruise-marks under his eyes so black-blue they looked more artificial than Dosh's makeup. The muscles of his jaw stood out in lumps. Poor Moke. He isn't really a nanny, he just made the mistake of loving both of us. I left him to it while I ran for a phone. I run the fastest.

• • •

I waited for the doc at the bottom of the alley. He's a Gooder, of course. All the guys on night duty are; you occasionally get a Prof during the day. Some of them are more self-righteous than others. We'd had this one before. He doesn't like me but I had no time to play to his hang-ups. I rushed him past Ole Yeller, refused to see him wrinkling his nose in the elevator and let him into the loft.

I'd been out twenty minutes waiting for the damned Bones, but Mokey was still sitting in the same place with a face like a wooden Indian. The Bones shoved him aside and got to work, with the same expression he had in the elevator. He had to use solvent to peel the shirt off some of the burns where it had really worked into the flesh. Mokey was standing beside me and I could feel him flinch at every tug as if the skin was his own. I felt creepy myself. There were red welts too and rope burns. When the Bones got down to his pants I turned away. Dammit, it's Dosh I go to bed with. When he's awake with all his cells going.

Mokey said, low and hurt, "No."

I nearly turned around and didn't.

Then he added, "Don't cut. If you wreck it he just has to work harder to buy more. I think this'll clean."

Then I did turn around and it wasn't so bad as I'd been scared it might be, mostly the insides of his thighs. The Bones was looking at us like we'd done it personally.

"Has it occurred to you that if he keeps this up some client's actually going to murder him?"

"Yes," Mokey said. "Every time."

He just sounded sad. Because that's how it is. Dosh is a tall, good-looking guy, he works out every day to keep in shape and his shape's damned something, and like a lot of hookers he practices katas regular because they know where they're heading. And mostly it's all right and some of the time he even laughs about it. And just once in a while he meets up with a psycho who is bigger and tougher than he is or who manages to sweet-talk his (or sometimes her) way past his guard and we have to call the doctor.

We're all racing against time. We know it. Either we get enough together to get off this Christ-forgotten planet while we're still young or we're going to end up under it before we've a chance to get old. Lecturing doesn't help. Umps haven't too many choices.

You can turn Gooder, put a peg on your nose and stick all you've got into convincing yourself you're improving the neighborhood while you bring up your kids to play the same way. You can lose yourself in Electronic Wonderland with decor by our award-winning pharmaceutical industry and pretend none of it's happening. Or you can try to work your way out. We're working. Mokey's a sculptor, Dosh is a whore and I'm a thief. It's a desperate remedy.

What was bugging Moke and me was that we should have known. Dosh drugs. We all drug. Sometimes three days in a row. You got to sleep.

You crawl up a wall with six hundred feet of space under your feet, you dive head-down in a service-duct with your nose against the metal and you never know if the damned plans are accurate and you're really going to come out the other end or if somebody's played a merry joke and there's a turn down there nothing human ever got around. Then they find your body when the smell gets too bad in the lobby. It happened to a friend of mine. So you get the shakes once in a while and you snort or you slap on a derm just to put some cartilage in your knees.

Or you go streetwalking by the spaceyards where the money's hottest, painted like Adonis and talking to everything on the block, not knowing what kind of crazy your next client's going to be. They're getting crazier every day, the whole world's going crazy. And you got to take your mind out to keep your smile in place.

Or you do monumental sculptures everybody comes to dinner recognizes as pure genius that ought to be standing in city squares or some guy's gardens with acres of green all around instead of heaped on the floor of a warehouse gets visited by nobody but rats. And you keep writing to the Design Council, which is a laugh, like most of our civil institutions. Umps are cattle, man. And you start to lose faith in your vision. Then you need something comes in a tube to put some hope and strength back so you can just keep doing it.

So despise us. But not out loud if you're only a Gooder yourself. Because we're all in the survival business together and nobody has the right to sneer at how someone else keeps their nose above water, not unless they first invented universal water-wings. And that I'm still waiting for.

And none of that excuses us for not knowing Dosh doesn't slug enough colored stuff to lay out a cow unless he's hurting badly. Too badly even to get home and ask for help before he hits the deck.

We stood hand in hand and watched the Bones working and didn't say a word. The Bones looked at us and then neither did he. And when he'd put his gear away and stuck a couple of new derms in different colors in place of the old ones and Mokey had put his aluminized survival-quilt on top of Dosh's blanket and some of the poison had gone out of the air, he looked Moke and me over and said, the nasty way Bones do, "You two should eat."

Then he banged his case together real bad-tempered and I led him back to the end of the alley and he hiked off like The Way the West Was Won. And I went back in to Mokey and we opened up my stale ribs and fritters which still weren't completely cold, but neither of us had the stomach to do more than mess them around. Even the beer we got out to console ourselves tasted flat.

So I ended up in bed with Mokey some time around dawn

and we began by lying together shaking, especially since all we had was my blanket and we don't steal heating power in the summer on account of keeping the risks acceptable, then we scored a blue each, then we got into the routine. But it wasn't exactly love, it was more like hugging your teddy-bear with a tiger in the cupboard. Some nights are like that.

By the time the sun came in grimy yellow through the layers of old age on our skylight we managed to fall asleep together. I don't mind sleeping with Mokey. He's hard and skinny and comforting and he's stupid enough to like me. But it's always been Dosh I was in love with. Always. Me with Dosh, and Dosh with Moke, and Moke mostly with his sculpture but me in between. Like the mulberry bush.

Bloody funny, right? Gets into our noses. Sometimes so much we have to toss for partners.

Some nights we can't stop laughing.

Morning in our place starts around four in the afternoon. There's damned little to get up for before that. The Gooders haul themselves out to their pretend work, their shops and offices and schools and clinics and workshops, by traditional after-breakfast, making like real pretend people. But on the Strip where life goes on all night you see the first early worms crawling out of their holes to get a coffee in before sundown, and the last late birds dragging back to their pads about the time the cits are getting around to lunch.

Glamour's after-dark material. When the sun's glaring orange over the dirty bubble of the dome you can see the trailing wires and crumbling façades in black clarity like the back of a television set. The stuff you only smell at night comes crawling out of gratings in ochre coils. If you look up, the stratus of smog sags like ragged veiling above a forest of masts and discs, and the El hangs over it all like a poised ax. Then the complexions that are interesting in the lights of the Floors look like Hansen's disease and the crusted glitter and sequins remind you of stuff you hope not to see in a hospital. The whole Strip stinks of gangrene.

I get poetic when I'm depressed.

After dark it turns into fairyland. Inhabited by the kind of fairies used to lead travelers into bogs and drift away laughing. You can hear them any hour at all, laughing their

14

dirty guts out every minute the neon tubes and arclights go on sputtering over our special particular Grimpen Mire. Where there's a road, sure, but you got to be a native to know it and if you do you're the kind of guy keeps a phosphorescent hound under a trapdoor in your back yard.

The respectable suburbs are worse in their way but we never go there. There's too much honest hope muddling its way to the cesspool and if they saw us coming they'd send for an exorcist.

What brought this on was Dosh. My kind lover who likes Moke better but never says so, and who keeps on laughing even when he's spent the night making love to dog-dirt. He'd been hurt before. Maybe as badly. But it was the first time he'd come around like something was broken.

Moke and I looked at each other and I could see he was terrified and he could see I could see it.

"Hey, come on," he said. Pleading. Mokey doesn't plead with Dosh. Like the truth he didn't want to take off Dosh's clothes without me was he understands the way things are only too well and he's keeping the gas tank away from naked flame. He does say yes, but only when they're both fit to understand what he means.

Dosh smiled, a pale sweet little-boy smile, and forced down another three crumbs like he was taking hemlock. He chewed them around for a bit to be nice and you could see him wanting to spit out and having to make his throat work to swallow.

He wasn't putting it on, either. I've never known him put it on. He was trying to eat to please us and there was something in there saying no and meaning it. And Mokey who'd gone out before midday and crawled at a Gooder bakery to get fresh bread and then crawled some more to get the butter, was on his knees by the side of his pad. He had dirty-blond stubble coming out on his jaw, he was gray with lack of sleep and he had a raw sore starting at his mouth corner where he never remembers his own vitamins. He was hollow at the cheeks and temples with willing the stuff in and none of it was going down.

Poor Mokey. Our desert genius. He usually feels better after he's angled a night with me. Today neither of us was feeling better. And Dosh looking like a grounded angel.

"Sorry, Moke. Ain't hungry. Later, maybe?" He lay back on the pillow and let his eyes drift to the ceiling. "Guess I ought to get up and dress."

This guy was talking to the love of his life, who was busting a gut to make him happy. And he had about as much chance of getting up and dressing as he had of growing wings and flying out the window. The tongue said it and the corpse went on lying there, looking up at the islands of damp on the plaster and seeing as much as a dead man.

"You don't have to, Doshky. We got plenty in the box. I cut a job last night and I got pay coming. Have a night on me. Hell, have two."

He smiled politely. At the ceiling.

"Pretty Cassandra."

That was scary. Dosh never calls me by my name and he's never in his life allowed I'm better looking than a monkey. And he's been clear all his life who earns half the money around here. Mokey's eyes were white-hot. The guy hadn't even noticed the quilt, and I've seen him touching it when Moke was out, with the edge of his finger, as if it was nearly as sacred as the owner and the touch might rub off and do him magic.

"You need sleep, man. We'll get the Bones back, get something for you. You're tired."

He didn't believe it and neither did I. Dosh went on smiling politely. "Sure thing, Moke. I'm a little weary below the waist. I'll get right up in a minute."

Maybe he was really looking through the ceiling, out to the blue fields of sky they say exist behind the smog. We've sure always wanted to see them. His eyes had a shallow soft shine as if they were made of china, or something deader and more precious. Lapis lazuli. They sure didn't look like they had human sight any more.

I could see the wheels turning in Mokey's skull like he had a glass forehead. He was considering an overdose and discarding it. The Bones had given Dosh a sedative, after he'd flushed out his system cleaner than the drain-man. It's what they do with us. Their contribution to human advancement. And then the wheels came around to my thought. Burnout. It happens. We've seen it. Sometimes it wears off, sometimes it doesn't. Sometimes people get crippled. Sometimes you end up spending the rest of your life feeding the guy with a spoon.

And I could read him wondering why it hadn't happened before. To any one of us. It's the random elements that fuck your calculations. We hunkered there over Dosh's legs exchanging thoughts like we were on the telephone. Only this telephone didn't need terminals.

"How's accounts, Cass?"

"No way. I had to dig out for Hallway and there was a pay-off for that spotty barman at Lavery's who got to remarking on my clothes. My nice djellabah with the stripes."

"He wants to sleep with you," Dosh said dreamily.

"He wants a knife in the gut. I offered it to him as an alternative."

"With pay coming?" Mokey persisted. "For one?"

Now that question gave me chills. We've agreed it's all or none of us. We're symbiotic. Space passage to somewhere worth living costs half the universe, which makes exactly one and a half universes for three of us and we've been working on it. One and a half universes, three guys, three tickets. Boom.

I gave it brain. "For one—maybe. Not this week. If I do another job. Hall's made the offer. I could take it."

"You don't want to," Mokey said.

"Never said that."

"I know you don't. Too close and a stinker, right?"

I didn't answer. The saw about wells hasn't changed and the truth was nobody in their right minds would touch that job. Hallway offered because someone asked him but he never sounded as if he meant me to listen. The Countess Irmana's country mansion, with enough armament to repel a planetary invasion and a sensor behind every geranium after you got across the kilometer of scorched earth between her and the highway. Forget it. Some people get to enjoy their loot in tranquillity. All it takes is money and spite. And the Countess Irmana's richer than Croesus and as sweet as a spitting cobra.

"Railroaded," Dosh said mildly. He'd changed his field of inspection from the ceiling to the skylight where the view's more interesting. Like a century of dirt, random patterns of bird droppings and a rust stain the shape of Asia and nearly the same size. "I won't go. All or none, right? How're we going to collect with Cassie dead? Who's gonna buy your tools, Moke?"

A flush rose on Mokey's cheekbones to match the reds of his eyes but his gaze didn't alter.

"I know. You guys work and I play welders."

"Moke, we're the jerks. You're the genius. Give me a day, okay?"

"All the days you want, guy," Mokey said with gentleness. "But I think it's time us geniuses quit gening and put some paint on. Cass, you can do facework. Make me a mug, huh?"

"No," Dosh and I said simultaneously.

"Listen, Moke, it's not just paint. You saw what Dosh hit last night and he's experienced. Damn it, he's a black belt in judo. You're going to get raped, and robbed after they've raped you. I'm not going to help you get killed. Do I have to lose you both?''

"The real trouble, Mokey, is you're honest,'' Dosh added in the kind of voice a nice grownup uses to a child when he doesn't want to hurt it. ''You're a straight decent guy makes sculptures. It's what you do. You think you can do my job like that? Could I do yours?''

"Yes,'' Mokey snapped back. "With practice. I mean welding, dammit. It's labor. I didn't say you weren't an artist. I didn't say I was going to be you. I don't have the equipment. But there's guys out there don't need art, all they need's a place to put it. Which, vulgarly, I got same as you do. And don't be superior about the physical. I'm strong enough to haul girders and people even say I'm good with my hands. I can use a knife like the next bum. We need money. It's time we all got on it.''

I opened my mouth and found I hadn't anything to say. I'd known these guys three years and I'd never seen either of them this way. Tough Dosh looking thoughtful and thoughtful Moke with a face like hickory.

"Hey, guys,'' I managed. "Don't panic. Moke's right you need out, Dosh. So we promised to do it together. Well, let's work both ends. It might even be efficient. I'll talk to Hallway about a job and we'll get you a fucking space-ticket. Then you can look for work—try acting, dammit, it's what you want, you got the physique—and Moke and me'll keep trucking. Hell, it'll cut overhead. Two sets of expenses and a place to go.'' I was improvising but for a moment I came close to even convincing myself. ''We're paying half what we earn on kickbacks. So we make some between us, then say Moke goes next. Maybe they buy sculpture. That leaves me on the take and both of you coining. Only one guy's risks and one outlay. I like it.''

"You're talking horse-shit, Cass. I haven't lost my mind

yet. The minute we separate we never see each other again. That's how it is. And don't contradict me.''

He didn't add, ''Or I'll slug you.'' Dosh has been going to slug me for arguing any time for three years. But he's always said it laughing. This time we hadn't the starving shadow of a smile among the three of us.

''And I'm not leaving you either,'' Mokey said softly. ''But we're getting Dosh out. And nobody's contradicting me, either.''

I looked blankly from one to the other.

''Tough fuckers,'' I said. And I stamped away into my own corner. To cry. Hell, I never cry. I quit the day my mother threw me out in the road for being dishonest, with all her Gooder uprightness and charity. Crying makes me throw up. After a while Mokey came and rubbed between my shoulders and I had to pretend I'd got dust in my nose. Then I did throw up which gave it away.

As if he hadn't known anyhow.

The Gilded Dog's what you'd expect from a place that hasn't the self-respect to call itself something different, but it was where I was coded for lunchtime (nine to ten in these parts), and Mokey came with me. Dosh had vanished into another electrical dream after a while and then got just plain unconscious and we'd decided to leave him sleep. We didn't reckon he was going anywhere and we had a quarrel to have.

The Dog's neon's blue with disconcerting white flashes, which makes everyone look dead most of the time and now and then shows them as they are for just long enough to make you think it was better the other way. Considering the food, when the lights have one of their petits mal it's better not to look down. You might see what you're eating. The entertainment's a person in more-or-less all-over gold paint waggling its bum and anything else it has depending on sex, in a big fishbowl over the bar and turning the brunchers off their vodka. Or it would if any of them were looking. Apart from that the Dog has routine obscene murals of over-endowed people doing boring things in multuplicate and a fair to good sound track.

A lot of people go there for the jazz, which is sometimes live and consequently sometimes worth the trouble. The rest of the time they go there because they've got into the habit. If Eustace the barman knows you he gives you the wink before the cops arrive, which information he gets from where you'd expect. He only rarely hits regulars with the Louisville Slugger he keeps under the bar. Not unless they truly deserve it. On out-of-towners, which is anyone from more than three streets away, he's kind of severe.

Moke and I had a table where we didn't have to look up the far end of the alimentary canal of the current waggler, which was a bonus since it looked pretty well-used even from a distance, and a portion each of Eustace's Special Steak-frites. They're guaranteed manufactured from real vegetable protein in a fairly clean warehouse by a pair of holistic Gooders with Navy surplus hydro tanks and a supplier who's a lot less honest than they are. Eustace likes Mokey. He's one of the few people who've had dinner with us and he has a nose for genius. That's why Dosh invited him. He was pretty sure himself but he wanted a second opinion. If I'm by myself I get a bar stool and the right to have anyone who bothers me against my will Louisville Slugged for free provided I ask nicely.

The music was canned which was a pity, because there was a guy on it played a mean trumpet. Moke was listening with concentration which meant he didn't want to get into this argument. I did.

"Mokey, we gotta talk this."

He grunted. "Uh." And took a big mouthful of fries to prove he couldn't answer even if he wanted.

Luckily I been dealing with refractory guys since I got busted for the second time at fourteen and I know the angles. The main one is it's no good letting them get away with it.

"There's no way you're going to walk street. I mean it. I'm not going to make you up and you'll make a pig's ear of it yourself, but that's not why. If I thought it would help I would. But lookit guy, you're going to get massacred. For one thing. I don't want to hurt your feelings, Moke, but you are not pretty."

"Uh," he said from around an even bigger mouthful of textured prote, meaning he still wasn't going to answer.

Seemed to me I'd hurt his feelings anyway. Hell, the stupid fucker keeps wanting to be in love with me and it's kind of depressing to have your best-beloved tell you you're ugly. I kept trying.

"Mokey, you're kind of sweet. What you aren't is pretty how that kind of guy means it. Don't run me around, dammit. Dosh manages though he's big because he does the Greek-god bit. The other thing they want is—something fragile. Little boy. Going on little girl. And you're neither. Dosh is crazy about you and that's because he's a serious person and he really likes guys. Men guys. You're a man-guy. You know, male of the species, no ass, like that? But to want that you got to be serious. When guys buy a lay for the night they're not serious except about getting a lot for as little as they can, unless you're a god like Dosh and you can ask god-money. You got to offer something—well, sensual. And you ain't got it, boy."

He finished chewing, slowly, his green eyes somewhere in the ultraviolet in the blue light, fixed on me.

"I'm not sensual, Cass?" He sounded sorrowful. I felt bad. I'd spent the night hanging around his neck panting and making noises. Saddish, but noises.

"For guys, Moke. Sure you'll appeal to the maternal

instinct in every dame got one to offer but I don't know women spacers are hot on the mother-bit. Anyhow most of Dosh's good payers ain't women. And the motherers aren't likely to hire you for the night, they're likely to want to take you home permanent and put some food in you. Goes with how you look."

"You never get that feeling, huh?"

"I'm a burglar, dammit. Anyway wouldn't help if I did. Next time you do what I ask gonna be the first."

He smiled at me with cute blue reflections off his teeth that made you forget his ultraviolet eyes. Then the fucking light changed and I was looking at my old Moke trying not to cry.

"I'd do what you asked any time you asked it, Cassie. Just happens this time's too serious to joke about."

"I wasn't joking."

Luckily the lights changed back and all I had to cope with was another face off the ghost-train.

"So what do you suggest, Cass? Burglary? Your bosses use a guy skinny enough to slide in windows and a head for heights to go with it?"

Hell. My bosses'll use anyone. There's no welfare in my work. Widows and orphans take care of themselves. My virtue apart from my beautiful character and striking intelligence is I'm skinny and small and can get around corners other dames can't reach, which also has the advantage I'm not very noticeable even walking around the place. So I sometimes get stepped on but not often fingered. Like up to date never, which is why I'm still in business. Also I'm real professional and very careful.

The problems I could see in my line were, one, even a skinny guy has more bone than a bim because guys just are bigger all over; two, the pros start training at seven when Moke was putting his first sewer-pipes into unnatural relationships; and three, the guy's incurably honest. I mean he's the kind who's liable to start feeling sorry for the mark in the middle of an operation and skin off leaving a Christmas card with his fingerprints instead of recognizing the redistribution of wealth's a social duty especially in an industrial oligarchy. Or closer to home, we need the money.

"No," I said.

"What then, Cass? Dosh got his load. Bones was right, it's a question of time before he comes home dead. I guess his crocodile just got around to recognizing it. Don't play dumb, girl. You know what it means. Even if he gets himself up to go back—and he may, he's stubborn as a mule—from now on he's asking for it. He's got the smell on him. Of the guy who doesn't care any longer if he dies. Maybe he already had it and you and I hadn't noticed. He's been doing a lot of cold green recently, you seen? It would explain how they got so well and truly to him. He's never been careless. Before."

I nodded reluctantly. I'd been thinking the same. He was right. It's what happens when people start to jive out. They really do start to broadcast some sort of a signal, call it a pheromone, says Come and get me. And the psychos start coming out of the woodwork all over the landscape.

"Yeah."

"So he's got to go. While he's still breathing. Arguments?"

"Nope. Only how you figure to make him."

His blue teeth parted in a smile so different from the guy I knew I nearly dropped my steak knife.

"No sweat, Cassandra. I will talk to the man. Just as often as it takes. And when it doesn't work as it won't, you and I are going to buy muscle. It's your specialty."

"What?" I got out.

"I said he's going whether he agrees or not. I've been checking the charter lists. There's a Saturn class merchanter out of Ashton port Wednesday, kind that takes cargo plus some passengers in third. About what we were thinking, huh? Calling at Titan, Pluto base and on out to the wide spaces. I figure we can get a ticket. You're due a payment. You know exactly how much. But I'd say the farther away the better. As far as the money'll take him. He can send a postcard when he comes around.''

I felt the steak I'd swallowed sticking in my gullet just short of my collar bone.

''You want Dosh kidnapped?''

''I want to save his life, Cassie. Then I want to save ours. Because believe it or not I need him as much as you do. I won't swallow this story we've got to break up if he goes. We don't have to let it happen. I don't believe anything has to be because a bunch of old maids says so. What happens is our business. Not fate or magic, what we do for ourselves. But I do think time counts and the less time we're apart the more chance we have of getting back together. That means I work. So the question isn't whether I do, it's what. And that, Cassandra, is the only thing I'm willing to discuss.''

Damn it, I felt as if my white mouse had just up and bit me.

''You'd really do that, Mokey?''

''Sure,'' he said. ''Wouldn't you?''

Around midnight a grubby kid in a torn shirt that showed its bare ass (and was the only way you'd identify it as male) slid in through the door and started slobbering around the customers' feet. I mean slobbering. It didn't have quite the right mouth. It may just have been surgical, the Beggars' Guilds are getting really high-tech these days. I was a bit surprised Eustace let it, he can be particular about vagrants.

Eventually it arrived drooling somewhere around my left ankle. I drew my foot back to kick it—you've no idea what I paid for these shoes—when it lisped out of its jutting fangs in a voice two demi-tones short of a dog-whistle, "You got code, mizuss?"

That settled that. I'd have put it at six. Close up it had to be nearer fifteen in spite of the undeveloped genitals, and that made it surgical okay and probably—damned certainly—Swordfish. Sword's a friend. If you believe piranhas are capable of friendship.

"I got you a kick in the ribs, short stuff," I snarled. "Piss off to Yuma, got it?"

It slobbered down the leg of my pants with a look of luxurious satisfaction that nearly did get it a kick up its half-grown you knows and snuffled off with its nose to the floor like it was following a trail of creosote. To the nearest public toilet probably. Mokey looked at me.

"Dessert?" I proposed. We were back on my territory.

"You want my early death?"

"Eustace's pie's okay. Same stable as the protein."

"Synthesized."

"Hydroponic. They're better with fruit. The steak's something they do because there's a demand. Try apple. Though the pumpkin's not bad."

He gave me a sinister look which could have been the lighting. "Coffee."

"As you like. Apple pie, Eustace?"

It came for two anyway. Eustace is like everybody, he thinks Moke doesn't eat. Maybe he's maternal at some level.

By the time we'd finished there'd been a change of floor-show, fresh coat of gilt and young male muscles disturbing the vodka. Something new. A short happy life was beckoning to it from the whole length of the bar, but it had sense and didn't answer. That's how Dosh survived.

Moke looked it over resignedly.

"Yeah," he said. "I see what you mean."

"Don't let it get to you. We all got talents."

There was a tug on my pants. The slobbery kid was back.

"Gim' money," it bat-whistled, its long gums exposed by the wrong mouth. It was a truly repulsive piece of tech and well up to Swordfish. The paw it shoved at me was pure Sword likewise, decorated with nails like shovels that looked stainless steel. With Sword all things are possible. I dug in a pocket and dropped it five cents.

It caught it in mid-air, turned it over several times and slapped it back at me. The nails were steel all right. It left with me five little nicks to prove it.

"Garbage," it whistled and did the four-legged bit out.

When it had gone I had a rectangle of cold shiny plastic in my palm. The stuff us Umps aren't allowed to have. That gets you real creds in a real bank and a real fifteen to twenty in the state pen if they catch you holding. I'd check it tomorrow. But I knew it would be right. My contacts don't cheat any more than I do. After all we've each got a tiger by the tail. I turned to Mokey.

"You drunk that coffee? I got a yen to go back home and snort a couple of lines. Then maybe we can watch a vid together. Don't think Dosh'll be running the conversation tonight."

He stood up, stretching skinny muscles. I guess he hardly ever sits still as long as that without welding something. I'd been worrying he was looking for things to weld in the Dog and I value Eustace's good opinion.

"Okay," he said agreeably. "But you're finding me work, Cass. We've a deal, right?"

I hadn't remembered we had. But I was afraid we were going to end up with one. My steak wasn't sitting well at all.

I've had my two guys for three years and there are three of us. It's how it's been and it's been good.

I felt the universe had just begun to unravel.

Which was because it had.

We didn't speak on the way home. Mokey likes to hold my hand but this time he mooched his hands in his pockets and occasionally dug at the joins of his teeth. Maybe he was hurt. Maybe he didn't want to reopen a subject he'd closed. We try not to bring our quarrels into the house.

"Pssst."

A hoarse whisper from under the steps. I knelt over the edge. Ole Yeller's like the blackbird, he'll whistle and sing but he's not hot on conversation. It could be his mouth but I think a lot is he's got out of the habit of humans. The only thing he ever says voluntarily is, "Bottle of red," and even in the liquor store he often just waves his card and waits for the guy to get the message. Which he does, being used to it. So communication means trouble.

"What's going down, Yell?"

"Snake-man. Upstairs. 'Bout half an hour ago."

His speech was further mangled by shortage of teeth but we say good morning so we usually get the drift. Mokey had joined me, his hair flopping into his eyes over his band.

"What kind of snake-man, Yeller?"

He shook his head in the depths. Didn't know, wouldn't know or knew too well and wasn't getting involved. But the label was harsh for him. Bad news.

"He come out yet?"

Negative.

"Any—uh—bad noises up there?"

Moke was worried. I could feel the tension in his arms as he cantilevered over. We'd left Dosh sleeping a couple of hours back. The door was locked, but if the guy had found it that way he should have left by now. So either Dosh had wakened and let him in or he was in there lurking somewhere.

Like I said, it's a warehouse. We've made a loft out of the top floor and Mokey stores and works on his big constructions down on the main deck, but that leaves plenty of holes for the rats. It's not a place you'd care to look for your worst enemy in the dark. And nobody we knew had a reason to visit us, particularly in the snake-man class.

That left two main possibilities. The guy was someone looking for me and probably someone I didn't want to know, or he was the same one who'd worked Dosh over with a hot iron, back for second helpings. Neither one made us feel any better.

"Uh-uh. No noise."

Mokey nodded and straightened.

"Thanks, Yell. See you for a full one in the morning."

If any. I didn't say so. I added my nod to the pile and set about unstrapping my high heels. I shoved the sandals into my bag and checked the knife in my sleeve. Mokey was already barefoot, he likes it that way. If the guy was listening he'd probably heard us coming but there was no reason he should hear any more. Moke slid the door open gently—we don't oil hinges for nothing—and we catcrept into the shadow.

The gate was across the elevator shaft, which meant someone had gone upstairs but not necessarily hadn't come down again. Mokey jerked his head and I nodded. Our main concern was Dosh. Provided he was alive we could have a snakehunt later.

He headed for the stairs and I took the service ladder up the side of the elevator shaft. Simple division of labor: he's stronger in a space wide enough to fight in, I'm the guy spends my life climbing buildings.

We don't use the service ladder often so the rungs were rusted and did my green silk pants no good at all. I wouldn't have minded my coolsuit but it's kind of a compromising item to take to breakfast. I concentrated on moving up quickly and quietly and controlling my breathing, trying to minimize the crunch of rust under my toes. I couldn't hear Mokey at all. For a bony awkward guy he moves real Indian when he has to.

I was looking into the shadows all the way up half-expecting a sudden searchlight in my eyes but there was nothing. A dangling cable, the hollow cage of the freight elevator, a dim quadrilateral of light reflected down from a broken window onto drifts of plaster. There isn't much metal any more, Moke's used the half-good stuff. The vague forest of his masterpieces rose up into the dusk of the roof like a metal lattice, an alien village, a puzzle for spacers.

If a human snake was using it as a jungle gym he wasn't manifesting. We met silently on the landing outside our door. The elevator was up with the grid open. The skylight let in enough sodium to see outlines and the floor was bare. No blood, no scrapes, no footmarks. No sound. The door was closed and it fits too well to let light out. Mokey hefted the crowbar he keeps over the entry like some people keep their key and lifted an eyebrow. It had a metallic glitter in the yellow twilight, picked out by a fine dew of sweat. I nodded back and put my ear against the door.

The muffled sound of voices, too obliterated to distinguish but more than one. I held up two fingers and let the haft of the ya drop into my hand. With the other I softly tried our oiled lock. The door was open.

Moke stepped swiftly past me, jerked it back and went

through fast. Battle formation. Inside he dived right with me on his heels, left. It's a standard maneuver, we practice. Step three is if it's a gun, drop and throw, if you aren't already dead. I have a dartgun but like the coolsuit it isn't a routine breakfast accessory. Consequently when you need it the bastard is naturally inside. I was beginning to think we'd all got careless.

Dosh stared with amazement from his pad. He was sitting upright against a pile of pillows, the aluminized quilt over drawn-up knees, his hands linked loosely over the outside. His hair was ruffled as if he'd run his hands through to straighten it and his eyes were neither china nor stone, they were eye eyes and brilliant with excitement.

Moke rose slowly from his fighting crouch and I fitted the ya back into its sheath. We both looked stupid.

The snake-man was sitting on a tool box by the side of the pad, one immaculate leg crossed over the other and our communal glass on the floor by his side. Dosh as host was drinking out of the can. The snake-man turned as we came in and gave us a white, perfectly engineered smile. The commando routine hadn't fazed him at all.

"And this is your group?" he said crisply.

I think crisp's the word. Brown and crackly. One of those loud confident voices that belong to guys who walk over floors very firmly, swinging their legs and stamping their feet in the absolute knowledge the boards wouldn't dare give way, and wait at the other end for someone to open the door.

A guy who's in charge of things.

He was wearing a gray rough silk suit that hung loose the way very expensive designer clothes do, with a paler turtleneck ditto. His boots had once formed part of a real living animal or maybe reptile, which had probably folded its paws and pleaded for the honor of getting worn by him.

He had smooth gray hair and eyes so like dry ice you expected them to give off a vapor.

A gray-all-over man. A snake if ever I saw one.

"Miss Blaine?" he beamed, standing in a single athletic movement. A rich, expensive move straight from an exclusive health club. He extended a white hand as cool and even as buckskin, with shiny nails flushed a delicate gray-pink. "Mr. Faber. A pleasure to make your acquaintance."

The hand felt like buckskin too, soft and suedey like you expected it to have fringe around the edges. I wiped my palm on the rear of my pants and stepped into the room.

Moke carefully closed the door and took a handful of suede with his sculptor's fingers. He looked as if he thought it might be poisoned. I understood that. Yeller seemed to be at one. What I couldn't understand was Dosh's radiance. Herpetology's never been his weakness.

"Mr.—er?"

The snake—a.k.a. Mr. Er—returned to his tool-box smiling. "Perhaps we could make ourselves comfortable."

We tried to conceal our gratitude. I sat on the side of Dosh's pad. His hands were twisted into Mokey's quilt like it was his lover's hair.

"How you doing, Doshky?"

He smiled, still with that uncanny radiance, his blue eyes luminous. There's nothing baby about Dosh's eyes, especially when he's in there with them. They're the color of sea in the vid-shows, greeny-blue with mauvish shadows in the deep bits, and anyone who falls in and doesn't drown qualifies for psychiatric guidance.

"I'm hungry. Had we bread and stuff earlier or was I dreaming? Or you guys eaten it, knowing Moke?"

That's a slander. Moke's the least selfish guy I know.

"We got bread. And stuff. Which could still be fresh. You want some, Mr. Er?"

I wasn't trying to be polite. I've never liked Aris, not

even the ones I do business with. But those do me the favor of hiding their faces.

"I'd love a cup of coffee. But by all means feel free to have a meal yourselves."

Generous of him. He was downright hospitable, sitting in our living room letting us use our furniture.

"I'll get it," Mokey said. "What's the deal, Dosh?"

"A proposition," the snake-man said, taking the reply right off Dosh's lips. Dosh turned me a rueful-happy smile. "A film-script. Coelacanth Productions. With feature roles for all of you."

"Uh-huh?" Moke was neutral.

For me Mr. Smooth-Hands's proposition was going through decontamination procedures before I even let it into my ears. The way Mokey was clanging dishware his weren't flapping either.

Then Dosh reached out his brown paw with the white nick near the wrist where one of his unfriendlier clients tried to saw it off and even the Bones couldn't get rid of the marks, and took my hand. His touch was apologetic and I recognized with a jolt under the ribs what he was telling me. His sea-colored eyes pleaded. Give me this. Please. I need it.

And I got the picture.

Three lots of guys on our paradise planet got the right to own money, the Techs, the Arts and the Aris. Of course the Aris got the most like they got everything, but they're willing to spread some about just to keep what passes for their sanity.

I guess life's awful tedious at the top with nothing to do all day but count your cash, plan your next facelift and admire your off-planet furniture. So they got Techs to keep the wheels turning, including the Prof medics keep the lot of them looking like this one, and Arts to stop them dying of boredom.

And that's where Moke and Dosh are at. The only way
you can be Ari is by choosing your parents right but you can
get to be Art or Tech by convincing one or more real people
you are one. Like Moke keeps trying the Design Council
though they don't answer.

I guess Dosh started wanting to act about the same time
he learned to stand since it seems that's when he started
walking around in his Mama's parlor curtains striking
poses. A good tart has a lot of the qualities of a good actor.
I think Doshky's survived a lot of warty guys with garlic
breath by resetting the film to something different, and
when he gets somebody he likes—and he has this bad habit
of liking people—he gives them the big love scene from
whatever vid's playing behind his eyes that minute and they
don't know what's hit them.

The decent ones pay him, sure, but it isn't pay he wants.
It's notice. Not look-at-me-I'm-one-hell-of-a-pretty-boy notice. He gets that all the time and it gripes him since he's
also smart, nice and can read and write. It's the notice
people give other people who have something special. Like
Mokey said, an artist. An Artist.

I guess he'd like to play Hamlet best but hell, he'd settle
for Rosencrantz-and-Guildenstern or the third Lord from the
left so long as there were upward openings. The trouble is
there're about thirteen million other guys with the same
ambition this side of the seacoast and they're all queueing at
the same offices.

He used to go and stand in line for audition. First as
himself, then he got the idea he was too good-looking so the
directors figured he had to be dumb so he made-up as a
heavy. Didn't make any difference. There's just too many.
He could probably go in full dress as Quasimodo and
nobody'd notice him from the other six million five hundred
thousand. After the first few million I guess all human faces
look the same.

So we decided to clear out. They have acting troupes out in the Big Black. Some of them tour which is what he'd really like best, showing his talents all over the inhabited Galaxy. And since they don't function with a captive totally unemployed society whose only purpose is consuming the garbage of the upper classes, there isn't the competition. Some guys do one thing, others are actors. Doshky's dream.

Sweet nice-tempered Dosh. And now some guy was offering him a film role on a plate and if there was worse news in the world you'd have to walk a ways to find it.

Because you got to know Ari films.

Aris live artificial lives. A lot of people would like to be them but I'm not one. What they do mostly is—you could say act. They act big guys, which they are, only among themselves they're not because everybody's much the same big (and the real bang they get is littling each other, which is what makes my employers rich). And they act young-and-joyous which is good acting plus good surgery, even genuine young ones. They're never so young they don't want to be younger. And the joy comes out of bottles and packets and cut multi-colored derms. Sitting on a planet's heavy, it ages you.

So they get a bellyful of acting, they do it permanently themselves. What they're short of is reality. Other people's. Ours.

So for one thing they watch us. Spy. Real people, real crying. Real love, hate, blood, sweat, tears. I suppose they got to love someone or something sometime but it ain't obvious who or what. Hate they know backwards. Comes cheaper.

But it isn't always enough. Everyday dramas get pretty everyday when you watch them all the time. Then they want something more, you know, dramatic.

Like a film.

Only since acting bores them they don't want an acted

film, they want a real film. With real people. Who get really hurt. That switches them on. Real people hurting. Ump people. Us.

Which puts the whole deal in the same class as Countess Irmana's mansion. You got to be insane to accept.

And Doshky was gripping my hand like a drowning man on the end of a spar, begging for it. He's not insane, poor little mec. Arts got to come from somewhere and a place they get found is on screen. If they survive. He is one photogenic guy and I guess he figured he had high survival potential. Look what's he's survived already. If the script wasn't too loaded he could be right. Even Aris got sentiment, they like to see the handsome guy get the girl in the last reel. That or a laser in the gut. One or the other.

That other bugged me. Dosh wanted the part and he might or might not come out alive. If he did, chances were he'd be set for life right where he most wanted. He'd certainly get cash. It's one thing Aris got by the cartload. Enough to go anywhere, do anything. Me, I'd rather have picked an off-planet touring troupe any day but without cash he couldn't get there. Nice problem, huh?

Then there's Moke and me. Neither of us is an actor and Mokey isn't even combat-trained. Our number for entering rooms where Dosh is being tortured's his only party trick and Dosh and me have worked hard setting that up. He just doesn't have an aggressive mind. Works it off wrestling girders. Or maybe if you're a dedicated builder wrecking joints don't come natural. I can throw a reasonably good knife and I know my way around a dartgun but Annie Oakley I ain't. I never fight if there's somewhere to run to, and running I'm good at.

I saw Dosh wanted it and in the way of things what Dosh wants I want for him. Except his life, goddammit, except his life. And I'd go a ways before I'd set Moke up for the hog-roast, likewise.

The snake was watching us, his dry-ice eyes moving from one face to the other.

"Standard contract," he said. Even his voice was suedey. "I think you'll find the fees satisfactory. We like to pay our figurants well. And in the case of—let's say, damage—we make sure the compensation's more than lavish."

"You pay off the survivors," I said.

His buckskin forehead got a pained look.

"My dear Miss Blaine, I'm talking a standard contract. Naturally we write in the legal details before we start, to make sure we've covered all eventualities. You must be aware Coelacanth makes various kinds of film, a good many simply diverting. I'm not at liberty to tell you what we have in mind except that it's an excellent scenario by one of our favored artistes. We don't want to interfere with the spontaneity of your reactions, which is what our audience values. But there's no reason to take a dark view. I can assure you of a lot of excitement with a rich reward at the end."

He fixed Dosh. "Your companion is interested already. I've been discussing opportunities for career advancement if the first trial should be successful. I think in his case the portents are promising, very promising indeed."

Damn him, he knew which buttons to press. Dosh's hand tightened so violently he nearly ground my bones to hamburger against the load of beaten silver Mokey makes me in his spare time. I tried not to yelp.

"Moke?"

He'd come back with the tray and was standing holding it, his eyes moving from one of us to the other. He bent to lay it on Dosh's knees and handed the reptile a coffee-cup.

"Hope you mean to eat," he said. "If I heat that again it goes out to Yeller."

Dosh nodded and grabbed for the spoon like a little kid

snatching a treat. He let my crushed knuckles go to balance better. "You got it. Thanks. Great stuff, Moke-o."

"Moke?" I repeated. I tried to keep my voice even. I didn't want Dosh to hear me begging for his downfall. The snake heard, of course, but fuck him. It was Mokey that mattered. He was our last chance. The one guy in the world who could say no to this damned suicide pact and make Dosh listen. After all the guy loved him.

Mokey was looking down, his brows drawn together. I could almost hear him thinking, but for once I couldn't tell what. The telephone was out of order.

He lifted his own mug off the tray, passed me mine and took his time about sitting on one of our luxurious top-quality packing cases.

He sighed in a deep breath and let it out.

"Sure," he said peaceably. "Why not?"

"You got to be crazy!" I exploded.

The snake was gone and we were having our private battle in our own time. Not that it would do any good. Our signatures were on the contract in his gray silk pocket and it's the kind of contract you don't break. Not unless you want one of the other kind, on you.

"Not necessarily," Mokey said. He was still being in charge. Blessed are the peacemakers for they shall get their heads kicked in. I was thinking about it. "We don't know what kind of film it is. Like the guy said, they make all kinds. Romantic comedy. Farce. Show-stuff, froth and cream pies. Humiliating but not lethal. And Dosh is the perfect romantic hero. Why waste him?"

"Because wasting people's what it's about."

It's what I wanted to scream. What I said was, "Supposing it's genre?"

You know films? You got these guys and they don't know it's a film. They're going ahead living their normal lives and they think tomorrow they're going to get up and go to their office or whatever like today. It's boring but ordinary. Then, boom!, this big green alien comes crawling out of the Frigidaire and turns them into catsup. It's genre. Or the vampire's coming through the window or some guy's dumped a corpse in the trunk of your copt and you're about to get accused of the murder. That's genre. It's what happens in films. Oh, you get singing and dancing. But did we look like singers and dancers?

One time they didn't bother with contracts, they just walked in and reorganized. It was funny as all hell watching the suckers' faces. Then the International Human Rights boys and girls got it up their noses and our local Aris found the fines prohibitive, so now they tell you and hand you a contract. Maybe it's even more amusing because now they got groups of guys like us sitting around shivering, not knowing what's coming down next but having a damned good idea they're not going to like it.

They call it suspense.

Like being in the haunted house. You're going around trying to act normal when you know any time something's going to come out of the woodwork and say Boo! And maybe it's a real giggly ghost, the kind lets you in for a few pratfalls and a lot of secret passages that lead you to the Lost Treasure of Blackhead the Pirate. And maybe it's really and truly Jack the Ripper, rattling his scalpels in your ear while you're sleeping and preparing to leave bits of people all over the landscape.

"The hell," Dosh said. He'd lost the flat look and was suddenly back in three dimensions and full color. He was practically bouncing on his pad. "Damn it, Cass, what are we scared of? You think we haven't been living a genre film all our lives? You're the safest of all. Tough, beautiful bim, why you shaking? You're set to be Heroine. Dammit, we ought to celebrate. We're edging in on the Art scene with enough cash to keep us in luxury for ever, and after it's finished we can do anything we like. Stay and enjoy it or space out and look for something even better. You and me show our talents, Moke shows his sculpture. You figure they aren't going to work it in somewhere? They wanted all of us. What you bet his next stop's an art gallery? And all we got to do is spend a couple weeks being usual.''

I didn't want to answer that one.

Knowing what I know about Ari thinking I didn't feel like speculating on what the next stop might be for any of us.

''Knock it off, Cass,'' Moke said. ''I'm going to bed. You guys want to argue all night, you're welcome. Just don't throw crockery. I feel like some sleep.''

''You want your quilt back?'' Dosh yelled after him.

''Keep it. It might warm the pair of you enough to shut you up.''

And he vanished behind his partition.

Dosh grinned at me like a beautiful happy shark and patted his pad. Often when Moke walks he sits and fidgets. Tonight I guess he felt able to be generous. He knew I'd given up for him. I reckon he didn't know Mokey had too. If there's one thing Moke's never wanted to do it's be a film star. Of course Dosh had no way of knowing what we'd been talking about while we were out. Me, I knew what Moke had done and why, only I didn't forgive him. But the trouble with insoluble problems is they're insoluble.

I dropped my pants and shirt and crawled in beside him. That was one nice quilt. It warmed us like an egg-cozy. It was almost like having Moke in with us. Actually we tried that but it doesn't really work. I get narky when the guys start coming on. Guess I've a naturally jealous tempera-ment.

''Dosh?'' I said after a while.

"Mmn?" He was nuzzling my shoulder, satisfied and sleepy.

"You don't figure they're going to find a way of splitting us up? It's the kind of thing appeals in the reptile house."

"Let 'em, doll," he murmured into my neck. "It's our lives. We don't have to do anything we don't want to."

It sounded very like something Mokey'd said not so long ago. I wished I was as confident as they were I had the world in my hands.

But that's men all over. Women's great virtue is we're nervous. Believe me.

The arch at the Midway had flickering lights and a grimacing face guaranteed to give kids nightmares. It was justified. What went down inside wasn't kid stuff.

Dosh and I skirted the Space Bowl where muscle-enhanced wrestlers threw dragon shadows on the dome like tarantulas mating, hairy deformed limbs twisting. At the Horror Ride next door the barker was handing out tickets, and derms in glinty packets like popcorn. A lot of the horror was do-it-yourself and clients who didn't make the exit turned up in the bay in the morning.

Dosh was wearing lime shirt, gilt pants and yellow boots plus a pirate scarf, which said holiday clothes and a kick in the privates for anyone who mistook his business. He'd taken forty minutes to dress and looked it.

We were following street rules: if the guy goes peacock, the bim goes guy. Otherwise they think you're hooking. So I had a black slide catsuit with an oily sheen, bare feet and earrings to my collarbones.

I also had a cartridge-belt over my hip with a waterpistol. Waterpistols are allowed so long as they aren't loaded with acid. Strip regs change without notice so if you're carrying you got to be ready to ditch at light-speed. The trick's to keep one step ahead of the regs. Mine was ahead, as of this morning. Ditching methods are among the states of the art that keep one step ahead of the cops. It's a game, with ten to twenty-five for the losers.

We were doing the guy-and-gal apache act and Dosh was enjoying himself. Too much for my taste. He was entirely too far up today considering how far down he'd been yesterday. I knew the effects of snake-bite and it looked to me he'd been bitten.

"Cool it, guy," I growled from the side of my mouth. It goes with the apache bit, nobody watches. "We're not on film yet far's I know. I'd say we were supposed to act normal. When they decide to hit I guess we'll notice."

"We got to be ready, Cass," Dosh snarled back. I haven't enough hair to pull, cascading masses being unhealthy if you spend time running for your life, so he gave me a fancy spin by my cartridge-belt. It was too fancy and nearly spilled my pistol and I kicked his ankle. "Anyhow, taking your girl out is normal."

"Not for you it ain't."

He forgot the apache long enough to give me a genuine Dosh smile, the kind that dims out the spotlights. "Then maybe we ought to make it. How come you always eat with Mokey?"

"Because you're never in. You hungry?"

"Yeah, but I'd rather ride the Loop before than after. Comes cheaper."

So that was where we were going. Well, he had that right. Anybody rides the Loop on a full stomach ends up buying two dinners. If they're not being removed in an ambulance.

"Sadistic bastard. Time you quit that job, you're catching bad habits."

His smile dimmed and almost went out. He caught it and had another try at outshining the neon. "Yeah. Haven't used them on you have I, Cass?"

"Idiot." The dim-out made me guilty. Bad habits weren't top of the bill right now.

I punched him where his gut would be if he had one, which he hasn't, and he did another apache swing. We were attracting attention but the right kind. The sort that envies your style without seeing your face. We've a couple of interesting routines but we rarely get to try them in public.

For a moment I really felt as if we were on holiday, then I remembered the damned film and started to dim out myself. The freshness and spontaneity of our reactions, yeah. They meant they intended to catch us in the toilet, which made natural functions itchy. Hence the waterpistol, though even I didn't know what the hell I meant to use it for. But it goes with apache dress.

We'd got to the dark tunnel of the Loop and my stomach flipped. Dosh likes the damned thing, I don't. I guess it's a male-female tic. He likes to be protective, I hate protection. Feel safer doing it myself, then I know it's done.

The tunnel's part of the scare. Instead of rippling electrics there's this low round entrance with ''The Loop'' written big in looping silver so everyone else's glitter reflects off it with a sinister shine. It's josh like the rest, of course. It's neither more nor less scary than the Midway's other attractions and any one's guaranteed to make you puke your guts up.

There's a rumor the government pays the proprios to have accidents. I don't believe it but it adds to the atmosphere. I don't say there isn't a death rate, but you don't need to engineer anything when your clientele's permanently bombed or otherwise out of its mind, and a quarter of it's gunning for half the rest. On contract or for personal satisfaction. We've a high personal satisfaction rate in Ashton. Moke told me once it's the principle of parsimony. Never do it yourself if you can get the marks to make it alone.

We walked towards the red glimmer of the pay-booth. Something semi-human rose under our feet halfway and bolted for the open but I didn't bother to react. It happens every time, the patron pays them. Dosh flourished his card—part of the apache deal is the guy gets to act macho without getting kicked—and the not-too-ugly silvered kid with muscles jerked his head inside.

The scariest thing about the Loop is the dark. If you could see or hear other cars or if you knew what angle you were at fewer people would end up bilious. You just get in your little car and shoot off into the black like a bullet.

The trajectories are coordinated at random. The number of tracks varies with the cars and they can get wild if there aren't many. It depends on the state of the force-field. The one thing you're sure of is losing your lunch.

Our car took off at roughly five gee into what felt like the fourth dimension, did a darting pirouette and slowed to a glide. The Loop loops. I've been with Dosh when my middle ear's been swiveling half an hour later.

The longer the glide the worse the descent. This went up forever. It doesn't necessarily even go up, it's the field-variations make it feel it does. You think you're going up and down when maybe you're only undulating in place. You make real gees though. I've got the scars.

We glided so far I thought we had to be scratching stratosphere. I reminded myself it's illusion and pandered to Dosh's vanity by wrapping an arm around his waist. The downgrade was a short wrenching swoop that had just begun to pick up speed when we pulled out and did a whiplash upward. Then we did it again. Several times.

"Doshky? Is this damn thing normal?"

"Guess so," his voice came back, a warm mouth close to my ear. "Probably not much of a crowd. The computer gets inventive when it's lonely. Hang in, kid, we gotta come down sometime."

"That's what's bothering me."

The car turned back upwards in a spiral, slow as

smoke-rings, hit the top of the grade and hesitated. I grabbed a mouthful of air and held it.

Then all the lights came on with a flash like magnesium and blinded the pair of us.

I squinted through slitted lids, blinking tears. The hangar we were in looked half the size of the Universe and we were scraping the dome with our heads. The floor was so far below, the tunnel where the cars were launched looked like a mousehole. The rest was emptiness, with Dosh and me with our arms around each other and tears on our faces floating in mid-air, and the walls a couple hundred yards away every direction.

Our car was the only one in the place. We could see maybe twenty ranged below like little dark bugs nosed to the edge of a minuscule platform. And all we could see between was distance.

I understand force fields in theory. You can't see them. In practice this one was maybe sparky or hazy or something, but the way it looked was just not there at all.

And at that moment the car finished its spiral, turned its nose downward and started falling. Dosh gave a grunt and his arms tightened enough to crush my ribs. I grabbed him back and hung on. Because both of us saw we were dead. Those cars don't just free fall, they fucking accelerate. Ours was headed straight for the floor with an aerodynamic whine and we must have been nearly supersonic.

It probably only lasted seconds but that floor was a long way away and I'd plenty of time to watch it coming. The one direction we were going was down. Then at the last instant, when I only wasn't screeching like a bat because my throat was frozen, the car flipped around, did a zig-zag a razor's width off the floor and began to climb again.

Dosh's face was rigidly white, his eyes almost purple with shock, a few broken veins red in the sclerotic. He was holding me but he wasn't looking at me. He was watching us rise.

Then I watched us too.

I should have expected the next move. Only I'd forgotten about force-fields. The car flipped on its side and kept on waltzing curvily towards the farther wall. It felt like the place swiveled around, toppled on its face and we went on heading for the new ceiling as if it didn't matter.

"Dosh," I said, Minnie Mouse at the end of a wind-tunnel. "Close your eyes."

His blue-purple look turned slowly as if his head and neck were all one piece, then he gave a functional nod. We gazed at each other to see we were really going to do it. Then I scrunched mine shut. Dosh sighed and pressed my head against his arm.

With closed eyes it wasn't any worse than normal. I never knew before why the Loop works in the dark.

When we hit the ground and unglued our lids there was a ghosty citizen with eyes as round as gooseberries at the bottom and he was shaking worse than we were.

"Hey, you folks okay?" he babbled, grabbing hold of Dosh's arm like an ambulanceman delivering a baby. He lifted him out and deposited him, and Dosh is a big guy and he was a little one. "Never seen that. Christ! Lucky you're both healthy. You are healthy, ain't you, Ma'am?"

I forestalled the lifting-out bit by shoving his hand aside and climbed out solo, but I admit my knees were tinkling like ice cubes.

"Yeah," I said. "What happened?"

"Computer-fault, I guess. She's set to put the lights on when the dome's empty. Cleaning, you know? But she ought to've known you folks were in. Ain't supposed to happen. Christ, if either of you'd got taken sick. Jesus! I could lose my license. You're sure you're okay, lady?"

"Fine," I quavered.

Dosh had his arm around me and I was proud of him. I could feel his body vibrating through my clothes but he was still upright and playing apache.

"Interesting experience," he said. "You got a mechanic?"

"Yes, sir," the pale guy said devoutly.

"Then I guess I'd call him. Next customer could be fragile. Come on, Cass, I'm hungry."

It was a lie, but the most gallant lie I've heard this year. And we almost managed to leave without stumbling.

"No film business yet, huh?" Dosh said, sucking his single malt. He's a beer man when we can't afford wine which is usually, but our Loop guy came running after us with a free voucher for a smart bar down the Strip where he had a soulmate and we were using it. We felt comfort procedures were justified.

"Not necessarily," I said, inhaling a lungful of prime cognac and admiring the color against the smart soft lights. Not like the Dog, real class with big mirrors and a fleet of cruising boys who rushed up with the bottle when your glass got to low-tide. "Could be what the guy said. Computer-failure. Happens."

He leveled a red-rimmed eye. "You don't believe that, Cass."

As a matter of fact I did. And the idea scared me worse than film-stuff. Because the film-crew presumably had an interest in keeping us alive until the end of the development, whereas the fucking computer could as easily have eliminated us while it was knotting up its reality. But I saw one thing clear and it made me uneasy.

Dosh thought it was film-stuff. And I was getting some insight into his reactions. He hadn't relaxed yet. He was sitting at the bar in an easy casual pose knocking back his malt like a gentleman, and anyone who didn't know him might think he was relaxed. But he wasn't. Every movement was a study in art. I guess I'd never appreciated how thoroughly he played through all his parts because I'd never caught him acting in front of me before. I'd always had the real animal.

But he was acting this time. In fact I was beginning to see he'd been acting all the time. There'd been a period back there when he'd thought we were really headed for the floor. He'd been genuinely scared, he'd genuinely closed his eyes. And when we got out he'd been genuinely shaking. But what he'd been doing, then and ever since, was act. The cool, unruffled hero, who passes it all off with a quip and winds up in a classy bar with just a touch of broken vein in the whites of his eyes.

It didn't make his strength and comfort less heroic—to give it you've got to got it—but from now on, Doshky was acting.

And me, I wasn't. All I was was scared. Out of my panties. And I didn't think the fucking film had even begun.

Back at the ranch the comforting sound of a screeching rasp met us at the elevator which meant Moke was in and being a genius. We peeled off at the main deck and went to check progress in case someone had turned him into a frog or something since we saw him last.

He looked as usual, skinny, dirty, half-naked and running sweat under his face-mask. The construction had got too big for the apartment and was developing little starbursts near the ceiling. One of these days he was going to build something so heroic we'd have to demolish the place to get it out. We lived in fear of his stuff coming through the floorboards as it was.

"Hi," Dosh said, still unnaturally cool and easy. "Anything going down, man?"

Mokey deliberately finished the piece of rasping he was

working on before he deigned to switch off, shove the mask back and slide to our level.

"Depends what you mean by down."

"Like what?"

Dosh's hero façade was in place but a quick flicker of something went across his eyes in a single blink like a station adjustment on a vid screen. I knew the name of it. Worry. Or if you prefer, screaming terror.

"Like this."

He dug in his jeans pocket—the back where various tools wore a hole long ago and now all he keeps there's paper—and produced paper. Uglified by close connection with Moke, which comes with the territory. Dosh took it and I had to climb his arm to read over his shoulder.

It had been a nice number in beige linen-weave with a gilt address at the top before it met Moke's jeans but the writing in real black ink by a real pen in a real hand—there aren't many left, these days of fancy voc-ops with a tendency to lilac squiggles—was still legible. It was addressed, incredibly, to Mr. Martin Faber at our apartment. It was the first I knew we had a street number. Nobody'd ever written to us before. It was also the first time I'd heard Mokey had a name other than Mokey. Somebody knew something we didn't. Ari stuff. Yeah.

It came from somewhere called Never which wasn't promising, plus what looked like a grid-reference which was less so. A three-dimensional grid which means private sat, longish coordinates which means way out. Heavy. It started businesslike and stayed that way.

"Dear Mr. Faber, I should be honored if you would call upon me at my home address, here above, to discuss your work in terms that may be advantageous to both of us. My yacht will be at your disposal tomorrow. My driver will call at your home at nine a.m., which I hope will suit you. I apologize for the short notice, but hope you will feel able to indulge me. You may wish to bring a friend.''

He was, Mokey's faithfully (a charming old-fashioned touch), and a fastidious black signature that looked like ''Hans-Bjorn Eklund.''

Dosh's brows were nearly up to his hairline. ''Friend of yours?''

''Nope.'' Moke was still being deliberate, which since he has a slow drawl at any time dragged it out around ten words a minute. ''Never heard of the guy.''

''To discuss your work,'' I said.

''Yeah.''

''So who knows you got work, apart from us and fifteen other fucking Umps?''

''And Swordfish,'' Dosh reminded me.

''Sword don't count, he ain't human.''

''Nobody,'' Moke said. He rubbed his hands on a bundle of wipes from his front pocket and fished in the port rear for a joint. He lit it carefully and dragged. ''Unless one of you got relatives?''

''Negative.''

''It's the thought-police,'' Dosh said. ''Alive and well and living in Ashton.''

''The what?''

''It's a literary reference.'' Dosh thinks I'm dumb. He's only half-right.

''Uh-huh. I really gotta learn to read.''

''The snake,'' Mokey amplified.

Sometimes he and Dosh throughline better than I do. Not that it hadn't occurred to me. I could feel that viper's buckskin handshake, like dipping your hands in cold grease.

''Film business,'' I said.

''Maybe.'' Moke was looking at the end of his joint with a finicky expression as if he just found a beetle in it—or as if he couldn't be sure whether what he found was a beetle or not.

"You going?"

Apparently he decided it wasn't a beetle because he put it in his mouth and took another drag. "Dunno."

"Well, you haven't much time, Moke-o. It's nearly two o'clock. If you're going spacing you better shower and get some sleep."

"Uh-huh."

He was still consulting the infinite. If that's what people do when they look blank and don't answer. There are other solutions but Moke's intelligent.

"He's going," Dosh said.

We both looked at him.

"Isn't he? If it's film business, let's earn money. I can't wait to get it and start packing."

"Check," I said. "Only you noticed yourself these guys got a real sense of humor. Where d'you suppose Moke's gonna find Never? Suppose the fucking rocket blows up. Or dematerializes or something equally hilarious. Dammit, Dosh, he isn't a fighter."

"You are. That's why you're going with him."

"Me?" I'd been meaning to propose one of us should accept but I'd thought Dosh would want to guard his best-beloved himself. "What about you?"

"Stay here and mind the shop." He was getting so damned relaxed I was beginning to think they were both half-conscious. "Make sure nobody puts these irreplaceable artworks in his pocket while you're gone."

"Ha," Moke said hollowly.

I'd have said the same but I could see ideas in a little balloon over Dosh's head. Sure, he thought it was film business. And he'd figured like me, they probably wouldn't kill us off right away, not in numbers, since they needed to get a story going.

I have known films start with half the cast evaporating in a big bang in the first thirty seconds but it was a fair bet not. So one, our hero was going to be the guy who stayed home alone and two, the reason he meant to do that was he thought if anything bad went down, home was where it was going to do it. Great. Make my day.

"Why don't we all go?" I said. Trying not to sound desperate. Nothing annoys Dosh like desperation. Little beaver eyes gleaming frantically, I could feel them.

"Because," Dosh said with patience, "we aren't all invited. Guy says a friend. And because, Cassandra, a good general guards his rear."

An even better general keeps his troops together was what I thought. But Dosh had that look again. If you wanted to know what role he was playing tonight the Good General was it. Anybody know how to stop guys playing heroes?

"So," he finished, grabbing one of us by each collar and running us towards the elevator, "what you guys get to do now is have a shower. Each. Or in pairs, don't matter to me." (It did. But in his present stance of soldierly self-abnegation he was going to be generous if it killed him.) "And after that you're going to bed. Until eight-thirty, which is six hours if you don't horse around. Go."

We went. Perforce. He's much the strongest.

But I noticed as I was sent sternly to my pad for the watch below we weren't saying a word to Moke about the Loop. Keeping up the morale of the troops, I suppose.

I wish I took to adventures like a Boy Scout to water the way guys do. My mother always said I took life too seriously.

I'd never expected to agree with her. On any subject.

I guess she'd have been pleased to know.

Never was an ugly chunk of rock that caught the light as we came up, drifting against the stars, a monument to the inutility of man.

There are sats and sats. From this high we could see a few twinkling below us. The cluster of globes that was the High Soul Mission, the long spindle of the Margarita Colony, two of the lazily turning wheels which acted as interstellar staging posts, a handful of sequins that said rich private enterprise. They were pretty. The planet below looked blue and clean, the clouds that grayed our skies making patterns of milky spirals that gave back sunlight.

And above, the landed estates of people who're too rich to have estates on land. Like Never. Hauled in from the Asteroid Belt at an expense that once ran nations and now sets up high rock-gardens.

It looked like the kind of flattish stone you skim over water, then a lump of darkness with mineral glitters, then as we came over the horizon there was a slash of green with the soap-bubble shine of a dome covering it with rainbows.

Never. An oval three kilometers along the long axis, one and a bit along the short, incongruous mathematics laid out on a hunk of cosmic rubble someone had stuck there and smoothed and planted with grass and trees to live like Earth where Earth and its inconveniences weren't. How perverse can you get?

But mankind's founded on perversity. Why do we do anything? If I had the money I might live on an asteroid myself. Building a world you can tolerate to replace the one you can't.

Our pilot, a bronzed type in aluminized overalls saying rich guy's pilot (real spacers wear stuff you wouldn't give the dog to pup on) who identified himself as Henry the one time he spoke, brought the yacht in to the landing port at the short end of the dome, put it right down on the painted cross and opened the lock.

I emptied my glass and checked my waterpistol not much caring if Henry saw me. Yacht trips are nice, in a luxury cabin with champagne and big windows so you can see the world go by out of sight and feel superior. Now I'd have to go and work.

Mokey'd spent half the trip catching up his sleep and the rest looking out morosely at the cosmos as if he figured he'd have made a better job of it himself. He unfolded himself stiffly, rubbed the back of his neck, dusted off the less wasted jeans Dosh and I'd bullied him into and marched to the ramp like it led to the guillotine.

Note that for him sudden death isn't a special worry. He regards terminal disqualification as an abstract problem and his own business as a series of practical ones so he doesn't bother to think about it. What was on his mind was first, the possibility the guy could be on the square, when he was going to have to explain his philosophy of form, and second, the likelihood the guy wasn't, when he'd waste several hours of time he could have spent at home making the neighbors' lives horrible with power tools.

He looked at me as if the whole thing was my fault. Along with the jeans he had a white shirt with most of its buttons and his lank hair hung over the collar. We'd vetoed bare feet so he'd put his shoes on. I guess his mother bought them before he left home. They were heavy, lace-up and hideous. Then we regretted the veto but we hadn't time to buy more.

I had black stretch leggings for fighting in, a red damasked tunic bunched at the waist by a silver belt to match my bag and soft-soled boots with some weight in the toe in case I had to kick.

Together we looked like Madame parading her wolf-hound or a guy operating a marionette, whichever.

Henry disappeared into an airlock stage left without bothering to say goodbye but a fresh bronzed and alumi-nized gonzo had materialized stage center with what looked like a golf cart so someone was expecting us. We ad-vanced towards it, me trying to look alert and deadly like a good gun-moll and Moke mooching. You'd have said he'd been sent to Sunday-school while the rest of the gang left with his football.

"Good morning," the gonzo called, which made him friendlier than Henry. He'd have to be if he meant to live with actual humans. "Jump in and I'll take you to the house."

We got a red leather seat each, me by the gonzo and Mokey in back, and the contraption trundled merrily off across the green acres.

The terraforming wasn't bad. The gravity was as near normal as dammit, the soil looked like soil and the trees were trees. Bigger and healthier than the ones at the Hindenburg Mall but it's hard not to be. A little scented breeze flapped the leaves a bit and bent the nicely trimmed grass. I wasn't sure whether the smell was real or decor. The dome was tinted prettily so the sky was only a few shades darker than normal and the sunlight was genuine. It was a real nice effect.

"It's a real nice effect," I told the gonzo.

He radiated like he'd done it single-handed. "You like it?

We wanted something that looked like home. Some people prefer specialized environments but I think art looks best in a natural setting, don't you?''

"Yeah, sure," I said.

I'd no idea if I did or not. I mean, what's natural? There were stone and bronze things scattered among the trees which had to be engaging Moke's attention and they looked nice, but then I seen stone and bronze things look nice in the city too. They do get blacker.

A snort from the back said Moke thought we were talking crud. And the gonzo took over my line.

"You think we're talking crud?" he asked politely over his shoulder.

Mokey isn't good at hurting people, it's one of his faults. "You got nice stuff here," he said, neutral.

"But not what you'd choose yourself."

"I use what I've got. Some of my stuff would look okay on grass. I'd urban plazas in mind where plain pipe sometimes looks better. Out here maybe they should be sprayed. Plastic. Red and blue, red and yellow. Primaries.''

"Of course," the gonzo said, still politely. "You'd do a different kind of construction for grass?"

"Maybe," Moke said, wistful. "I began working in welded metal because it's easiest to get in Ashton. I'd a couple ideas for cast stone. Big. Kind of quarry look, half rough, half polished. Anthropomorphic at the edges.''

"Interesting," the gonzo said. He kept on steering the golf cart, towards a big glassy house in the distance. I couldn't tell by his voice if he was interested or not.

"What're you looking for, Mr. Eklund?" Mokey asked.

I did a double-take and looked at the gonzo closer. He was middle-sized, thinnish, limp yellow hair, big nose, pale eyes. Mouth not badly shaped, very white teeth. Plain but intelligent. A bit like Mokey. His aluminized suit wasn't much different from Henry's. His hands on the wheel had polished nails. Apart from that he could have been the gardener.

I had to hand it to Moke. Sometimes he's a lot smarter than me. When he bothers to think about it.

"Why don't we discuss it inside?" Eklund said. "After lunch? And perhaps you'd like to look at my collection. I've some African ethnic that's quite appealing and a selection of Sternbrunners. I fancied you might like Sternbrunner."

Which made Eklund not so dumb. Sternbrunner's a guy Moke talks about. When he does, which is mostly when he's drunk. Drunkish. He's got a puritan streak, Mokey. He does a couple derms sometimes but he has this objection to falling down. Grates on our friends.

"Uh," he said. Which I guess was gracious consent.

Lunch was a scene from a sitcom. We sat around three sides of a crystal table the size of a golf course on Eklund's terrace, which looked across acres of grass starred with sculptures. There were terra-cotta urns of flowers rioting about. I'm not hot on flowers, which are in short supply in our neighborhood, but these had spraying petals in bright colors, unlike for instance the indoor arrangements of Mrs. Waller-Gurney which ran to pale fleshy things that smelled like a graveyard. Nature gives me hay-fever. I liked his version better than hers.

Eklund sat at the head in his spaceman suit, Mokey sat about fifty yards on his left in his old jeans with his clunky shoes digging into the carpet and a bigger gap in his shirtfront than I'd noticed when we counted the buttons, and I faced Moke from the other side of the ninth green.

The service was robot, an Ari habit, but polished. I spent the first half of the meal watching for the domestic to slip the mickey into the whatever and gave up. Not even an Ari mickey-finns Beluga caviar. The champagne Eklund opened himself and I heard the tales you did about the hypodermic through the cork and the host taking the antidote before, and if you want my opinion they're for vids. You ever pushed a hypodermic through a champagne cork?

I figured he was a humorist when he called the robot Henry. I wondered if the pilot patronized him too or he just called all his domestic appliances the same.

Moke ate like he hadn't seen food in a month which made it a shame. I'm not sure he can tell caviar from cornflakes. It isn't ignorance, it's the call of higher things. Eklund had his Sternbrunners laid out around the terrace and Moke was too busy sizing them up to watch his plate. They looked to me like bulgy bronze hunks with owl eyes in unexpected places. I could have eaten without them. Moke was fixated. I think Eklund found us both funny.

Toward the end of the caviar Moke said suddenly, "Who designed your domestic?"

Eklund paused with his fork in mid-air looking as pleased as a guy found the Rajah's pearl in his breakfast kipper. When he smiled his nicish lips made a more attractive display than you'd expect.

"You noticed."

"Characteristic. Never seen his stuff in spun steel."

I took a second look. Owl eyes, one higher than the other, and something odd around the armpit. I should have known. I'd thought there was something weird about the damned thing but domestics always strike me as threatening unless I've a good Hallway jinx on the fuckers so I try not to look. I suspect it's a common reaction except maybe among Aris.

"You're not afraid of it getting damaged?" Moke was saying.

"I try to avoid wild parties." Eklund's smile was wicked. "I'm a trial to my neighbors. But I find celebration destructive to art. Henry's a private indulgence. I've standard models for routine."

A way of saying we, or rather Mokey, were getting the

celebrity treatment. The idea sent a little thread of cold down my neck. I was back to feeling paranoid. Aris do not behave like that to Umps. I sneaked a look up at the awning but it looked exactly like an awning. No concealed ninjas, no poisonous reptiles of whatever sort, no toppling urns. I sneaked a second look at the floor. Octagonal tiles, high-class decorator, with a turquoise zig-zag around the border. If there was a hidden trapdoor I couldn't see it.

"Trout, Miss Blaine?" Eklund offered from first tee.

The hell with it. I decided we weren't getting killed until after lunch. I gave Henry my plate.

"That is truly great stuff. I guess you must've spent"—I thought he was going to mention money and get us thrown through the airlock—"a lot of your life on that."

I guess Eklund had thought the same because he'd tensed a bit but when he heard the conclusion he smiled sweetly.

"I think you could say that. But with me it's business as well as pleasure. I keep my private collection here but I also run galleries." He gave us more sweet smile. "A short chain—three. But in major cities of major planets. That's why you interest me, Mr. Faber."

"Me?" breathed Moke.

"Certainly you. Your work's interesting and remarkably mature for a young man. I sell works by the great but it's a poor patron of art who can't spend some time and trouble on the young. That's you."

"Me," Moke breathed again. His ugly shoes were sunk to the ankles in a priceless carpet, his raggy jeans made a charming contrast with the silk wallpaper with birds and flowers behind him. His shirt had lost another button when he'd pulled the neck in a moment of exaltation. He looked like an ape from the gutter and his face shone with the radiance of the seraphim.

"Let's go on the terrace and talk, shall we?" Eklund said. "I'm sure you're hungry."

We went. Henry (by Sternbrunner) was laying out crystal glasses as we sat. I stared at the Earth above me as the guys got down to business and it looked as pure as a pearl in the glittering space.

As we sipped our wine the flat skipping-stone of Never moved around its orbit into twilight.

When we got back Dosh was waiting at the main gate where the traxies zip out and start to accelerate before they take off for the higher levels, and the exit ramp leads out to the moving walkways. It was dark and the port looked kind of exciting and exotic with the big floods pointing at the sky and the lighted windows of the control tower. The passenger lounges were outlined in ripple neon and the blinkers of the traxies changed color as they zizzed past.

I could tell from the exaggeratedly casual air he had as he leaned against a bollard he was still in character, the cool tough guy waiting it out while the villains got lined up behind the trash-cans. That was two days in a row I hadn't zapped my pistol and I was hoping to keep up my average so for me they could stay there.

"Hi, boys," he said in his cool tough-guy voice. I liked it less than the Dosh I knew. "Interesting day?"

"Depends on your attitude to guys eat caviar from three-kilo cans," I said. "Arty but quiet."

He looked disappointed. "No excitement?"

"Sure. He's offered Moke a big exhibition with off-planet options and maybe a commission if he likes his sketches. And we may've sold the teepee if he can have it sprayed."

Dosh frowned. I thought real. "On the up and up?"

"Who's to tell? He sounded sincere, but don't they all?"

"Mokey?"

Our genius scuffed his shoes on the concrete, adding a few scratches to their un-beauty. "Got hot stuff. Sternbrunners you wouldn't believe. Things I only seen in books. He's got corn."

"But you don't believe him?"

Moke looked down at his shoes.

"It's just the way it adds," he said at last. "I'm not in Sternbrunner's class."

"You're in your own," Dosh said with violence.

"Yeah." Mokey scuffed some more. Then he lifted his head and grinned. "You noticed the line of guys queueing down the street for it?" He shook his lank hair. "Would've been nice if it'd been true. Let's go and eat."

"Then you—" Dosh began.

I grabbed his arm and shook it.

"Leave the guy alone, huh? It's a fucking heart-breaker. Moke would sell his soul for an exhibition. Takes a nice sense of irony to offer it as a joke. Let's go eat."

"Yeah, right." Dosh went after Moke and grabbed him around the shoulders with a silk-covered arm. "Why don't you shuck the shoes, country boy? You look like a rambling wreck from wherever. Born on the bayou. There's a real pretty trash-can over there provided free by the city fathers. It's only grateful to use it."

I had first-hand knowledge of the effects of Dosh being sweet. Mokey grinned a shade less palely and kicked the shoes off like he was getting rid of leg-irons. When they hit the deck I was shocked to see his heels were two enormous blisters, one ripped and bleeding. The stupid bastard had been playing Little Mermaid all day.

We made a ceremony of dumping the instruments of torture in the receptacle provided and hopped the walkway in the direction of the Dog. As we skipped belts my two guys were wrangling. Dosh was determined to buy Mokey a pair of trainers that fit, Moke was explaining the reasons he'd rather walk on his own skin. Dosh was getting eloquent about broken bottles and abandoned hypodermics.

By the time we were lined up against the rail of the fast lane with the rushing air whipping our hair over our faces and the dust from the freeway below blowing up into our eyes, it seemed to me things were back to normal. For the moment.

I looked across at the flowing neon of the city and thought with a kind of nostalgia how nice it had been when we'd nothing to worry about but living until tomorrow.

That reward stuck up in front of us like a glass mountain and we were doomed to climb it.

Damn. There's no such thing as easy money. Not even if it falls from the sky on your head. Ours more or less had. And look what it was doing to us.

We quit the walkway where the runoff slid down to the Strip and took to our legs. It was maybe three blocks to the Dog and we were looking forward to a row of Eustace's specials. Dosh had dropped back to joking, contented to have Mokey docile under his arm, and Moke was letting him be doctor. His repartee's less than warp-speed but he grunts in as many tones as a Chinese flute. I was walking behind them neon-gazing and listening with one ear, recognizing Mokey needed it and was getting it and feeling something like tranquillity.

When a sharp cut-off scream from an alley turned all our heads like they were on strings.

Down in the shadows was a pile of scuffling bodies with edges that glinted, and a bare pale leg stuck out from under. I had my pistol in my hand almost as soon as the first echo but Dosh was faster. I guess you develop reflexes in his job. I've a nose for trouble but he works on clairvoyance.

We pelted down the alley like the Charge of the Light Brigade and probably just as dumbly. The glinting edges were prostheses, and they can be anything from razor-blades to laser-canon. And the whole deal could be Swordfish, who takes badly to being muscled in on. But bare pale legs aren't quite his style. He prefers the male of the species and in numbers. Though it does depend on the price.

Dosh hit them with his full weight and a lot of hard science. He practices martial arts but on the Strip you don't neglect plain dirty fighting. The combination's a winner if the other guy isn't too many and too heavy.

This lot were amateurs. There are a lot about. Unwise, on Swordfish's territory. They have short unhappy lives. This lot were lucky to get a first thrashing from Dosh. He's big, he's strong, but he's neither surgically enhanced nor psychotic. All he did was whale the tar out of them.

They had the prostheses okay but not much sense of how to use them and only rudimentary alterations, like hooks and chains. You don't actually get much further unless Swordfish is in on it and he picks his soldiers. This lot looked like routine muggers. Dosh pretty well fixed them single-handed while Moke and I stood behind and cheered.

I let off a squirt would be sending one to his dermatologist in the morning by way of showing solidarity but it was just helping them on their way. They were already going. Mokey, in a similar spirit, tripped the one who made the mistake of coming too close and delivered him a good kick to a bad place, which wasn't too much hindered by his lack of shoes since Moke has damned hard feet.

They they were gone, whimpering as they went, and we were winners of the field. There had been four unless one had run the other way when he saw us coming, so the odds hadn't been too uneven. I stuck my pistol back in my belt, Mokey rubbed his foot on his other jean leg and Dosh, looking frantically handsome with a thin line of blood down the side of his jaw where a loose chain had caught him, bent and chivalrously offered his hand to the victim.

She drew back for a moment, scared of us. We were three, two of us a lot bigger than her, I had a gun and we'd all just been showing violent tendencies. Dosh is used to cases of this sort, male and female. He bent down and stretched a reassuring hand, making the sort of noises you make to a dog. The girl looked at us with huge frightened eyes, tried to pull her torn smock over undeveloped breasts and drew her knees up to her chest.

"It's okay," Mokey joined in, leaning over my shoulder. "We're straight. Well," he grinned, and he has an innocent infectious grin, "straightish. Let's get you out on the main drag and see what they've done to you. Come on."

She made a whimpering noise and looked at Dosh's hand as if it were a new invention.

"Yeah, come on," I urged. "How much did they get? Look, you can't go around like that, you're going to get raped by the next seven guys you meet. We're going to eat. Come and we'll look after you. You can have my tunic, I'm fairly decent underneath."

"Hup." Dosh grasped her by the wrist and pulled.

She was a skinny kid maybe sixteen or seventeen years old, in a brief shiny carapace that had hardly covered her narrow bum and now covered almost nothing. It had had interesting cut-outs which had joined in one big rip that threatened to divide the thing in two.

I undid my belt and hauled the tunic over my head. I'm small and skinny myself but there was going to be room for her and her sister. Luckily I'd a camisole underneath that would last through Eustace's without getting us thrown out.

"Here," Dosh said, calm and winning. "Try Cassie's shirt. She's healthy and it's clean."

The child put out a hesitant hand and took it—not from me, from him. He helped to work it over her head. It came down to her knees but it didn't look bad. Apart from her skinny figure and huge eyes she had a shock of gilt hair that stood up like a dandelion clock and the effect was sort of fey.

"Right," Dosh said, the confident big brother in every line. "We're going to the Gilded Dog. It isn't as bad as it looks" (that was a pious lie) "and we'll see nobody bothers you. What's your name?" he added, carefully artless.

"Mallore," the child said in a low clear voice, still shaky. "Are you sure?"

"Sure I'm sure."

She paused, then smiled at him. She slipped her little fragile hand into his big warm one and he wrapped his arm around her. Moke added his as reinforcement from the other side. We took to the road again. Two guys with touching arms, me behind and Mallore right in the middle.

Hell, she was a scared little kid. Not even I could be jealous. I went back to looking at neon and tried to pretend I wasn't cold. It would be warm in the Dog, anyhow.

We went in rank. Four of us.

The Dog was its jumping self. The lights jumped, the clients brooded over their vodka and the gilt goldfish gyrated drearily.

In the blue light the kid looked even frailer and more juvenile than in the alley. Her skinny arms and legs stuck out of the edges of my tunic like the feelers of a hermit crab and the dandelion hair surrounded her pinched face in a fiberoptic aureole. Her eyes, wide and bright in wells of shadow, looked almost black. I figured she was on something more than usually weird. She seemed to have no irises. When the next white jump showed her for real there was a narrow periwinkle ring around the huge pupils. She looked terrified out of her mind.

Eustace gave her a nasty look but he recognized the rest of us and let Dosh lead her to a table in one of the corners where if people fall over you you're allowed to slug them because it's got to be deliberate. Mokey went to negotiate steaks which is wiser when Eustace is having a mood, since he has a taboo on poisoning Moke that doesn't necessarily extend to anyone else.

Dosh and I shoved the kid towards the rear into the big paper leaves of a palm where she couldn't get trodden and set about calming her.

"Let me buy you a drink. What'll you have?"

The kid jittered. "Coke," she said in a tiny voice, gazing at her hands. They were as narrow as bleached twigs, her nails done a silvered azure that looked terminally cardiac.

I resisted the impulse to ask if she wanted it in liquid or powder form and mouthed Moke the order. It wasn't my business how she took her caffeine. The rest of us had it straight. He nodded and resumed his summit conference at the bar.

Dosh was looking protective and helpless at once. Holding the hand of the weak comes naturally to him, especially if it's female—look at the problems I've had—but hysteria makes him uncomfortable. In spite of the tough guy act he's better at taking it than handing it out. I was willing to whop her if she needed it but he wasn't any readier than he ever is and I could see him watching her face and my hand with equal nervousness. Her mouth had a small wet droop suggested she might open it wide any minute and start screaming.

It seemed to me we'd all had a hard day. Getting mugged's no fun, but hell's teeth, what was the little connasse doing alone in a dress would switch on a stuffed gorilla two streets off the Strip? You can't ask intelligence from her kind but you don't have to take imbecility.

I said to Dosh, ignoring her, "Take it there's nothing serious at the farm?"

He shook his head, disgusted. "Quiet as the tomb. Been bored out of my mind all day. Was glad to see you guys walking out on your legs. I'd begun to think the action was where you were."

"Only the psychology. No time-bombs in the basement?"

"Not when I left. Yeller keeps an eye out."

"It's the only one he's got."

The kid was looking at us as if we were crazy. The Strip

has that effect on people if they aren't used to it. I was beginning to think she couldn't be.

"Another routine day."

Mokey arrived back with the drinks, three coffees, one juice-bulb and a handful of cutlery wrapped in paper napkins.

"Food coming. Steak and hey, it's our lucky day. Tonight we got plastic onions."

"I told you, Moke, the veg is okay. It's the prote's home-made. You put the mojo on Eustace again."

"Think the guy's in love with you," Dosh said gloomily.

"Then it ain't reciprocated." He smiled at the kid. "Don't let these guys get to you. You got sore bits? Barman's got a first-aid pack, asked if we could use it. Want anything strapped?"

The kid slowly and shyly drew back my sleeve like she was baring her virginity in front of Sword's whole crew and showed us a small scrape on the point of her elbow. The elbow was sharp as a skewer and she'd probably left a corresponding groove in the road surface. There was nothing soft about any of her angles. She looked as if she was built out of whalebone and piano wire.

"You need to clean that," Dosh said. "Cass, how about you take Mallore to the washroom? Maybe she'd like privacy."

What he meant was if uncovering her elbow cost her that amount of pain, God help us all if she'd got grit in her bum.

As far as I was concerned this kid was showing every sign of growing into a major ass-ache. Okay, she'd been scared. I could relate to that. She'd been rescued by three completely Strip types, no problem. Since then we'd clothed her, cuddled her, led her to lights and company and were in the act of buying her dinner. Seemed to me the fragile-lotus-bud act could get switched off any time now.

I'd already seen one flash of her periwinkle eyes that

suggested she'd have pulled the hysterics on Dosh if they'd been alone, but she wasn't because she'd read in my eye I was the swat type. Now she was going coy on Moke because she was getting sympathy.

I was willing to bet if I was fool enough to lead her to the washroom she'd lie on the tiles and howl like a wolf until she'd reduced Eustace's clientele to overcooked mush, then she'd let them take her home in an ambulance. Feeding her dainty drops of cognac on the way while a pack of big strong guys supported her in their muscular arms. I met 'em, you get 'em, but you don't got to like 'em.

"You seen Eustace's washroom?" I said. "Get me the pack and some alcohol and I'll scrub it off right here. Don't look lethal."

I thought that would knock out some of the nonsense and it did. She pulled her sleeve down in a hurry and said in her tiny girly voice, "Oh, no, it's only a scratch. It scarcely hurts at all."

Of course that got the guys going and we had to let our steaks get cold for fifteen minutes while the both of them fussed around her dabbing at minuscule bruises with wads of cotton and spraying nuskin delicately over the rougher angles. She didn't actually scream, she made the kind of held-breath whimpering noises that tell the world you're suffering torments but you're too fucking brave to complain. In a pig's eye.

I let them get on with it and ate. They looked at me reproachfully but I'd figured that was how they were supposed to look. What was interesting me was finding what particular asylum this desert flower had escaped from with the intention of taking her right back soonest. Christ, we had troubles of our own.

"Ask the kid how she got here," I said to Mokey who was repacking the remains of Eustace's emergency pack. They'd used enough spray and wadding for a field hospital.

He made a rueful Moke-face that said, "Why don't you ask her yourself?" and hinted he'd made a good guess why not. He has this nasty habit of mind-reading.

"I've run away," the kid said, as if it was Mokey who'd asked the question. She spoke up into his face, anyway, her pink quivery lips maybe three inches from his mouth. Her cute little voice was quivery, too. Then she turned smartly to take in Dosh in case he'd come unhypnotized while she had her back turned. I figured I could dislike her given time.

"I've never been here before. It's awful. Frightening. Is it always like this?" The quivery lips made a brave little mouth and resumed quivering. "I had to come but I didn't know it would be so frightening."

"It's not so bad," Dosh said in his warmest big-brother deep-tenor. Guaranteed to enliven brass monkeys of both sexes. "You're safe. Why did you run away?"

The dandelion head turned down. She didn't have to keep her big unirised eyes on them now, she'd a captive audience.

"It was my daddy. He—he—"

Her miniature voice wobbled and broke.

"Who's your daddy?" Mokey prompted when it began to look like the mechanism had run down.

"You wouldn't know him, we don't live here. He's—We're—"

"You're Aris," I said brutally. Someone had to feed her her lines or we'd be here all night.

"My daddy's a Technician." Softly. "He manages the furniture complex at East Meadow. I live—I used to live out on the edge of the country with him and my stepmother. That's why I ran away."

Another break in the melody. I remember a friend telling me the fascinating thing about Chinese music isn't the notes but the rests. You spend your time waiting for the next plink. Like water-torture, only more musical. Her family had to be real Chinese.

"Which of them raped you?"

It was meant as therapy, I figured she had us all going and it might bring her to the point.

She bent her fiberoptic fluff a bit further and whispered, "Daddy. Almost every night. For years. Years and years." She lifted her tiny face and there were big salt drops welling from the all-pupil eyes and running down to the point of her chin. "To begin with I thought perhaps it—happened. To everyone. Then I found it didn't. I saw a vid. It gave a number. I was going to call it but my mother—my step-mother caught me. She asked what I was doing. I told her a lie, I was afraid, but she guessed anyway. Then she told my daddy and he hit me with his belt. He hit me a lot. He enjoyed it."

Her insect shoulders hunched, bent almost double under the damasked silk as if someone was beating her right there. A single hiccupping sob jerked her narrow bones.

"And my stepmother stood and watched. She told me I deserved it. Because I was a liar, she would tell everyone I was a liar, they all knew my daddy was a fine man. She said if I went around telling stories like that they'd call the doctor, the mad doctor, and have me sent away. Somewhere special for mad people who say things like that about their fathers. So I was afraid. And I let him go on and on because I was afraid of him. But after the whipping he gave me it all got worse."

Another more violent sob. "I think he found he liked it. I used to cry and cry, I screamed, I held on to his legs and said to him, Daddy, daddy, don't, it's me, you're hurting me so much . . . He used to get excited, he'd grunt and pant like he was running, only worse, and then he'd do—it, again. Over and over. He really hurt me, he hurt me so in the end I couldn't bear it any longer. Then yesterday they went out, him and Mommy—my stepmother. She makes me call her Mommy but I hate her, she hates me. She knows, I'm sure she does, she likes me to be hurt, they both do. So yesterday when they went out I broke the domestic, the one they leave to look after me. I got one of daddy's big wrenches and I hit it and hit it until it didn't move any more. Then I ran away."

She lifted the huge welling eyes. "I took a public traxie, I had a little money in my card. I thought I'd come down here where there are so many people you can get lost and find somewhere to live and look for something to do. Among decent people. I've heard there are decent unemployed people, you can do anything. Work in a shop, or a cafe, like this."

She looked around. "Well, maybe not quite like this. I didn't imagine it like this, on the vids it's different. I thought there were respectable places you could go and—work. Where nobody gets beaten or made to do—horrible things like my daddy made me. I don't mind working, I don't." Her voice, sanded with tears, was tragic. "Only those boys—they stole my card. So now I've no money and nowhere to go, and I can't go back."

Her voice had risen almost loud enough to be audible at six feet. "I truly can't, I'd rather die. I would, I think I'd kill myself. And now I've no money and nowhere to go and I don't know what to do." She turned the periwinkle-ringed darknesses from Dosh to Moke and back again. I didn't rate the treatment, being a nasty guy. "What am I going to do?"

I knew the answer to that as well as she did.

"Eat your steak," I said roughly before either of them had a chance to actually fall on his knees while begging her to come and live with us. "What's the use of real fake prote if you let it get cold? And you probably won't see onions again this side New Year. You better get used to it."

The guys looked at me with two pairs of hurt eyes, one

blue, one green. I glared right back. A real public enemy,
that's me.

I sleep with Dosh unless he and Mokey have a private
arrangement, or he's out, or Moke's looking more than
usually plaintive. Tonight I stood around while they fell
over each other to offer Mallore the use of the shower, point
out grazes they hadn't nuskinned yet and apologize for our
packing cases.

The brat went on shivering, clutched my shirt around her
like a nun's robe, creasing it in the process, and carried on
so much at the smallest glimpse of skin anybody'd think she
was still in diapers. You can take my word she wasn't.
Finally they got her Mokey's towel and Dosh's bathrobe
and she spent the best part of an hour using enough water
and power to hose out the Augean stables and bring the
electricity company down on our necks.

Nobody noticed it was me was half-naked for God's sake,
and that after a long day's wining, dining and spacing either
Moke or me could have used a bath ourselves. I put on a
sweater and waited for the end of the circus.

And when it came, damn me if she didn't shimmer out on
the tips of her toes like Peter Pan and wrap herself around
Dosh so tight I expected to see him turn blue.

"I'm frightened," she whimpered.

Personally I'd have laid one on her and given her reason.
Dosh fought gallantly for breath, wheezed a couple of sweet
nothings in her winkly ear and carried her to his pad like
Rudolph Valentino. That left Moke in the middle of the
floor with the expression of a kid just saw his best enemy
take off with his roller-skates and me on my crate. The
inside of my expression felt like sophisticated irony. I can't
speak for the outside, not being able to see it.

I cut things short by slamming into the shower for a
three-minute splash and retired to my personal pad to be

mad in private. Considering the squeakings and heavings coming from Dosh's corner of the floor, privacy was difficult. Mokey went on standing looking lost and deprived, then he dropped his jeans and took to the shower himself.

I waited for our little lost lamb to whimper as a sign she'd never seen a naked guy before, and she did. There ought to be a law against being so goddamned predictable. Especially considering what she seemed to be up to with Dosh, not to mention the story about Daddy. Maybe Techs do it with their boots on.

When Moke came out he slunk damply away to fetch his quilt. I suspected him of wanting to heap it on the goddess but apparently he just felt in need of survival. He lugged it across to me and showed signs of being about to get in.

"Go away, Moke," I snarled.

He stood there looking forlorn.

"It's cold," he said.

"Right. That's what that thing's for. You switch on the heating element, it's that red dingus on the side."

He hunkered down like a nesting stork and perched his narrow ass on the edge of my pad, hugging the quilt around him.

"Can I stay, talk to you a bit?"

"No. I'm asleep."

I closed my eyes. He stayed there, knees to his chin, his forehead propped on the folds of his quilt, until I damned near was asleep. When I hadn't moved for a minute or two he cautiously slid in beside me and wiggled his bony carcass into the bit of space I'd left. I pretended not to notice. He really was cold. Hell, the guy had been getting stretched all day. I rolled over and put my arms around him.

"Okay, but it stops here, right? I'm not going in for his 'n hers both sides of the floor to the rhythm of a drum, it's a damned orgy."

"I'm just cold, Cassie," he whispered.

"You believe that kid's story?" I whispered back.

He seemed surprised. "Sure. Don't you?"

"God knows. For all I know every Tech in the place does it. Haven't many upper-class acquaintances."

"She's so young."

"Yeah, I know. Wears off."

"You're mad," he diagnosed.

"Who, me? Now why would that be?"

"I don't know," he whispered after a pause. Guys can be awful fucking dumb. "It's just— Cass, aren't you frightened for her?"

"I'm frightened for all of us. Why her in particular? Looks to me she found one warm Dosh to cling to. Aren't you jealous?"

He thought about it. "No. I mean the film. What are we getting her into?"

"Deep question. Wish I knew what we were in ourselves. Meantime, looks to me like we got to be four. I told you what I got against communes?"

"What?"

"There's always somebody left out. Want to make bets on who?"

He shivered against me. "I think they're asleep."

"Great. Let's copy."

We lay together under his quilt with our arms around each other, like Hansel and Gretel in the big bad forest. It was a long time before either of us got in any dream time.

Morning dawned fair and fine about three hours later with a lot of thumping, splashing and giggling, male and female. I tried to ignore it. Moke seemed to be unconscious. When I smelled burning bacon I gave up and rolled out on the floor, gray and groggy.

The first thing I saw was Peter Pan flittering around the

room in my best oil-black catsuit with my silver belt and
boots knotted and screwed into dashing shapes above and
below. Her dandelion hair was crackling with joyous
electricity, attracted by my hand-made crystal earrings
which were whipping and tinkling like leaves in a storm. I
could make some educated guesses where she'd found her
face-paint, too. Among other things it was the wrong color.
I'm dark.

I got up from the boards in one swoop of sheer levitating
rage. It's amazing what adrenaline can do for you. One
minute previous I'd've sworn I wasn't going to be fit to
crawl for half an hour. I got to her in three strides, got the
belt off in a single furious whip, unzipped the suit with the
other hand and started emptying her out of it. She squealed
like someone was gutting a pig. When I thought about it it
wasn't such a bad idea.

Mokey sat up in bed with his hair tangled over his face
just as Dosh came bolting out of the kitchen with the skillet
in his hand and they both rushed to the rescue. Of, naturally,
Mallore.

I'd go a long way before I'd kick Dosh in the personals,
so I gave him it on the kneecap instead. It probably hurt me
more than it hurt him but like all berserkers I don't feel it till
later. It's one of my few fighting advantages given my size.

"You guys interfere and I'll fucking kill you."

Moke let go my arm and backed off. He was pale.

"Cass, she didn't mean . . ."

"The hell she didn't. This is girl stuff, keep your guy
noses out. Any bim helps herself to some other bim's
fucking wardrobe, she gets her ass whupped. It's in the rules
and she knows 'em. If she don't she's learning. If you want
to die, come near me."

"She hasn't any clothes, Cassie!" Dosh yelled, full stage
volume.

''Wrong. She has a whole slew of mine, but give me thirty seconds and I'll fix it.''

I resisted the temptation to take out her earlobes along with the earrings and unhooked them, keeping her head still with a fistful of her hair. When I'd finished I guess Dosh could be said to be correct. I smeared my hand across her over-painted mouth to complete the job, which also put a temporary sock in the squealing, and let her drop on her ass on the floor. Then I stood panting.

''You guys were saying?''

Dosh had got hold of himself. He was breathing almost as hard as I was but he had the sense to keep it down.

''Cassandra, this child is naked.''

''Right. I just naked her. Was it you gave her permission to go through my closet?''

He flushed. ''I showed her which it was.''

''And you told her she could help herself to anything she fancied.''

He was looking the smallest bit hangdog. I read that one right away. He hadn't. Even he knew better. What he'd done was not stop her and hope the storm wouldn't break. Now he was trying to make me feel guilty. I didn't.

''Cass, she was wrong.'' Moke got in fast before somebody could make things worse. ''Only it's true she hasn't any clothes. She should have asked. But won't you lend her something so she can go out?''

''No,'' I said. ''If she'd had any common decency I would've. Since she hasn't, she can go out the way she is. May cure her of whinnying every time she shows her ankles. If you'll excuse me, I'm going to tidy my closet. I'm subsequently going to put a lock on it. Anybody got any objections?''

It seemed no one had. I went, boiling down slowly on the way. My belt was ruined. The boots might recover and they might not. The suit would survive once I'd washed her out of it. The underwear—gray lace—had got torn in the disagreement and I slung it in the garbage on the way past. I had to see the closet before I got really mad. And worse.

That cow had been through it like a dog down a burrow. No wonder Dosh was embarrassed. He had to know how it would end. All my stuff was piled on the floor and twisted into heaps, shoes, clothes and jewelry mixed together. My makeup containers looked like she'd excavated them with a mechanical digger.

But the worst was, she'd been through to the back and she'd come within an inch of taking the boards out. I didn't know why she hadn't. Maybe Dosh stopped her. But if she'd gone one inch further she'd have come on what nobody touches. My working gear. My dart-gun, my ya, my credit-cards, my coolsuit, which rates twenty years in itself, my private stash of blue. Everything that could send me down for the rest of my life.

I sat back on my heels and thought. As soon as our unwelcome guest went so did my things—to somewhere nobody was going to find them. Hard on the guys, I'd trusted them. Even to use my stash if they needed it. No more.

And okay, it was a dumb place to keep it. I saw that. I'd relied too much on Yeller. I hadn't expected a spy inside the house. From now things were different. Worse. Much. But different. I started untangling my clothes and putting them back on hangers.

When I'd finished clearing up and got back to the main loft properly dressed and mostly cooled down, Mallore was finishing up a plate of bacon and eggs that would have sunk a farm-hand and poking her pinkies out while she did it. When she saw me she faked terror and hid behind Dosh, who was fool enough to let her.

She was wearing a pair of clean but raggy jeans that had

to belong to Mokey, slashed off below the knee which meant Moke wasn't going to have a use for them when he got them back, and an embroidered Cossack shirt that was Dosh's favorite. I decided not to comment and dropped a slice of bread into the toaster.

Moke writhed on his case and Dosh shoved his last mouthful of bacon down and got up. I noticed there was no place set for me. Dosh's ultimate sign of disapproval. I was less than totally crushed but I did have a couple of thoughts for the future. I figured getting mad now was playing into her hands. I poured myself some coffee and sat on the box he'd vacated.

"We," said Dosh emphatically, "are going out. To buy clothes. For Mallore."

I waggled my fingers without turning around.

"Have a nice day."

I could feel him tensed behind me waiting for me to apologize, or kill someone, or maybe scream for the fire department. When I did none of those things he drew a deep breath through his nose like a horse and went out with dignity. At least I guess he did. The door banged quite hard.

Mokey took in a long gloomy sigh.

"Cass, she was wrong. But go easy, will you? She's only a little girl."

"Sure," I said. "How old would you make her?"

"Sixteen? Fifteen?"

"Let's suppose she's the same age as Juliet. That makes her six years younger than me. You know what I was doing at that age?"

"Time," he offered, without smiling.

"Nuts. I'd learned better. I was apprenticed to Razor, working the uptown fur trade nights and serving in a bar days."

"Yeah. I'd left home too. But I guess rich kids are protected."

"Maybe. But unless that fey little magpie learns some manners, protection's what she's going to need. From me. I learned, you learned. Does she look feeble-minded?"

He sighed again.

"Okay. Pass the word to Doshky. Wasn't me started the war. All she has to do is grow up and I won't lay a finger on her. If she doesn't I'll play schoolmarm and teach her. Am I unreasonable?"

His look spoke for itself. I was sick and tired of the lot of them.

"I'm going to buy a lock," I said. "For my closet. Don't tell anyone, but even if one of you breaks in again there'll be nothing in it. See you, Moke."

"Cassie," he said half-heartedly.

I didn't look back. There are some things you got to stop at the beginning.

We had a good lock on our door. In three years of living together we'd never had a lock on anything else. The locks came in with Mallore.

Among other things.

I was heading for the public Clean-Op with my catsuit under my arm when I noticed something four-legged and the wrong shape scuttling behind. It wasn't exactly hiding. It was just entertaining itself by evaporating into doorways every time I turned around.

After a couple of looks I identified it. The deformed kid from the Dog, the one that carried messages. I turned sharply at the next intersection and did a vanishing act myself. When it crawled around the corner sniffing for tracks I came out like a bullet and picked it up by the back of the neck.

It was a good precaution. It kicked furiously and just missed my eye with its claws.

"Looking for me?"

It turned its wrong-shaped head and grinned with animal teeth, strings of drool hanging from the corners of its mouth.

"Why look you?"

"That's what I'm asking. I'm waiting for the answer. How about I carve you to shape, short stuff?"

"Look you," it admitted. "You call code tonight quart eight, listen good."

"Wasting your time, Rover. No codes. Auntie's busy."

It turned unexpectedly intelligent hazel eyes. "You better listen. Or bad things happen, okay?"

"Sorry, Rover. Bad things already happened. You tell your bosses. No codes. Not safe, double plus ungood, you receiving?"

"Receiving. Boss not, tell you."

I dumped it on the pavement. It was making my wrist ache. "Give him my love. Make space, Cuddles, or I'll give you a boost-assisted take-off."

It drooled down my pants leg and took off an inch ahead of my boot. I wiped off my pants and resumed the road for the Clean-Op. A missed code was all I needed. What I didn't need was a genetically engineered werepup to tell me how the bosses thought. They paid well and resented refusal. Enough to buy contracts sometimes on recalcitrants.

But getting filmed in full burglary wasn't going to do any of our careers any good. It was a subject I just didn't care to discuss in the middle of the street with an animal didn't necessarily understand English. You can never tell with genetic remakes.

The Clean-Op dealt with the catsuit, though three machines were out of order again. The Strip's getting more run-down every day. If they don't watch it we're going to stop attracting tourists.

I paused at Adelaide's window by the corner of the Mall, half-thinking of replacing my lace and half of buying the kid some functional pants. I knew what Dosh was likely to get.

After breakfast I'd fished Mallore's dress out of the garbage to look it over (we don't run to recyc, we have to haul our own trash cans out for the local truck) and it was what I'd thought. Heavy satin in beetle-back colors of green and gold, barely long enough to cover her ass with large holes in eloquent places. Torn to shreds, but it looked to me there was a structural weakness somewhere because solid fabric shouldn't rip so easily. I'd heard of it as entertainment but not as worn by gentlemen's daughters, even if Daddy was ill-behaved.

I dropped it back but I was puzzled. I figured I'd get her some jeans anyhow. I didn't go with the idea of her wearing Moke's and from the dress I reckoned she had as much natural taste as a blue-assed macaw.

I was leaning into Adelaide's holo-display when Sword-fish spoke in my ear.

"Moved into the upper classes, Cassie?"

I didn't bother to look around. The most you see of Swordfish if you're lucky is a pair of evil eyes about six and a half feet off the pavement.

"What makes you think that, Sword?"

"Hear you refused a code."

"Correct. Tell the guy I'm saving his life."

"He'll be touched."

"Sure he will. Tell him at the same time we're being fucking filmed, killer. Unhealthy for all of us. No codes until it's over, okay?"

"I think you'd have done better to refuse the film," he said gently above my left shoulder. I had a cold flush. I hadn't thought they'd call muscle so quickly or Sword would buy the contract. Stupid of me. Sword would buy a contract on anybody. I don't say even his mother because I'm not sure he had one.

He felt me flinch and laughed.

"Not today, Cassandra. I'm just warning you. As a friend. If you aren't taking the code you'd better lay in artillery. It's a cold climate this week."

"To use on you, Sword? I'll make it expensive. Listen, it ain't my choice. I live with guys. You know that."

"I know. Told you it was a mistake. You'd better live with me, we're a good couple. Make it very expensive, Cass. Whoever you use it on isn't going to come cheap."

"Thanks. Appreciate it. Just wish you'd teach your messenger not to dribble."

He laughed again farther away. "Any time. See you, kid."

The voice was still receding. When I turned around there was nothing to be seen. I don't know how Swordfish lives permanently in a coolsuit but there's a lot of things I don't know. What I do know is you don't take his warnings lightly.

I abandoned Adelaide's, to the disappointment of Adelaide, who'd been making a give-you-a-discount sign out of the window. I signaled, "Later," and headed for the alleys behind the hypermarket. Hallway arms all of us. If he's in the mood he can nearly make odds equal. But nobody's ever equal with Swordfish. It's what he gave up being human for.

You wouldn't notice the armory if you weren't looking. It's a dingy door with paint that might once have been wine and now looks like old blood, squeezed between a junkshop and a thrift shop full of second-hand clothes, of the sort you wouldn't want on your baby. There's a bell-push by the side with a faded slip of card with "Hallveg" lettered in ink so yellow it's barely readable. Hallway sometimes pretends it's his name. Some people believe him.

If you push the bell and he recognizes you, the door leads on to an enclosed tunnel under the thrift shop that comes out in a yard full of trash cans where the neighborhood dogs have a toilet. A set of dirt-encrusted windows covers a workshop with a crooked sliding door in galvanized zinc. The door doesn't slide any more but if Hall goes on recognizing you he'll open the service-hatch and let you sidle in. It's so narrow you have to. That way he gets fewer nasty surprises.

He's a youngish guy so elongated he looks like a basketball player, with an innocent face, mild blue eyes and mechanic's hands. He wears scrubbed-out blue coveralls and whitened tennis shoes like a theater-nurse. But he sees himself as a surgeon. A pathologist of navy-surplus this and that, a lot of which maybe wasn't surplus before it got liberated. Nobody asks him where he gets it.

To my knowledge he's never used his own merchandise in his life, being a conscientious pacifist, but he helps other people stay alive. I think that's how he sees it. And anything he sells is functional. He's careful of the lives in his hands. It's nice. The other thing about his conscience is he only sells to private citizens. Like me, and Swordfish. Arming the House is for professionals. His medicine's being better than they are. Believe me, he is.

He let me in and I picked my way through the dogdirt to his door. It always takes me aback how quietly efficient his machinery is considering the state of the outside, and how clinical he keeps his workshop. You really could use his bench for an operating table. Hell, it's probably cleaner than the hospital. Hallway's a craftsman.

When I came in, he was sitting at the back on a lab stool doing precision surgery on an anonymous black box that might have done anything from locating lost lambs to firing torpedoes. His head was covered by a helmet bristling with sensors that was plugged in at both wrists, his fingers tipped with micro-tools. I hitched my rump on the edge of a table until he'd finished.

Maybe ten minutes later he put it down, removed his finger-extensions one by one and fitted them back into their dustproof case, then shed the helmet. He unplugged the wrist-jacks, removed the cable from behind his ear and put the whole issue back onto its stand. Then he turned around.

"Hi, Cass. Another job already? How did the stuff go?"

He's always concerned things should work properly.

"Great, thanks. Matter of fact that's the trouble. Got offered another job."

He shook his head, disapproving. "Too close. You didn't take that Irmana thing?"

"No way. That is I don't know what the offer was. I just refused."

His pale eyes darkened. "Protective artillery?"

"Such is Sword's recommendation." I let it hang a moment. "I'd've come anyway. We're stuck with a film contract."

He whistled. "Hard. You couldn't turn it down?"

"My mates couldn't. I'm beginning to think one way and another I need personal protection."

"You want advice?" He lifted a brow. "Hire Sword. Before someone else does."

"Not stupid. But I hope it's not that bad. What you got I could use myself?"

He wandered around his cases looking thoughtful.

"Navy laser-rifle? You got an ear-socket? Latest thing. Short of implant surgery, which comes expensive. Jack her in and point. She does the rest."

"Fire at will, huh?" I said sourly. "A bit showy around town."

"Wrong," he said. "She's made for sniping. Comes apart, fits in a case would go in your handbag. Knowing your handbags. Wouldn't even weigh you down. Cero-fiber alloy, hardly know you're holding it. Nearest thing yet to point your finger and zap."

"Contract-gun, right?"

"Listen, Cass, if you think there's someone with a contract walking behind you, you better be at least equal in fire-power. If you won't hire Sword. I told you, this won't match up to a service killer with a neural targeting program, but it's the next best. You won't meet anything hotter on the street. If you would I'd've heard."

"What do you get if you're caught carrying?"

He grinned briefly. "Don't ask. You need this baby or you don't."

"Let's look."

When I left an hour and a half later my bag was hanging heavy. It wasn't wholly the rifle, which was everything Hallway said it was, it was three gas grenades and several bits of gadgetry we'd talked over on the side. My credit card balanced by being lighter. It's lucky I go in for bags the size of mail-sacks. If you get them made in golden calf, they hardly ever search you.

This time I did call on Adelaide and she gave me a satisfactory discount on two pairs of jeans, two sets of navy-blue lace ought to blow Dosh's mind if he still had one, and an acid-green shirt that happened to be there. After my discussion with Hallway I needed the discount.

At the end of our alley I saw Moke staggering towards me from the other direction. He had a sack on his shoulder anyone else would have had sent by carrier and a strong list to port. Mokey's got this thing about owing us because he doesn't pay rent. If he only knew, Dosh and me are waiting for him to make his first two or three million to live off him for the rest of our lives. So okay, it's slow coming.

He got level and let the sack hit the pavement. It looked like cement, it smelled like cement and it sounded like cement. I made an intelligent guess.

"Cement."

"Right." He wiped a gritty wrist over his sweating forehead and sat down on the load. He looked tired. "Going to do some work for a change."

"For a change." I fished his package out of my bag. "Catch. Bought you some jeans."

He brightened.

"Hey, you didn't have to. I understand . . ."

"No, you don't. If you think it's an apology, think again. I hate to see your ass hanging out on that bimbo's account."

The overcast came back. Low-pressure area over the Azores.

"Don't be hard on her, Cass. She's only a kid."

"She's a cute statuette in pure spun sugar. Can't you see she's got you guys dancing the polka? She's making you into a circus act. Knowing Dosh, I got a pair for her too. She can wear them while she's doing the dishes."

"Cassie . . ." he said pleadingly.

"Cassie, what? You figure I'm going to devote myself to painting Mademoiselle's toenails, or washing out her smalls for her, maybe? If she's living here she can work like us."

"I'll do it," he muttered.

"No, you won't. Fucking Wendy can do it. Getting her hands wet'll be good for her. This is the real world, Moke."

"I wonder sometimes if it can be."

Me too, as a matter of fact.

"Back to the ranch, Martin. Before she reorganizes the place so there's no room for you and me."

He gave me a pale grin. "Damn Eklund. Nobody's called me Martin in seven years."

"Hard, hard."

"You're right though, Cass, we're changing. I don't like it."

"Me neither. Who said we're paid to?"

"Wish we knew what this damn film's about and when it's starting."

"Thought it had."

"Eklund?" He shook his head. "I don't know. He's got real art."

"Probably has real artists. Gun artists and camera artists. He's an Ari." I jerked my head at the cement. "That's for him?"

"Thought I might as well. Maquette." He rose wearily

and hefted the sack onto his shoulder. "Got some ideas. I've
wanted to work in stone."

"Way to go, Moke. If he doesn't buy it, we'll hang it on
the City Council."

He smiled sadly. "Yeah."

We turned down the alley in step, him leaning one way
under his load, me the other with my parcels. We came to a
stop at the same instant.

Our door was open.

We went up the steps at a run. Halfway I heard a groan
and braked. I doubled to lean over the edge. I could see
broken wood, and a spreading pool of something sinister.

"Moke, where's Dosh? Get up there, fast."

I vaulted to the ground and ducked under the arch.
Yeller's back was turned to me, spikes of dirty hair showing
over the collar of his mud-colored coat. Something dark and
sticky was crawling over it and pooling out into the area.
The stench was appalling, filth, excrement and something
else, sweet and heavy.

I knelt beside him.

Mokey arrived two seconds later, his bare feet crunching
on the boards of what had been Yeller's living box. "Let
me."

He bent and turned him gently over.

"God, Moke."

Yeller was limp as a doll and his face was a color I've
never seen. I rarely stay to watch them die. Yellow-gray
under its dirt, with a sheen like melting wax. It had a slack
innocence like he was sleeping, that wiped out his deformities and left him with the ghost of someone else showing
through from another dimension. A guy who'd been young
once and had once been handsome. His breathing was
horrible, an animal grunting.

I felt sick. He'd been harmless, and so badly hurt already.

"Ambulance, Cass."

"I know, I run the fastest. What about Doshky?"

"This guy's going to die without help."

I thought maybe he was going to die anyway. But I was already running.

I beat the wagon by maybe five minutes. When I got back Dosh was half-lying on the steps, his face pale and his yellow hair slicked down with blood. A dark stream was rilling from under the towel pressed to his scalp. His exercise tights were torn and his eyes black with shock. But he was alive. There was no sign of Mallore.

"You okay, guy?"

"Yeah. Give Moke a hand, Cassie."

I slid over. Mokey was bending by Yeller's body with a basin and a pile of torn linen that was our best sheets or all Dosh's working shirts. Or both. His knees, the water and the sodden rags were crimson.

"Hold the bowl will you, Cass? I daren't move him. It's a medic job. His skull's fractured, and God knows what else."

That was obvious. There was a shallow indentation like a saucer in his temple and a torn flap of scalp above his one eye. Mokey was pressing pads of folded linen against it, trying to stop the bleeding. The pads soaked through faster than I could fold. The blood went on pouring like a tap.

"Where're the fucking medics?" Moke snarled, throwing a handful aside and snatching another wad. "He's losing more than he's got."

"Coming."

You could hear the undulating howl blocks away. Moke dragged a gasping breath and pressed harder.

The noise seemed to get through to Yell, wherever he was. He gave a louder grunt. His one eyelid flickered and lifted enough to show a line of white like an old billiard ball.

Then it sank under its own weight. His twisted mouth moved.

"It's okay. Yell, it's the good guys. Hang in there." Mokey had his lips against the crusted brown-stained ear, his hand holding the pad. "We'll get you out."

The lips moved again and Yeller found a thread of breath to give himself a voice. He whispered one word.

"House."

We supported Dosh into the elevator. He was on his feet and the derms on his throat were strictly medical, but he was groggy with concussion and shock. He leaned on us hard.

"They took Mallore."

"How, Doshky?"

He sighed, leaning back against the wall. "Three guys, maybe four. I didn't see. I was doing my exercises when someone knocked. Mallore went to open it—guess she thought it was one of you. I yelled but it was too late. By the time I got there she was screaming and they were carrying her out. One guy holding her arms, one her legs. She was shrieking and kicking and they were swearing at her. There may have been another outside. Then someone shoved a scarf in her mouth. I ran across to jump them and someone else hit me from behind."

He made a parody of a grin. "Guess I was lucky, or I'd be going Yell's way. They can't have hit hard. But I was out for a while. When I came around it was a bit before I could make myself get up. Legs didn't work. I was still lying there when I heard someone coming. Thought it was them to finish me off, but it was my old friend Moke."

Mokey slid the gate back and guided him out onto the landing. "They've turned the place over, Cass. You've never seen such a mess."

I thought maybe I had. Messes I'm an expert in. "Poor Yell."

"Right," Dosh agreed. "I guess he tried to warn us. Not even his business, trying to help. Turds."

"Two guys holding, and her struggling. That's a full-time job. So someone else to do the gag. And at least one behind you. That's four."

"Yeah," Mokey said. "They knew where to come and they knew there were several of us. Guess Dosh was lucky to pass out before they fixed him too."

We'd got to the door. I poked my head in and looked around. Turned over, yeah. There was hardly a thing in one piece. Even our packing cases. Matchwood, like Yeller's. Clothes and bedding scattered.

"Yell said House."

"Yeah, he did."

"Look that way to you?"

Moke shook his head doubtfully. "Don't know how House looks, Cass. Don't have your experience."

"Looks damned queer to me. House is recognizable and I'd guess Yell's had my experience. They don't smash things up for entertainment. Just if they have a point to make. They could have smashed Dosh's head in as easily as Yeller's, but they didn't. Sorry, Doshky," as he shuddered. "That was a nice scientific sap. Neat tap, nasty headache, you're going to need a date with a hairdresser."

He had a shaven patch in his mane where they'd grown his scalp together.

"Fuck the hairdresser."

"If you must. Point is, they could've done the same for Yell, 'stead of caving his skull. He's not as young or mobile as you. Don't add. Looks plain brutality. Then they turn the place over, after they've taken Mallore away. Don't smell of House to me. Not unless someone paid them for something specific. House does things neatly."

"Yell could've disturbed them," Mokey offered. "Maybe they had to shut him up fast."

"Sweet Moke, you know anyone come down here to stop a Donnybrook? *Especially* if they saw they'd have to stop a Donnybrook?"

He shook his head. People our way have awful bad eyes and ears sometimes. It's a survival instinct.

"They came for Mallore," Dosh said. "The rest—you could be right. It could be a warning."

"Who from, lover? It's a good idea to leave a note, when you want somebody not to do something. Enough to kill for it."

"Her father?"

"Could be. But if Yell's right, that makes him House. Not what one expects of a respectable Tech. Even a bent one. They're real snobbish people."

"Maybe he hired someone."

"Not a lot of someones in this business, Doshky. It's specialized. At this level."

Moke groaned and sank down on the remains of a bed-pad.

"So what are we going to do?"

"Do?" I said. "Ask Dosh, kid. We're going to get her back, of course."

I stood in the doorway and looked around. The Dog was as usual. The latest beauty was in the fishbowl and he was still keeping his distance. He had a future. At my shoulder Dosh shifted.

"So?"

"Patience. I'm looking for the kid."

"What kid, for Christ's sake?"

"My little mate with teeth. Who drools. You don't find Swordfish by whistling. Sit and try to look normal. I'll talk to Eustace."

He did. Looking normal was beyond him but he ordered a beer and tried to look like he was drinking. Mallore had got to him. He was wriggling like a worm in a jar. I glared and he tried to sit still.

We'd got him to the hairdresser after a quarrel, on the grounds that being shaved was romantic but attracted attention. So the outside of his head was as usual. It was the inside that had me worried. He still had a couple of derms under the collar of his shirt, but that was so ordinary at the Dog no one was likely to notice.

I slid onto a stool and worked at catching Eustace's eye. When he saw I really wanted him he finished polishing the four square inches in front of his nose—he hates people to think he comes because he's called—and wandered in my direction.

"Yeah?"

Eustace's manners are uniformly charming. It's a mistake to take them at face value.

"Anise and mint, Eus. And a word."

He grunted and made with bottles. Then he jerked his head at the far end, where a space seemed to have cleared. I've never figured out his signals to his potmen but they work. I took my glass and wandered in that direction like a dame who's lost someone, but not of importance.

At the end I mountaineered another stool and leaned towards him.

"I'm looking for Sword, Eustace. You seen his kid?"

He polished the bar with concentration, his meaty face expressionless apart from its normal veneer of hostility.

"Bad idea unless you really want him."

"I really want him."

"Does he want you?"

"He's going to. I'm just waiting for the chance to lay big bucks on him."

"Why'n't you go sit with your pretty friend? Looks like he's got piles. Tell him if he wants a bath, toilet's down the corridor."

"Wrong. His trouble's at the other end."

But I went back to our table. It was true Dosh gave the impression of more swimming in his beer than drinking. He'd poured a puddle in front of him and was making ring patterns on the tiles.

"Knock it off, Doshky, people are looking. I said make like normal. Eus is on it. Try to keep your ass still, huh?"

He made an effort and took a sip like a kid being heroic with the ipecacuanha.

"I'm scared, Cassie. What do you think these guys are doing to her?"

The same song he'd been singing all afternoon. I gave him the same answer.

"I don't know. But the best way to stop them's professional help. Dammit, we don't know where to start looking. Unless she told you something she didn't tell us."

He shook his head miserably.

"She talked about dresses, and parties, and her pony. Sounds like a big house in the suburbs. She didn't say where and I didn't like to ask. Could be anywhere."

"Okay. Keep still. And don't annoy Sword, he's jinky. I like you alive."

He returned to his glass. The way he was forcing it I wasn't sure I blamed Eustace for taking offense. His beer's bad, but not that bad.

About a quarter of an hour later I noticed a warm damp patch around my left ankle and looked down to see Cuddles slobbering lasciviously over my shoe. I used willpower to restrain the kick itching in my thigh muscles. I needed the brat. It grinned at me with all its teeth, knowing damned well why it was getting away with it.

"Looking for someone?" it dog-whistled.

I noticed sometimes its speech was less Man-Friday than others. It probably got off on driving people crazy. If you looked the way it did you probably had to take amusement where you could find it.

"Correct."

"You don't wanna kick me?"

"If you look hard, you'll see I'm restraining myself. That's because I'm looking for someone. If I don't see him fast, the situation can be rectified."

"Nasty," it said with approval. "Come. Five minutes. Not him."

"We're in a hurry, short stuff. I don't have time to run errands. He comes, because it'll save me the time it would take to come back and explain. I don't offer big bucks for nothing."

"Sword won't like it," it said happily.

"Let me and him sort it out. Five minutes. Go."

It went, taking a detour to scare the shit out of a pair of tarts trying to turn an honest trick at the bar. In the Dog it's a waste of time anyhow.

Dosh and I stepped into the street five minutes later. There was nothing and nobody in sight.

"Little bastard's cheated you," he snarled, pulling fretfully at his collar and nearly dislodging a derm.

"He plays games, Doshky. Thinks he's a fairy from the bottom of the garden. Let's make like tulips."

We strolled slowly down the block, a lover and his lass. At least, I did. Dosh had forgotten he was a great actor tonight. He moved around like he had ants in his pants. I had to grab his arm to keep up the illusion and prevent him doing a four-minute mile in some useless direction.

At the next corner a whistle came from a doorway and I made out our kid. It looked like it was cocking its leg on the holo-display. When it saw we'd noticed it frisked off four-footed, moving surprisingly fast.

"Stay this side," I said to Dosh. "Don't want anyone to think we're with that."

"I'm not stupid," he snapped. The only time he says that is when he is being. I wrapped myself around his arm and tried to look like we weren't running.

The kid led us along the Strip, onto the main drag and down the next entrance ramp onto the walkway. It had a hell of a good time out there, changing lanes like a mad monkey and terrifying pedestrians every three steps. It had the makings of a pre-adolescent sex-maniac. It was happy to terrify anyone, but it preferred pretty ladies, especially in the kind of skirt you can stick your nose up if you're at knee level. I'd've kicked its surgically implanted teeth in. Most of them shrieked like steam-whistles, and I'd hate to tell you how the little shit reacted.

After a couple of miles of entertainment it turned back to the slow lanes, got onto the old-ladies-and-weight-carriers' strip between off ramps, stood poised on the edge—on two legs for once—and glanced back to see we were ready.

"Watch it," I said. "Here we go."

When it dived it nearly took me by surprise. I didn't see an exit. But I have faith in Swordfish. I grabbed Dosh's sleeve and we threw ourselves blindly into the dark.

We landed on dusty tarmac and stood to look around while we cleaned off. A gap in the rail, scarcely more than six feet wide, led into a black passageway with something that thumped at the end. The kid whistled from the darkness in front.

"What the hell's this?" Dosh hissed.

"Looks like a service tunnel. Keep going. If somebody's about to kill you you'll never know. Sword's efficient."

"Thanks," he said sourly.

We groped in the direction of the whistle. The surface was even beneath our feet. The sides felt like concrete. Behind us the lights of the walkway threw stroboscopic flashes the length of the tunnel, giving glimpses of bare walls, whitish concrete above our heads, some kind of barrier in front. The rumble of the walk drowned all noise except the rhythmic thumping up ahead.

"You come?" the kid whistled near my knee.

"Yeah. Dribble on me and I'll kill you."

It made an edge-of-hearing sound that might have been a giggle.

"Through here."

A slit of cold glare opened in our faces and the kid's skinny rump slid through in silhouette. I grabbed Dosh's hand and followed. A door slammed and we stood blinking.

The high-ceilinged room stretched in front to an unseen distance. The thumping was loud and came from all around us. The machinery was covered with protective casings like mechanical mountains that filled the place almost to the roof, and dials and colored warning lights flashed from their sides. The main light came from the ceiling, where shadowless tubes furrowed it from end to end.

It took me a moment to make sense of it, then I realized we were in a walkway maintenance-station with the city above our heads. The rhythmic thumping hit our ears from both sides as the strips circulated behind us. With that knowledge I could see we were in an entrance bay, and the big room also stretched away backwards on both sides under the walkway itself.

The kid was standing on one leg looking self-satisfied and scratching its left ribs with its right toenails. The sight was repulsive. It grinned like a shark.

"You explain to Swordfish now. Thataway."

It jerked a steel-clawed thumb to the acreage behind us where the walkway crashed. I signaled to Dosh.

"Thanks, Fido. Remind me to kick you on the way out. Your manners are disgusting."

Its grin widened and it began to lift its leg. I turned away before it had a chance to finish. Dosh padded at my shoulder, looking apprehensive. He knew bad places but this one was bad, bad.

We walked between the rows of machines while the thumping grew louder. Behind the entry bay the chamber opened out into a space as wide as a football field with a sharp drop in the ceiling where the returning belt of the walk ran overhead. There was still more than enough room to feel lost.

"So where the hell—?" Dosh muttered.

"Hi, Cass," the smooth voice murmured in my ear. "Thought I said to come alone."

I controlled my reflexes and turned. The eyes were in the usual place, just behind my right shoulder and six and a half feet off the ground. They were sharp, cold, and dark gray. The rest blended so perfectly it was scarcely more than a ripple in the air, and that because he was breathing. He doesn't always. He trusts me.

"Hi, Sword. This is Dosh. We got problems."

"The knockout," his warm deep voice diagnosed. "As opposed to the genius. If you had to bring him your problem's serious. You know my feelings. Let's hear it."

Dosh was bristling, but it's hard to get mad with a guy you can't see. It's a psychological disadvantage.

"We've lost a lady. Very young, very rich, very pretty, you get the picture. We'd like her back."

"Your guy would like her back." He has a habit of getting inside my head drives me nutty. "What do *you* want, Cassandra?"

"The same. It could be House. They wrecked our apartment, sapped Doshky, damn near killed Yeller. Maybe did, he's still out at the hospital. Took the kid. We don't know why, there could be bad answers. It's a rush job, is why I'm paying high. Like now. Tonight."

"Her father's crazy," Dosh supplemented. "God knows what he's doing. They could be torturing her to death. They've had her hours."

The cold gray eyes stayed with me. "Killed Yeller."

"Smashed his skull. Pure brutism, he's harmless. From the kid's story, guy really is out of his mind. We got to get her."

"Doesn't sound like House," he observed.

I didn't say I thought the same.

"Yell said House. Dosh saw four guys, maybe more. Neatly sapped and the place turned over, professional. Nothing in one piece that would break without power tools.

Took the girl, turned the place over while Dosh was out on the floor.''

"They had House weapons," Dosh put in. He was strained. "Gray suits, artillery. I didn't see much, but I saw that. We're not asking you on a pleasure trip. We could do that ourselves."

I motioned him to shut up. Sword doesn't need told. "We don't know where they've taken her. That's the main problem. Apart from manpower. She chattered about a house in the suburbs, but it could be the same place or different. No address. I've stuff on my card. Name your price."

The eyes looked down, expressionless. He'd never once glanced in Dosh's direction, though that didn't mean he wasn't listening. "It'll take numbers. Can't do this kind of job without help."

"As many as you need. Up to my limit."

For an instant the eyes crinkled. "You can't afford me, Cassie. This one's for Yeller." Then they disappeared. He'd turned away. "Dribble? Get Wings."

The deformed kid had crept up behind us, smiling slyly. Now he moved like he'd had a shot of electricity in the backside. He vanished like a streak.

The eyes came back, icy. "I don't suppose you guys would stay at home? Okay. Your entrance, half an hour."

I knew we were alone from the feel. We walked back towards the entrance. Dosh was shaking.

"That guy gives me heebies."

"He means to. But he's the only person I know can save Mallore."

"If anyone can," Dosh murmured. He sounded tormented.

Seemed to me that crack was my heart breaking.

Jumping belts and pounding pavement to our crash took twenty minutes. Mokey was squatting on the floor using a mousse-bomb on the remains of bed-pads. He'd knocked together some less-wrecked crates and dug up a couple of new ones. Considering we were promised riches, we hadn't kicked the economy habit.

He'd really cleared the wreckage. We were short of clothes but the place looked habitable. He'd been working like a dog. Worry takes some people one way and some another.

"I fixed the shower," he said. "How's things?"

He looked gray and tired, smeared with half-liquid patches of mossy rubber.

Dosh had cleared up a lot during the run. Admiration does him good and he'd been getting it. The prospect of action helped too, whether he believed in it or not. The Competent Hero was back.

"Ten minutes. Get some clothes on, Moke, it's going to be cold. How late's your friend likely to be, Cassie?"

"He's not. When Sword says half an hour he means thirty minutes."

"Sure, he can fly," Dosh growled. He began to toss over his wardrobe for hero clothes. "This do?"

"Darker and heavier." I was skinning on my coolsuit, hood thrown back so as not to get stepped on. Invisibility has disadvantages. "Got a jacket, Moke?"

"Have mine." Dosh threw a black leather number with buckles across, and looked gratified when Moke grabbed it and started doing up straps. I thought Mallore had driven Mokey out. Seemed not. "What's that, Cass?"

"Mind your own business." I slung my sports-bag on my shoulder. Reversed, it was invisible. "You guys got metal? If it's House they'll be tooled. Want my dart-gun?"

I figured it had better be Dosh. Moke doesn't like things that go bang. Dosh stuck it awkwardly in his belt and I made an adjustment in the interests of his virility. I hadn't known he owned brass knucks, but he collects surprising things from clients.

Moke was strapping a nozzled cylinder over the jacket. Exceptionally, he was wearing shoes—torn tennis numbers I hadn't seen. Maybe he'd been to the dump. "What's that, Mokey?"

"Door-opener. Thirty minutes. We going?"

In the street there was a rippling of the air, subdued movement. The only thing I could see was Cuddles, cocking his leg against our step, but breath brushed by from half a dozen directions.

"You ready?" Swordfish said very close. I located his eyes in front of me, which meant he hadn't pulled down his filters yet. "Put your hood up, girl, you look like you've been guillotined. Got something for scent?"

Mallore's dress had gone from our trash can, which meant someone being careful. But my torn lace hadn't.

"She's worn this. But she isn't likely to have walked."

"Didn't think she had. Dribble?"

The horrible kid lolloped over. He grabbed my panties in a grimy paw and buried his nose in them, grinning with the whole of his slobbering mouth.

"Pretty, pretty," he dog-whistled, leering. I took Sword's advice and pulled my hood up. The eyes above me vanished.

The kid skipped back to the door, pants between his teeth, lowered himself to his belly and put his mishappen nose to the ground. I thought he was enjoying the local dog-piss but after a couple of casts he came down the steps head-first, his ass cocked. Blurred color shimmered around me. Dosh and Mokey, to one side, looked tense.

The kid wove his way to about six feet from the bottom step, snuffling like a vacuum cleaner, circled on the spot and straightened to his hind legs. He had to file the panties in his armpit to speak.

"Was here. Carried out door, walked last bit. Four, five people, fancy perfumes. Some went down, came back. Two, three copts here, two today. She got in front, went up."

Dosh groaned. Mokey's face tightened.

"Wings?" Swordfish asked.

A black box appeared about three yards away and hovered. It moved backwards and forwards.

"Kenobe, sports job." I recognized the snarling tones of Sword's lieutenant. The box gestured. "Ruhr-Wiertz Donner behind, went same way same time. Traces of a Yamashita, light copt, couple days old."

"That would be the snake-man." I felt Sword looking. With his emendations he could probably see me. "The film guy. He was here a few days ago, had some kind of light copt. I heard it. Must've parked around the corner, because Moke and me didn't see it."

"Scrub the Yamashita," Sword said. "We want the Kenobe and the Ruhr. Got a heading?"

"Dead on. We going?"

"Sure. Move, guys."

Blurred air flowed towards the mouth of the alley and out onto the Strip.

"Right, wild boys," I said. "We're taking the fast belt to the 'burbs."

"No copt?" Dosh asked, disappointed.

Swordfish laughed from over my head. "You want them to hear us coming? With the uptown traffic this time of the day the walkway's nearly as fast. I run an attack group, not the fucking airforce. When you get on the belts, take the main lane to Meadowlands. That's where Wings has them located. Watch Dribble. Be in touch, Cass."

Dosh and Moke took off after the scuttling dog-child.

"All the same," Sword whispered, "those are damned

peculiar copts for House. And Dribble doesn't get things wrong. Your kid walked out herself.''

"Drugged?" I whispered back.

"All things are possible."

A soft scuff and he was gone. He leads from the front.

"Meadowlands," Dosh panted, as we jogged towards the ramp. "What are they going to do? It's a big 'burb, scattered, fancy plantings. I had clients there. Minor Ari. How'll they trace the copts?"

"Navy 'scope. Wings has identified their emissions and he'll have them registered. He's tracking. He'll pick them up, if they're within a mile or two. They could've changed direction in the air. But they wouldn't expect us to scope them. I bet we find them."

"What if we don't?"

"Sword's very inventive."

I didn't say what I thought. What was bothering me was the same had got to Swordfish. A sports copt and a heavy limousine were damned peculiar vehicles for the House. They're serious guys. I'd have expected an armed gunship, possibly masquerading as a cop-car.

This deal had an air of evil frivolity that didn't amuse me at all.

Jumping a walkway in a suit isn't a major leisure activity. I ducked between knots of cits, avoiding heels and elbows. Ahead of us Sword's pack smoked through like currents of air. Dribble stayed level with my knee, I suppose by scent, and Moke and Dosh kept up with him.

Dosh got his usual share of admiration. Moke, oddly enough, moved just as fast and stayed nearly invisible. It doesn't matter how many buckles he wears, he isn't a guy people notice.

Towards the 'burbs the foot-traffic tailed off. The copt lanes still cut swathes through the twilight with an occasional bluebottle caught in the glare, but the homey guys heading for their wives and martinis had mostly got there.

At Meadowlands terminus we cut out of the complex with its mall and copt parks and headed towards the winding drives of the 'burb. It was almost dark. The glimmering roadways curved into a sea of evergreens and flowering bushes. There was a scent of pine and exotic blossom. It was cold. This was a countrylife dome designed to give the illusion of living under the high stars, and the air had a nip. It had to be cozy in front of a log-fire.

There was no one about. You don't walk in the dark at Meadowlands. Every house has its own acres of wood and stream guarded by sensors, dogs and domestics, with a camera in every bush.

Swordfish caught my arm. Dribble came to heel and the guys turned back, afraid of stepping on someone.

"We've a location. Three lots away, a mile across country. Does your boyfriend know the place?"

"I've been here," Dosh said. "Where've you located?"

A slink of zips and a long-fingered hand disengaged to point.

"Three streets, maybe five properties between. I'd rather stay on the highways, but we could lose hours. These roads go every which way. Don't try to guide us if you can't, I'd rather do dead reckoning and corpse a few dogs."

"There's a turn-off about three hundred yards ahead. Visited a guy there."

"How was he?" Swordfish asked with detached interest.

"A swine."

"Figures."

The hand flicked at the breathing dust around us and vanished.

Dosh grinned nervously and set off at a trot. From the soft pad at my heels Sword was behind and his pack following.

"She said Papa was a Tech? Isn't Tech country." His voice was pitched for me.

"Dosh's dates were Ari. They needn't have taken her home. Might be better not if there was screaming. Techs live closer together."

"You wouldn't hear much screaming here."

"And nobody would lift a finger if they did."

"Perfect," Sword concluded. When there's screaming where he is, he's usually the cause.

The road curved and forked. Discreet paths led away into the foliage, occasionally broken by a high gate. Once a dog barked and fell abruptly silent.

Dosh stopped at an intersection. The lane ahead led uphill. The main path curved back the way we'd come.

"How far now? I don't know where these go."

"Wings?"

"Quarter of a mile." The black box showed near the snarling whisper. "Good enough."

"Okay. Thanks. Move, guys."

We turned up the hill. Stands of pine, ivy, blooming magnolias. Things that smelled. On Ari ground small roads say wealth, privacy, nasty things in the undergrowth. A snicking of weapons went with us.

I reached in my bag and found the rifle-case. I fumbled for the pieces, snapped them together and slotted in the jack. The landscape came into sudden focus, every leaf clear as moonlight but washed of color like an old film. Red targeting lines bracketed my vision.

"That to kill me, Cass?" came Swordfish's velvet whisper.

"You're kidding. Hallway told me it'll outshoot anything except a neural implant. You telling me you don't got that?"

He laughed and his tread moved past me, taking his troops up front. I could see his coolsuit rimmed in faint light, tall as a tree and sleek as a hunting leopard. Others flowed in his wake, not all human. Twenty at least. He'd brought the hounds okay.

Wings stopped at a gate. I grabbed Moke before the pack fell over him and he halted Dosh. The dog-child lolloped past, giggling in ultrasonics. The gate clicked and we poured through.

Wings stayed to close it and I grabbed his arm.

"Don't do that," he snarled, whipping around. "Want me to kill you? You filtered?"

He was wearing shades; you need them to fight in coolsuits. Stops you shooting your friends.

"I can see when the gun's jacked. What about my guys?

We're cooled, they're not. They're going to see them coming.''

''That's the idea. They walk to the door. We follow. You got objections?''

He ran me up the path, his hand brutal. His gun, a heavy close-combat job with an ugly snout, banged painfully in my ribs.

''A million. Suppose they shoot before they send out the butler?''

''Why should they?'' He was trying to sound innocent. His voice wasn't made for it. ''Your lay's been here. Aris have visitors.''

''Not without arrangement.''

''They've a bim locked in the cellar. How do plain-clothes cops grab you?''

''Do they look like plainclothes cops?''

''Why not? They're in, it's a cop trick. Anyhow, Sword's running this. He didn't want you. Since you're here he'll use you.''

''He's too kind.''

''Correct. He broke a rule yesterday.''

''He never breaks rules, at least his.''

''He turned down a contract,'' he spat in my face. ''On you.''

I felt cold. He jerked me faster. ''How did they take it?''

''How d'you think? Now we got to kill them. Before they kill us. You better be worth it.''

He let go abruptly. The door was ahead, Dosh on one side and Moke on the other. I heard him crunching away behind and the swish of leaves as the bushes closed.

''Cass?'' Sword's light-rimmed silhouette turned towards me. ''Stay with these guys and cover them. Once you're in, give us two minutes. If you have to shoot, relax and leave it to the gun. She's a pedigree killer. Don't let him draw, he'll shoot himself in the foot. Two minutes. Ring.''

I prodded Moke. He raised his hand to the bell and held it.

The house was long, high and making like a manor, with rows of windows and fanned steps. It stood on the crest of the hill, with a sharp fall of ground behind giving a view of the edge of the dome and the mountains beyond. Bushes and specimen trees broke the lawn in front. There was no light anywhere. Nobody answered the door.

Moke pressed his thumb down again. His eyes caught a glint from the sky.

"You there, Cass?"

"Yep."

"You sure it's the right place?"

"Yes. There's a pad around the side and the Ruhr-Wiertz is on it. I don't like Wings, but he doesn't make that kind of mistake."

"Okay. I didn't want to break and enter on strangers."

He abandoned the bell and tried the door. It was locked. He knuckled it gently. It looked like wood, oak or something rich and rare. It gave back a hollow metallic echo. He grinned and unslung his cutter.

"Thought it might be. Stand clear."

"Moke. Keep to the center. These doors can have nasty surprises. If they have, they're usually activated near the edges, especially by the lock. Watch it."

"Okay." He was adjusting the pressure, fiddling with the aperture. "Look away."

Just in time. I'd forgotten how blue-white a cutting-flame is. My target lines flared dangerously and the gun jumped in my hand.

"Down, Rover. Not yet."

"Cassie, if you're waving that gun you'd be nastier without the suit," Dosh whispered.

"I'd also be more visible. Get out the darter, take off the safety and make sure it's a bad guy before you shoot. And keep her high, I'm going to be in front of you. I hope you know where my head is.''

He laughed sourly. "That's right, you're covering us."

"Yeah." I was trying to sound tough. I wouldn't have minded someone covering me.

The door was marked by a line of white-hot metal that smoked and slobbered. Moke finished the first cut and turned the nozzle down.

"Heavy bastard," he murmured. "I think they're trying to keep us out."

He was neatly in the center, just wide enough to let us through. The hot line hissed and dribbled around the outline of a square, the edges cooling to charred red. Then the lines joined and the slab fell heavily in.

"Okay, guys, welcome to the robbers' cave. After you, Cass."

"Keep behind, Moke. Let the guys with guns do the work."

"No way." He'd reslung the cutter and was readjusting the nozzle. "You seen what these can do at close quarters? Just lead."

My pacific Mokey. They never stopped surprising me.

I stepped through, avoiding the red-hot edges, and landed in ankle-deep carpet spread over black-and-gold tiles. The carpet was black too and felt like real fur. If there were that many sables in the world. The slice of burning door had done it a lot of no good. The place smelled like a slaughterhouse already.

The smoke wasn't alone. It mingled with an odor of incense almost thick enough to see and dancing light-figures that started on the walls and undulated into the middle of the room to improve the scenery. The designs were of the kind they call artistic, read incredibly obscene.

Apart from the fur and the art, the place was tastefully bare. A low table in the middle supported a vaguely oriental brass tray with a statuette in gold and ebony to match the light-figures. Quantities of gilding in wedding-cake relief on the ceiling culminated in a floating chandelier shaped like a dragon breathing smoke. The smoke wasn't necessary. The air was thick enough to bite out in chunks.

There was nobody around.

''Are we sure it's here?'' Dosh hissed.

''More and more. It's too damned quiet. Keep the gun up and watch. What do you bet there's a basement?''

It seemed logical. There were no lights but there were people in there, I could feel them. Staying still, but being alive. My instincts said down. I catfooted across the hall, taking a detour around the brass tray, and located a set of velvet drapes among the cavorting coils of light to one side.

I used the gun to poke them open. Another door. Moke moved up and tried it. Unlocked, opening on a room choked with ottomans, cushions and silk carpets. It had a sound-tape of the gasp-and-moan kind with meaningful chords. No one, though someone had been smoking a hookah recently. I hate Aris, they're so boring.

I backed out and made for the rear. More drapes, moved by a draft from behind. I repeated the gun maneuver but this time the heavy velvet opened on space and a set of wide marble steps leading down. A gilt baluster went with them for the infirm, the weak and the stoned.

''Robbers' cave, Moke? This way for the ghost-train.''

It crossed my mind if Sword and his crew were turning over the upper storeys they might find all sorts of interesting things, most of them with no clothes on, but we were going to be awful lonely down there by ourselves. I caught that thought at the other side and stood on it. Hell, I was supposed to be professional. I'd been passing myself off for it long enough. I bracketed the bottom of the flight and started down.

Our feet were quiet on the smooth treads. The guys were

locating me by the moving gun-barrel, keeping close on my heels. We'd make a nice group for anyone with cute ideas and a blaster. The steps took a turn at the bottom and went on down, towards another lighted hall. It was real White Rabbit stuff. I stood and looked around at the doors.

No curtains, just doors, half a dozen spaced around the walls, all painted black and picked out in gilt. There was another expanse of fur with its own brass tray and obscene statue filling the hall between. Another smoking chandelier, maybe an Eastern demon, hung in chains above.

"Which?" Dosh whispered, moving his gun-muzzle nervously. I could tell like me, he felt human people in there somewhere.

I turned my red targeting-lines to the chained demon—a profoundly repulsive object—and felt the barrel rise with them. I wished it gone. The hiss and clang as the laser sheared neatly through the chains and let it down on the table with its nasty statuette was resoundingly satisfying. Moke and Dosh jumped backwards and burning oil began to spread over the fur rug. It stank even worse than the one upstairs.

It got the door open. One of the two at the foot of the stairs. A startled face looked out, with a fez above and a red velvet jacket below.

"Thank you, Cassandra," Swordfish said, stepping past me. "Like sounding brass or a tinkling cymbal. I couldn't have done better myself."

I wondered how long he'd been behind us. Quite likely all the way. He brings his clients back alive. When it isn't his mission to bring them back dead.

Mallore was in the room. So were the guy in the unnatural clothing—who was shy a pair of pants, revealing the full inadequacy of his personal endowments—and four anthropoid types in black velvet smoking-jackets armed with a variety of toy tools. Such as a little gilt whip, a red-hot branding-iron with a tiny heart on the end, and a set of handcuffs decorated with silk flowers. Plus a nasty-looking force-pistol each.

Sword's a professional. His courtesy requires the other guy should raise his gun before he mows him down. They did and he did.

Mallore let out a pitiful little scream. So did the guy in the fez. I thought his was the realer and more pitiful of the two. Dosh crossed the room in a single bound, hurdling a couple of bodies, and took her in his arms. It was real touching.

Moke had turned away and I suspected he was being sick, but he was out in the hall waiting for reinforcements. There weren't any. If there was anyone around they were keeping quiet. Some misshapen coolsuits lounged on the steps and given their artillery I thought the inhabitants, if any, were wise.

"This your bim?" Sword asked, prodding Mallore in her skimpy chest like a dubious puppy.

"That's her. Is she dented?"

"Nothing sticking-plaster won't fix," he said indifferently.

He raised his laser and pointed it at her feet. Mallore screamed again, with much more depth of feeling. He gave her a couple of short bursts that sectioned the chains that held her on the lush velvet couch where she seemed to have been being ravished—spoiling the couch some—and turned to the guy with no pants.

"This house yours?"

The guy shook his head dumbly. He could hear the voice, he could see the laser, but he was nowhere with Swordfish. Sword finds this entertaining.

"The bim?"

Another shake.

"Got any wild urges to immolate yourself in her defense?"

The guy seemed to be having trouble with the long words. He looked blank for a moment before shaking his head so hard I thought it would come loose at the hinge.

"Then take your pants and go," Sword said. "Or not, if you like it that way."

But he said it to the guy's vanishing back. I don't know if he liked it that way or not but he didn't stay around to look for them.

Swordfish shouldered his gun, which vanished like the rest.

"You think of any reason to stay here?" he asked. Dosh was cradling the sobbing Mallore. Moke was screwing down the pressure-valve of his cutter. I seemed to be plain in the way.

"Not a one," I said.

"Then let's go home. This place stinks. And I wouldn't hire their decorator."

Nobody tried to stop us leaving. Nobody asked us to sign an insurance declaration. Nobody even asked us to pick up our garbage.

We filed out in an orderly way, stood in the garden while Wings hot-wired the Ruhr-Wiertz—he was brought up as a copt-pilot, don't ask what went wrong—and crammed in. The overflow did the same for the sports job. I suppose the lower ranks walked. We abandoned the copts in an all-night park near the spaceport where the owners would or wouldn't find them in the morning and headed for the Strip.

Dawn was breaking when we got to the Dog and Eustace looked at us with disapproval. Dawn's latish for him, he goes to bed with the first cock. He handed us out greasy bacon and eggs and drinkable coffee anyhow.

Sword had gone. He brought us to the door of the Dog and left for where he leaves to. We exchanged words before he went.

"Not much hurt, your lady."

"That's what I thought."

"Odd place for—what did you say, a Tech's daughter?"

"Check, and check."

"Don't suppose the guy in the hat was Daddy?"

"I'd supposed not."

"Yeah."

"Yeah," I repeated. "Got contacts in films, Sword?"

"I got contacts everywhere."

"Uh-huh. If you hear anything—"

"I'll keep you informed. 'Night, Cass."

"Thanks, man."

"It was for Yeller," he said sweetly. And vanished.

I'd shucked my suit in the copt with invisible guy-bodies crawling all over me. Now I felt dirty, tired and bad-tempered. I went back to join my personal gang. All of them. I wasn't sure I hadn't felt safer wriggling around that damned copt full of deformed hounds. At least I knew whose side they were on.

I dropped onto a chair and reached for a fork.

"Okay. Nobody talks to me until after breakfast." I looked at Mallore, tiny and trembling in a miniature smock some people would've been ashamed to wear to a beach party. "And then we talk plenty. You better believe it."

"I was afraid," Mallore whispered, casting a look at me. It was all the fault of the ogress, obviously. "I thought you'd be mad at me."

Moke and Dosh fell over each other to chorus how much they could never be that. Me, I wondered what there was about being rescued from muggers to make people so damn-all mad.

"It wasn't true," I suggested, by way of getting the party back on the ground.

"Well— Not quite."

Meaning not in the smallest detail.

"The place is a whorehouse."

Her enormous eyes said she wasn't accustomed to my nasty crude language. I didn't bother to point out Dosh had spent his life in the same line of business without needing to call a spade an agricultural engineering appliance.

"My daddy is a Tech. When Mommy died he got married again and my stepmother didn't like me. She's young enough to be my sister, she's afraid he compares us. I make her look childish. So she sent me to boarding-school. But I hated it and ran away. I met Mr. Williams at a party. He's a friend of daddy's and he'd always been kind to me. When he knew how hard things were he told me I could come to him if I needed help."

118

Her trembly lip trembled. She had to be one of the world's all-time bad actresses. The guys hadn't noticed. They were hanging on her words like crows on a gallows. Me, the suspense was killing me. Wondering whether I was going to die of boredom or not before she got to the point.

"So you went, and surprise, surprise, he was a mackerel."

"What?" she squeaked, her cat-mouth hanging open.

"A pimp. One of those guys who buys little girls and sells them to big johns with tiny pricks."

She gave me a blast of flowery eyes venomous enough to say she'd have killed me if she could. I'd just snatched an hour-and-a-half of her best lines.

"He shut me up in that house with those nasty pictures and things. There were three or four of us, I didn't really see the others." Her tinkly tone was meant to slaughter me. I was really slaughtered. "Our clients were gentlemen. That's what he said. I suppose they were rich, his prices were enormous. But—"

I could see we were having another interruption of service. Tremble-break. I was getting into the swing of playing emergency generator.

"And you found rich guys aren't any nicer than poor guys when they're in bed with a tart."

The next blast would have sent me up in smoke if I'd been susceptible to liquefaction. Luckily after seven years on the streets my skin's blastproof.

"They did horrid things. More and more. Mr. Williams was nice at first, he tried to choose me young men or some of his friends who were kind and gentle. But later—" She contemplated another pit-stop, got a glance at me and changed her mind.

"Later they got more and more—perverted. They wanted to do—things. You saw. So," the little pink mouth set itself bravely, "I waited till afternoon when we were supposed to be asleep, and crept downstairs. I'd tried before but it was the first time the door was open. So I crept out and came into town. Then it was what I told you. Except I didn't have a card. I didn't have anything. I was looking for somebody to give me work, but people didn't like my dress.''

More work with the lips. ''It wasn't my fault. We didn't choose our dresses. Mr. Williams made me wear it. If Cassie would have lent me something, I could have tried to get a job.''

Nasty old me. And the word Please freshly wiped out of the language.

''So you walked all the way to Meadowlands terminus in that dress and came into town by the public walkways, and nobody noticed until you started asking for work?''

I was being truly polite. I'm often polite when people don't steal my clothes. Also I was preventing myself saying ''In a pig's eye,'' out loud on account of I could see Dosh and Mokey weren't ready for it.

''I suppose I was lucky.''

I appreciated that. She was one hellish lucky little girl. I wasn't sure our luck was equal to hers.

''And they followed you and killed poor old Yell, just to get you back?''

She bit her lip. ''It was—revenge. To stop the other girls thinking we could get away. They were going to make an example of me.''

Seemed to me it was us they'd made the example of.

''Naturally you've no idea how they tracked you to us?''

She shook her dandelion head.

''Not in the least. I suppose people like that have detectors and things.''

''House people.''

She turned me blank periwinkle eyes. Her pupils were almost normal so whatever she'd been on had worn off for the moment. ''What's House?''

"The mob. You know, like the vids, gangsters? Guys go around in big copts mowing each other down with rocket-launchers, like that?"

Vigorous nod. "It could be. Very queer people came sometimes. Frightening. I thought Mr. Williams was afraid. Sometimes I was terrified. That's partly why I ran away."

"You're with us now," Dosh said. "We'll keep you safe."

It was her cue. She'd been waiting for it. The big eyes turned my way.

"Well—if Cassie doesn't mind." They filled with crystal tears. "I don't want to spoil things for her."

"Cass doesn't mind at all," Dosh said in a big all-male voice. You could tell Cass had better not. "You're not spoiling anything. We want you."

"Well—" Another of those irritating pauses. "I'd love it. You're so kind." The eyes took in Dosh and swung to make sure Mokey didn't feel left out.

"Only— Maybe you won't want me. If you don't, you've only to tell me and I'll go. It's just, it could be— dangerous."

"Dangerous?" Moke asked carefully.

The blue eyes shone at him like headlights. "Yes. I'm afraid. Terribly afraid. That they may—try to pay you out again. For helping me. They're awful people."

And she broke into a storm of whiffly little sobs that had them both on their knees like Mother Homeland and her Children that used to stand in the square in front of the central station. Before an Ari party blew it to smithereens, probably in mistake for their birthday cake. It's never been put back, which is a wise move. If they'd needed I could have supplied them the models.

Personally, having the choice of Peace or Victory, who used to flank the lady—one with corn-sheaves, the other with a particularly unconvincing sword—as my share, I ungratefully chose not to be either. I sat on my crate in my corner cherishing my own slogan. Which ran, "In a pig's eye." Periwinkle, if you insisted.

Not the things that went bang. I believed in them too well. The rest of the story. I couldn't wait to hear Sword's version. The guy may not be human but he's honest. It seemed an attractive virtue.

"You aren't getting much credit for leading the rescue-party," Moke whispered ruefully.

Since he'd only made two pads out of the ruins of three we were doubled up and Miss Dandelion had pitched in with Dosh. Who showed no inclination to pitch her out again. Maybe it was for the best. I'd have hated her corrupting Moke and I'd personally prefer to snuggle up to a Black Widow spider. Dosh is a career whore. I'd never been jealous of his clients. But he'd never gone mushy over them either.

"Forget it, Moke. I was invisible. And maybe I don't rate credit. I'm beginning to think I just killed four guys who didn't deserve it."

"They nearly killed Yeller."

"Maybe. Then they should've got hauled up in the usual place and handed twenty years. But we don't know it was them."

"Mr. Williams?"

"If there is one. That place wasn't defended. There was nobody around but the four goons and the guy with no pants and he was scared out of his prostate. That sound like a big bad House boss? Mr. Williams seems to be the Little Man Who Wasn't There."

"You don't like her, do you, Cass?"

"Should I?"

He murmured, "I don't like this. Any of it."

"Nor do I, kid. Go to sleep. Maybe somebody'll kill us, then everybody'll know we were right."

"It's what I like about you. You're comforting."

"You can always go out there and make a threesome, I'm sure Miss Cutiepuss'll make room for you."

"Don't be nasty, Cassie. I only just got you to myself."

"Hey, somebody wants me."

"Didn't you know?" he said sadly.

I put my arms around his lean neck. Sad Mokey. That made two of us. And Sword, who'd turned down a contract because he wouldn't kill me. Maybe three. One big round of laughs. No doubt we'd all get the chance to split our sides in the morning.

I was suffocating in my dreams. Beastly dreams, tracking Dosh through the world's biggest department store where the salesfolk told me my card was out of credit and the elevators went up instead of down. Eventually time ran out and my legs were caught in molasses and I knew any minute now he was going to give up and leave with Mallore. And finally I'd run out of air, like I'd run out of love and money. I wasn't surprised, but my lungs were burning and I was dragging for breath.

"Cassie! Wake up. Come on."

Mokey was shaking me violently, his hands digging into my arms, his voice rough and hoarse. I slapped at him, half-awake. There was a roaring noise all around us and a flickering glare that hurt my eyes. My throat was raw, my eyes streaming. I was coughing, still in the grip of suffocation, drawing in great breaths of air that burned and choked me.

"Cassie! On your feet. Get up and run."

He was still tugging, coughing himself. There was some reason I couldn't see him clearly though there was light, too much light, coming and going redly. I came around with a jerk.

What was between us was smoke, blue and swirling, with boiling clouds of black pouring through. Tongues of flame licked up through the floorboards, red and yellow, edged with soot. The loft was on fire.

I stumbled to my feet, staggering, blinded by tears and with my lungs searing in my chest.

"Where's Dosh and Mallore?"

"I don't know. This place is a million years old, it's going up like a bomb. I don't know if we can get out. Come on."

He wrapped his aluminized quilt around me, thrusting random handfuls of clothing into my hands. He was coughing too much to talk, his eyes red as coals, streaming as badly as mine. I grabbed the stained T-shirt that came nearest and wound it around my nose and mouth, trying to get a flap of quilt over him before he roasted.

Clinging to each other we staggered through the thickening fumes towards the partition. Just in time. As we got to the other side the floor fell crashing in behind us in a cloud of sparks and flame and the fire sprang up to the rafters with a roar and started eating the roof.

At the end of the loft the boards were hot beneath out feet, the wood beginning to char. Twisting tendrils of flame curled through the spaces between. A muffled figure groped towards us through the smoke, head swathed in towels.

"Christ! Let's get out. Elevator's too risky, we might just make the stairs. Give me a paw, Moke. Here, Cass."

Dosh grabbed me by the waist and lifted me across the burning boards to the other side. His arm was around Moke's ribs, half-carrying us both. As we reached the clearer area by the stairs there was an explosion behind that painted the wall with blue-white shadows. The floor shifted and I thought for a moment we were going through into the raging mass of fire below.

"Fuel-tanks," Mokey choked. "Should've remembered."

"What could you have done?" Dosh's face was seared under the towel, his broiled eyes blue on red. "Move it, guy."

"Mallore?" I managed through Moke's T-shirt. It helped, but not much. The smoke was still blinding my eyes.

"Out here. Get on down, Cass. We'll stay with you."

I groped out onto the landing. Mallore was out there, wearing one of Dosh's shirts and a towel around her head, wielding a scarlet cylinder on the roaring funnel that had been the elevator-shaft.

"Come on!" she cried, grabbing my hand. "We've still got time. Run!"

Moke swept her up in a blackened arm and we rushed the stairs together. Miraculously her extinguisher was still spouting. Without it we wouldn't have made the ground. The foam kept the steps clear long enough for us to fall out in a huddle into the open air and lie in the street coughing, dragging oxygen into dried-out lungs.

While we were still falling down the front steps the staircase went up with a noise like a blowtorch and we saw the metal risers standing for a moment in silhouette against the fiery light before the whole thing crumpled and slumped out of sight among the fallen beams and blazing debris.

For a minute or two we were content to breathe. Then Dosh dragged himself to his feet painfully, in sections, as if his skeleton wasn't too well articulated, and gave a hand each to Mallore and me.

"Keep going, guys. This whole building's about to fall in. Could take the rest of the street, it's all old property, she'll jump the road and cook us from behind. Let's get out."

Mokey copied, moving like an old man. Still weeping and

coughing we made it to the mouth of the alley and out into the main drag. As we got there we heard the ululating wail of fire-sirens.

They were uncommonly fast on the job. Downtown Ump property can burn like a Roman candle before the guys get out of their beds. Our local Gooders do what they can but they lack the equipment. I'm expecting the whole Strip to go up one night, and nobody's going to give a shit.

"Where to?" I choked.

"The firemen will save us!" Mallore exclaimed.

She'd dropped her extinguisher down in the hole that used to be poor Yeller's home and she was trying to fluff up her hair with sooty hands.

Moke and Dosh saved me the trouble of explanations by turning on her as one.

"Not here, sweetheart," Dosh wheezed.

Moke seconded. "They'll stick the blame on us. We're legally squatting, even though we pay rent. Property doesn't belong to anybody. You pay the guy could make most trouble if he turned you in. Guys like us haven't any rights. If they don't nail us for arson, they'll claim illegal destruction of property on account of our cooking-stove, my gas, anything. What you do after this is disappear."

Mallore opened her eyes wide—they were bloodshot, but nothing like the red-hot embers the rest of us had, we looked like a row of Halloween lanterns—and made a little O of her mouth.

"But what shall we do?"

"The Dog," I proposed. "Eustace won't be delighted, but he may let us doss on the floor."

"Especially if we pay," Dosh agreed.

I stood still. My heart stood with me. "But we can't, Doshky. Everything I had was in there. Card, tools, clothes, rifle, coolsuit. Do you see me explaining that to the bank? I've an account and no way in."

He looked at me gravely with red-coal eyes. ''Me too. Clothes, makeup, money.''

We both had the same thought at the same time. I got in first.

''Oh, Mokey.''

He turned us back a gray face smeared with soot and reddened with scorching. His green eyes in their rings of blood were steady.

''So the whole fucking exhibition was a fake. Time I moved on to something new, you can't weld metal all your life.''

We were silent. There had been seven years' work on the main deck of the warehouse and it was there the fire had started. We'd lost tools. Moke had lost everything.

Dosh had tears in his eyes, and they weren't fumes. He put a burned arm around Moke's shoulders and we started off in dirty shuffling procession for the Gilded Dog.

Eustace didn't waste time arguing. He shoved us into a storeroom out of sight of his cleaner customers, handed Dosh the first-aid box and jerked a thumb to the rear.

''Shower's out there. Rinse around after you, I use the fucker myself.''

That was an argument for also rinsing around in front of us. We used everything and did a sort-out of our clothes. Everything stank of smoke and most of it was burned.

Mallore came out best with her inherited shirt and her jeans which had been beside her bed. Dosh had jeans, undershirt and damn all else and Moke and I were sharing two grubby T-shirts and a pair of pants—his. Since his T-shirt was long enough to cover my ass I settled for his and left him mine, which looked picturesque, and the pants, which had holes in unexpected places.

None of us looked remotely respectable. Eustace looked

us over in silence and handed out hash in the storeroom. We got the message. Even the Dog didn't sink that low.

"Well?" Dosh said, after a longish pause while we ate silently.

"Guess we look for work, guy."

"Sure. I'm really going to turn tricks in this rig."

"I don't know," Mokey said, considering. "Nice show of muscle."

"Done rare. Dammit, I need clothes."

"We all do," I said. "I can't work without kit either."

"How does waiting table grab you?"

"Fuck, I been there. What I need is to see Hallway."

"Well," Moke said with decision, "I already offered Eustace my services slinging hash. He's agreeable, in exchange for his storeroom for a couple days and the price of pants all around. It'll tide us over."

"Yeah. Tide's real low right now."

"It's all my fault," Mallore said unexpectedly. She sounded less whiney than usual, even slightly intelligent. "I told you I could be dangerous. I'm afraid somebody wanted me."

"Obsessive, your old man."

She caught Mokey's arm, making him wince. There was raw flesh under there. "But you've got to be serious. He's mad. Not sane. He could do it again. I'm afraid he will. Again and again, until he's killed me. He'll never let go."

Her halo of white-blonde hair stood up against the light. She looked like she might be going to throw another fit of hysterics.

"Hey, guys, don't panic," I said. "Hell, there's a contract out on me, too. Missy isn't the only guy who's popular."

I caught Mokey's expression. Like mid-winter in Siberia minus the northern lights. Dosh simply looked blank.

"Guess I forgot to tell you. I turned down a job. Other commitments? Contract was offered to Sword and he nixed

it. So now his own ass is on the line and he's pledging his
time to eliminating the man, but there's likely some street
muscle already bought with a line on my butt. Makes for
interest, huh?''

Mallore's eyes had got back the wide staring look.
''Somebody's really trying to kill you?''

''That's right, sweetie. It's a common pastime around
here. Now my tools've gone up in smoke I'm a sitting duck,
until I cut another deal with my armorer. Feel like moving?''

She sat still, transfixed, like a little pink-eyed rabbit.

''Nobody's moving,'' Dosh said roughly. ''We're hanging together. You think me and Moke can't look after you
two dolls? We'll take care of you. Trust me.''

Oh, boy. I was all for beefing Dosh's self-image but it
looked to me he was taking the hero bit for real. Protect us?
Him and Mokey, one card-carrying pacifist, one nice actor
who was having a nervous breakdown day before yesterday
and never did figure out which was the hot end of a
dart-gun? They were going to save the lives of sweet
Mallore, the lady of the House with the firebug friends, and
poor helpless little me? I looked at him with compassion.

''Lovely Dosh,'' I said.

I hoped to hell Swordfish had his ass in overdrive.

I waited table after all. With a checked apron provided by
Eustace on top of the T-shirt and a pair of shiny heels
left by some lady of the streets. I appeared in public, got my
backside pinched and kicked a couple of asses without
being arrested. People who knew me either did or didn't try
ribald comments depending on whether they hoped for a
future or not. Most politely failed to recognize me, which
was just fine.

Moke worked in the kitchen with the dedicated patience
he gave whatever he did. Dosh started carrying trays, then

got into a conversation with a spacer who was cleaner than most and no drunker than many and disappeared.

Mallore stayed out back indulging her crise de nerfs, or whatever it is high-class tarts do when confronted with the grimy realities of life. I guess it would have been unreasonable to expect her to copy Dosh. I wouldn't wish some of the Dog's clients on my worst enemy. Not even on Mallore. I did think she might have helped Mokey with the grill.

That took us through the afternoon and a lot of the evening, and I never realized how hard Eustace works. Considering he usually does this himself with two potmen and a domestic. Moke's bacon was better than the domestic's but that was the only noticeable difference.

Around six, to the sound of early cocks in distant backyards and late whores exchanging abuse in the street, we retired to our storeroom. Dosh flopped on a pad with Mallore resting against his manly chest from whatever mental labors she'd been working on all night. Moke and me parked ourselves separately on a couple of old chairs thrown out of the main room as too battered even to be re-gilded.

It could have been worse.

That's what I thought. Until six-thirty, when Eustace put his mean cropped head around the door with a look on the bad-tempered slab of raw ox he uses for a face so like pity it scared the shit out of me.

"Got word in from the fire department. Some guys I know been working your place."

"Yeah?" Mokey asked.

"Cops say it was arson. Incendiary grenade on the lower floor, fixed to go up at ten. Which is when decent citizens are earning their honest bread, and you guys are doing God knows what. Proprio's not amused. Old building, title mix-up, no insurance. He'd like a return on his property, if it has to be out of your hides. I'd move your asses elsewhere, I was you.''

''You want us to go now, Eus?''

Eustace looked Moke over.

''Nah,'' he said. ''Just telling you. You got grief coming, all of you.'' He paused and spent another look on Mallore. ''About her. She was mine, I'd send her to the country. Some mean guys about.''

I saw Dosh's arms tighten. And Moke's jaw.

Well, great. Some days it never stops raining custard pies.

When I got up I called on Adelaide. Dosh had split last night's takings between Mallore and me. I guess spacers are generous. Then there was my share of the advance from Eustace plus a night's pay for waiting tables. Mallore wanted to come with me but I put her off. Pink sugar frills are another department and I had business to do.

I was too disreputable to rate a discount—you notice people only give discounts if you look rich?—but the money stretched to wide satin pants and a tight jacket to match plus what goes under. Adelaide clucked her tongue I was buying underwear again. I guess she thought I'd a kinky boyfriend. I didn't enlighten her.

I glommed over a pair of really slick boots but I hadn't enough money. I stuck with the tarty heels and let Ad disapprove of me. She put the boots on a shelf in case I came back.

Then I dumped the singed T-shirt and set out for Hallway's. If you're stiffing a guy for credit it's a good idea to look like you can pay it back some day.

Hallway was in operating posture but he paused long enough from doing open-heart surgery on a night-lens camera to hand me a chip.

''Message from Sword. There's a deck over there.''

The deck had Military written all over it. Something else

132

that fell off the back of a battle-cruiser. I slotted in the chip
and gave the program a thumbprint. That's trust coming
from Sword. He rarely settles for less than retinals and often
wants genotype. But Hallway's an exception to most things.
The message was short and sour.

"Query Mallore: Birthdate classified, over forty. Registered Art actress, a.k.a. Nimbus. Eight years porno, sixteen
big screen, popular Ari vid prods. Specializes female leads
mid-budget adventures, high body-count, eats her mates.
Watch it. Trojan War following? Sword. Ends."

"Uh." I sat and looked at it, wondering if there was any
point in doing it out in hard-copy and waving it at my mates.
I decided not. They wouldn't believe it, Dosh least. I'd been
too successful playing ogress. What more natural than that
Sword and I should get together to slander the little kitten?
We're known to be much of a muchness. After all, he and
Razor brought me up.

"Trouble?" Hallway asked, squeaking up behind in his
clean sneakers.

"You could say. Me and the guys are playing a film.
What does mid-budget adventures, eats her mates say to
you?"

"High body-count," he said promptly.

"Yeah, that's Sword's version."

"It's a formula. Handsome hero, gutsy heroine, lots of
twists, bloodbath finale, they get to kiss against a studio
sunset. Special effects highly rated, especially the death-
scenes and emotionals."

"Which are?"

"Hero's or heroine's, depending on the star. You don't
catch them?"

"Never had a taste for snuff movies."

"I've a professional interest in the technicals. Their arms
aren't bad. You can pick up points."

"You don't have to apologize. What are the other main parts in this formula?"

"Depends. On who the other actors are. Commonest are Hero's Buddy, the sympathetic young guy gets to die bloodily couple of scenes before the end to give the hero a reason for wiping out the rest of the cast, and Other Bim, the bitch of the piece, comes to a bad end. Stepmother, hero's ex-girlfriend, whore, criminal, like that."

"And what's her usual choice of bad ends?"

"Any end that's bad. Sometimes she gets to take the shot meant for one of the guys and dies in his arms, sometimes she gets come-upped and disappears in a police-copt, sometimes she just loses everything. Occasionally she makes a heroic renunciation and walks into the sunset in the other direction."

"Thanks. Sounds delicious."

That sorted that out. Mallore/Nimbus was heroine, clearly. Dosh was the guy got to kiss her in the last scene. Nice for Dosh. I was pleased he was hero, but I'd've liked him to kiss a woman, or even a man, rather than a green mamba. Not so nice for Mokey and me. I could see what we were getting.

It also explained why the fire in the loft had started under our pad rather than theirs, and a couple little points had been bothering me. Such as how Mallore had come to have a nice red fire-extinguisher in a building hasn't had as much as a sand-bucket in a century. Not to mention the prompt arrival of the fire-engines.

"Suppose you'd got slotted for Hero's Buddy or Other Bim," I said carefully to Hallway. "What do you figure you'd do?"

He scratched the back of his ear, where his mask tends to gall him. "I think," he said after a pause for thought, "I might just alter the script."

"A man after my own heart. Listen, Hall, we've a problem. We got burned out."

"Yeah, I heard. So did Sword. Why he was asking after you."

The bush telegraph works as well in Ashton as in any other part of the jungle.

"Dosh and me are in a bad position. We've each got money in the bank and neither of us can get it out, because our cards were in there when it went up."

"Illegal, of course."

"Naturally. Right now we've got what we stand up in. I'm standing in mine, he's got one pair of jeans and a singlet. Great for lion-taming. Not so good for high-class soirees."

"Which he attends."

"Nightly."

"You don't know your account number, I suppose?"

"You're kidding. I got a photographic memory. You know my business."

He grinned. "No problem. Give me fifteen minutes with that deck and I'll get you all the money you need. You're going to have to draw from my account though, unless you want to risk a pick-up."

"I'll take the pick-up, but shift all you need into your account anyway. I'm about to require a couple pieces of equipment."

"Sure. Give me a list. Then I'll do the transfer."

"You're a treasure, Hall. And while you're at it, give me a rundown on how film companies get their images."

"No sweat." He pulled up another stool, doubled his long legs with the heels of his sneakers wedged on the highest rung, and sat down to lecture. He looked like a praying mantis in mid-sermon. I didn't take notes, but I listened hard.

• • •

On the way home I called at Adelaide's and paid for the boots and a big bag to match. Ad looked self-satisfied. She knows I hate to disappoint her.

I'd got to a couple hundred yards off the Dog when I registered a faint steady pad behind me. My neck hair lifted. It didn't seem a good idea to parade my arsenal down the street so I wasn't carrying. That can be a mistake.

I used the next window to glance behind and saw exactly nothing. Meaning a guy in a coolsuit. I waited for a little clot of people coming in the other direction, stumbled right into the middle so we had a moment of confusion while we sorted out and apologized and scooted into the nearest doorway.

"Primitive, Cassandra," Swordfish said in my ear. "Fire shook you up?"

He caught my arm and turned me down the alley by the side of the Dog which is so private even the cats avoid it. I think it's something Eustace puts in his trashcans. I took up a casual attitude against the wall, like a guy meditating on fate—a lot of guys meditate on fate in Ashton—and tried to look alone.

"Yeah. But not as much as your note. Thanks."

"Pronto. I've been having bad feelings about that house job."

"So've I. Those gorillas didn't draw very fast."

"Very slow. Did Miss Cutie actually have heart-shaped burns on her behind, or is the question indiscreet?"

"You know she didn't. And no little gilt whip-marks either, before you ask. If I'd been smarter I'd have looked more closely first time, but she was making such a screech over her bruises I got lost in being pissed at her."

"Maybe you were meant to. To stop you seeing she hadn't any."

"I'm disgusted. I've been dumb. That little cow's really set me up. Wearing my clothes, turning over my wardrobe, messing with my makeup, hopping into bed with my guy, then waiting for Aunt Cassandra to react as programmed and show up on film as Miss Jealous Girlfriend, Ashton Strip. I ought to have a blue satin sash. I guess the muggers were fake. It would explain why we got a famous victory with so little sweat. Prostheses they didn't know how to use."

"Like gorillas who didn't know how to shoot. I'm wondering if those irons were even loaded."

"Don't blame yourself too much. They were, I looked."

"Then the guys weren't. Doubt if they'd held a gun before." He paused deliberately. "I dislike wasting professionalism on film-extras."

"That's how it looks to me," I said unhappily. "I think they were ready to stage a fight, even kill some of us. But they didn't expect you."

"They expected a male whore, a limp-wristed artist and a little girl hardly bigger than Miss Cutes of Hollywood. They underestimated you, Cass. They thought you were an un-serious person. They didn't think you'd show up with a professional assault group."

"Shows my cover's effective."

"So now what?"

"We run a raid on the house. With armed support. Dosh hasn't suggested it yet, but he will. He's really getting into the hero part. Consequently we've got to play it. As it happens, it suits me. I've fixed the deal with Hallway."

"Good. Where and when?"

"Sorry, guy. I want your help, I don't want you. Get me some mercs."

An interval of silence so intense I wondered if he'd evaporated. Then his filters lifted to show mid-air eyes, dark and hard.

"They know your capacities now, Cass. I doubt if it'll be extras with guns they don't know how to use this time."

"So do I. That's why I want professionals. But not you. I'm going to rewrite this fucking scenario, and when I do things'll blow sky-high. Guys'll get arrested. Maybe me. Get me mercs and make sure they understand the deal. I want guys who'll do as I tell them, stop when they're told and who're in for a minimum-loss operation. When we find ourselves up to the shins in cops they can shift any way they like. But until then I'm in charge. No smart-asses. Do it for me."

"I could do that myself," he said with soft bitterness. "I'm minimum-loss if I know what you want. My guys follow orders and we'll do what you want done. We'll also bring your butt out in one piece. Don't fool around, Cassie. This stuff's serious."

"I know. I got four lots of guys gunning for me at the last count. Ain't sure there's enough of me to go around."

"I'm failing to laugh. Name them and I'll switch them off."

"Sorry. If it was just me I'd take it. But we're stuck with this film and I can't risk Dosh or Mokey. Another op like the last and they could lose everything. Nimbus-Mallore's begun to figure I'm not what I seem. So I want it clear it's me. And nobody but. That's why I want mercs. Get them, it's all I want. Please."

"Even I'm going to have trouble busting you out of the State Penitentiary, Cassandra. It has truly righteous security."

"I'm touched you'd want to try. But Moke's life's on this. Please do it."

The silence lengthened.

"How many?" he said at last.

"About twenty again. Combat-trained, no berserkers. And no coolsuits, I want this on film and I'd rather they didn't shoot each other. The only people I trust in cool are yours. And guys who'll obey orders.''

His eyes looked down at me, blazing with something I didn't think I wanted to understand. Then they turned curtly away.

''Right.''

''And, Sword?''

His receding steps paused and the eyes turned back. I saw in them I was right.

''Don't come yourself. Promise. I value you.''

It was a low blow. It just happened, in its way, to be true. The eyes tightened, then turned away.

He hadn't answered. But I thought I'd got through. Now all we had to do was do it.

When I got back to the Dog and aproned-up for my shift I looked at Mallore with new eyes.

Forty? Then she'd spent a world-class fortune on rebuilding. Anybody would have sworn, looking at her curled purring on Dosh's knee, she was sixteen at the oldest and fluff to the backbone. There were two glances of the eyes, private to me alone, that could have belonged to anyone old enough to really hate.

I wondered if Dosh would end like that too when he finally got his longed-for career. An elegant portrait of Dorian Gray who stayed gruesomely young while the rest of us grew up? I'd never thought about it before, though everyone knew vid stars never wrinkled or grew gray. Now I did I found I didn't like the idea.

Miss Muffet had spent her share of loot on velvet bullfighter pants, an embroidered tunic-of-lights and a pair of little kid slippers with pompoms. She'd had her hair re-dandelioned. She looked ready to win both ears and the tail, probably mine.

If I hadn't known I mightn't even have asked how she

managed to get so much out of less money than I had. What was clear was she didn't mean to wait tables.

I did, if only to show gratitude to Eustace. Moke and Dosh looked hopeful and I gave each of them an enigmatic smile. Miss Mystery needn't get away with being the only guy on the set with secrets.

Dribble edged in around two when the Dog's at its jumpingest and bit me on the calf. I yelped and lashed out at him but the little bastard had zipped away.

"Get me a doc, I need rabies shots!" I yelled.

Nobody took any notice. This stuff's routine for the Dog.

"You be nice, I you card got," the vile object whistled. Its English got more mangled every time it opened its nasty little mouth.

"Be damn grateful I don't have a gun down my stocking or you'd be fucking dead, meatball. Come within six feet and you're dead anyway," I snarled. As a matter of fact I had an eight-inch ya with an edge like a razor but that was a surprise. For the next guy tried to pinch me.

"You ain't wearing 'em. Nice legs. Lovely."

"You going to tell Sword you tasted, or you leaving it to me?" I asked evilly.

It got a cautious look and sidled nearer. "You not tell Sword?"

"Not if I can have the pleasure of gutting you myself. Come to mama, baby, I wanta fillet you."

"Card?" it whistled plaintively, following me back to the serving-hatch.

"So give."

"Not if you're gonna fillet me," it whined, abruptly recovering its education.

"You want a gold medal as well? Hand the fucker over. And next time you come around you better bring your vaccination certificate or I'll call the pound and tell 'em you don't have a collar."

"Ha," it said hollowly and thrust out a grimy paw. When I glanced down there were two cards in my hand, one mine and the other Dosh's. Hallway'd been moving.

"Thanks, Fido. Try the kitchen and maybe Moke'll give you a bone. But not when I'm there or it's liable to be yours. And tell Hallway thanks, if you can remember such a hard word so long."

"Pronto," it said, in exact if ultrasonic imitation of Swordfish. And disappeared.

The next time I saw it Moke was feeding it. He's nicer than me.

Dosh was late back in the morning. I thought he'd found another generous spacer but he'd been having a private lesson with the boy from the fishbowl. Eus keeps four behind the scenes painting and gossiping, two male, one female and one dubious. The young fresh one made eyes Dosh's way while one swayed and the other carried trays, and they finally disappeared to exchange professional secrets. Or something.

I never bother Dosh about his private life. It's never serious. Mallore had got bored flaunting her embroidery around the storeroom alone and looked put out. I sneered at her quietly. If she hadn't been so damned lazy she could have been out there getting her bottom pinched and her legs chewed with the rest of us.

He came back finally looking self-satisfied and said he didn't want breakfast. The rest of us were digesting Eustace's moderate coffee and disgusting croissants. By the sweet fresh smell of his breath I'd have said the young beauty had shown his appreciation in kind at one of the breakfast-bars on the Strip. Since Mallore and I'd consumed his last night's work between us, I didn't quite feel we'd the right to complain.

Mallore felt differently and pouted.

"You smell of cinnamon," she accused. I guess field rations are hard when you're accustomed to fresh bread from cooing domestics. On the other hand, seemed to me she was getting paid, which was more than we were, or only at the going rate for unskilled kitchen help. Eustace is charitable but not crazy.

Dosh blushed. Moke and I rushed in.

"More coffee."

"More sugar."

"They don't taste so bad if you dunk them."

Dosh sat on one of the wrecked chairs and took up his own fate.

"Look, guys, we got some money, which means we can do something. We can't go on like this. They've tried to kill Mallore twice and I don't want to wait for third time lucky."

"Cassie seemed to think it was meant for her," Mallore squeaked, with a glint of malice.

"It wasn't," Dosh said with confidence. He and I linked eyes. We both knew it damned well.

"Why not?"

"Because we're alive. Cassie's acquaintances don't leave anything to chance."

"They don't shoot all around the scenery, either," Moke observed. "They're paid for one, not the whole crew. It's considered sloppy work in the trade."

"You're joking," Mallore declared bravely.

"If you say so." I looked at Dosh over the heel of my croissant, now well set in the west. "What had you in mind?"

"Pre-emptive strike." How I know my Dosh. His eyes, only the slightest bit pink, were blue and earnest. "Provided Lorey's sure it's Williams."

"I'm sure," she said, nodding her flossy head.

"And we'll find him in the same place."

"Oh, yes."

"Can you be certain?" Mokey asked seriously. "If I'd had a visit like the other night I think I might have moved out."

"What Moke means," I expanded, "is the house wasn't defended. Which means either a coward or someone unserious. Neither usually stays for Act Two."

What I wasn't saying was that if this Williams really existed and was in his right mind, he had to know by now that we were a) alive and b) hostile, and he'd be expecting a return with reinforcements. But I guess the script didn't allow for our being intelligent. Umps are allowed animal cunning but no brains.

Mallore opened her huge eyes. Her pupils had expanded to fill the space available and the lines of blue around the edge were almost invisible. I wondered if she was as spaced-out as she looked. She'd had all night to hit any chemical combination appealed to her.

"He's a very bad man," she declared, with the solemnity of a cuddly white mouse explaining the habits of the tom next door. "Last time he didn't think Doshie would be brave enough to rescue me. Now he knows what he—what you're like, he's going to have a real army."

She grabbed Dosh's arm with hysterical earnestness. "Oh, Doshie, you're so truly brave. But please, please don't go. Something awful will happen, I know it will. I'd rather die than get you into trouble for me."

Procedure for driving men to battle, Number Two. Number One you hand them their shield and shut the door.

Dosh, the heroic mug, reacted as all knights in shining armor are paid to—or, in his case, not. He showed a profile pure as steel, eyes like sapphires and a jaw like they draw in comic strips.

"We're going to deal with Williams once and for all," he declared. "Then we can sort things out peacefully. Listen, Lore, we're expecting money soon." (As if the little sweetheart didn't know.) "We're going to move off-planet and start again. We'll buy a ticket for you too. Then none of us will ever have to worry any more. Right?"

I'd be ashamed to have some guy explain me things like I wasn't out of playschool yet but clearly my ideas ain't universal.

"Ooh, Doshie. It's a dream, but it's wonderful." Our screen queen elocuted a juvenile quaver. "Do you really think we can?"

"We will," the strong man assured her strongly. I thought it was a good thing Auntie Cass had made arrangements. "Cassie?"

"Sure," I said. "I can lay on a friend or two."

"Moke?"

Mokey answered the call to the colors with a preoccupied nod. "Yeah, sure."

"Then that's it." Dosh was too deep in questions of strategy to notice the grayness in the Moke-weather. "When, Cass?"

I was touched he still turned to me for battle plans, even if he'd chosen Bo-peep for his partner at patacake. "Tonight?"

I saw hesitation in Mallore's eye and for a second I was afraid she meant to explain her director hadn't got the props together, or maybe her dress wasn't ironed for the big scene. But Dosh was in the grip of heroic enthusiasm and she shut up.

"Sooner the better. Before they've time to organize their defenses. Time, Cass?"

"I can get some guys at the Meadowlands terminal towards midnight."

"Great!" our military genius decreed. "Don't worry, Lorey. By this time tomorrow you'll be safe."

Mallore smiled, pale, small and terribly indomitable. "I hope so. But I wish tonight was over and we were all safe. I'd feel better."

I left Dosh to tell her all the reasons she didn't need to bother her little fluffy head, which seemed to satisfy both of them, and got on the case of my favorite sculptor.

"Something wrong, Moke?"

He smiled with the bloodshot green eyes that went on examining the world with unchanged intelligence while his skin got grayer and the furrows between his mouth and nose deepened every day.

"Apart from being burned out, cleaned out and worked out?"

"Don't horse around, Mokey. There's something."

He sighed. "I had another letter from Eklund. His chauffeur brought it this afternoon. Offering me a date for the exhibition."

I felt a squeeze of rage and pain like a sudden mouthful of lemon juice. "Naturally, he hasn't the slightest idea you haven't anything to exhibit. What did you say?"

"Thanked him, and said I was sorry but my work wasn't available any longer." He squinted ruefully. "What else could I say?"

"Right."

But its sheer cold cruelty sickened me. Swordfish is supposed to be short on human feelings? Nobody in the world deserved this less than Mokey. I was nearly as fretful as Dosh to see darkness.

In the afternoon I decided to gum down my nerves by giving Eustace some extra labor to make up for not being there most of the night, and started a session of washing and polishing I hoped would carry him through. Mallore lounged against the mahogany in her moonlight suit and watched me, less with criticism than in simple astonishment.

"Cassie," she said carefully, "were you serious about people wanting to kill you?"

I'd finished the mirrors and was in the act of hoisting myself up onto the bar to have a go at the goldfish bowl—which was probably something got forgotten from among the labors of Hercules. Since like all goldfish bowls it was highly convex, I had to hang on to the rim with one hand and lean well outwards to get at it with the spray.

That's what I was doing the exact moment I saw light wink the other side of the road.

My combat-training's been whopped in by the best masters over quite a lot of my childhood. I dropped like a ripe coconut, swinging an arm to take Mallore with me. Her gasp for once was unacted and totally adult.

We lay on top of each other in the shelter of the counter as teardrops of molten glass drooled down onto the surface I'd just finished polishing and formed lumpy lakes there, to an autumn smell of beeswax and woodsmoke. A few of the larger pools overflowed in sparkling icicles over our heads.

We're both small and the counter overhung at the top, so most of the drops that got as far as the floor simply left blackened spots on the planking. Except the three that burned neat holes in the skirt of my apron and left me beating at the little flames at the edges.

I waited for the remains of Eustace's fishbowl to finish collapsing and for the laser-artist across the street to call it a loss and vanish. Then I lifted my head cautiously and examined the damage.

"Sure," I said. "Why do you ask?"

For the first time in our acquaintance I thought Mallore

was genuinely frightened. It gave her quite a different look, like an intelligent woman with a career in films.

Almost human.

I hoped Eustace was insured. This kind of stuff wears out your welcome faster than blackbeetles.

"You going like that, Cass?"

Dosh sounded mildly outraged. He was fastening a black shirt over matching pants with leather jacket to come. Moke had settled for a dark jump over a sweater. Mallore looked resolute, with only the slightest tremor of her brave little lip, in a dashing velvet blouson over her suit of lights. She looked as warlike as a pixie in drag.

Dosh had wasted half an hour trying to get her to stay home. If he'd known, a matched team of saber-tooths wouldn't have kept her away. I wondered at what point in the action she was slated to take off the blouson and reveal her splendors to the camera. As soon as she had a bleeding corpse to nurse on her knees, no doubt. I wondered which of us she had in mind or if it mattered.

They were tooled to the eyes and I was letting them try out for weight. I meant to carry the damned arsenal myself, being the only guy with a bag big enough, but I figured we'd better make like real. They could need them.

Dosh was wielding a darter as if he'd seen one. I'd shown him the only things that mattered, where the safety was and how to avoid shooting off his personal parts. Mallore was handling a nasty snubbed repeater with skeleton grips that went charmingly with her get-up. If you were making a film, that is. In real life I wouldn't have trusted her to carry it from here to the table without killing someone.

148

All the guns were on stun, which I hadn't mentioned when giving instructions. Only Moke didn't seem ravished. He looked down the muzzle of his disruptor with the expression of a guy who'd found it in the soup. He'd have been happier with his cutter, but that was a pool of metallic slag somewhere in the ruins of where we used to live.

The hardware was Hallway special, wicked as the devil to look at, lots of flash and little flame in practice. The only guy with killing capacity was me because I'm the only guy I can rely on not to panic and use it.

"Sure I am. What's wrong with it?"

"It's visible?" Mokey suggested.

Sweet Moke. This scene was already written, and the way it was fixed we could probably process to the door in a cade of lighted floats with baton-twirlers and carnival dancers without anyone seriously trying to stop us. I didn't see any reason to wear pirate pants and a brilliant hair scarf. I could move in them, and so long as I was cast as Bitch I might as well look it.

"You guys know what a coolsuit costs? Took two years' work to pay for the last." I didn't actually tell them that was five years and fifty B & Es back. "If you've finished primping, gimme the tools and I'll load 'em. There's no point being picked up for carrying before we get there."

"I suppose people don't stop you?" Mallore asked, all melting innocence. She'd got her nerve back since she felt her feet on her own ground.

"As a matter of fact they don't, doughnut. Who'd think a little girl in disco gear would be carrying for half a platoon? Protective cover depends on what you're protecting. Trust me. Somebody stops me, I'm liable to panic and drop my bag over the railing. It's expensive and puts the operation back a night. But try reconstituting what was in a bag when it's gone four miles under a fast strip. I might hit a drugs charge, and they'll find I smoked hash night before last. It's to laugh at. Get your asses together, we're going belt-hopping.''

Last time Dosh and Moke practically had to carry Mallore. She was busy being shocked and couldn't be expected to stand single-handed. I was interested at how clumsy she really was on the belts, as if she'd never hopped before. I wondered what backgrounds her previous adventures had had. I should have asked Hallway.

She passed as a drunk bim being lifted from belt to belt by her boyfriends and I acted private enterprise. That suited me. If we got stopped, they were innocent as a spring dawn and I knew the way out.

I stuck close to the rail, swung my bag prominently about and generally played little tart going to big date. I had some cold twitches around the solar plexus of the sort I hadn't had since I ran my first jobs for Razor at fifteen. I hoped it wasn't a bad sign. I don't go in for entomology.

Plan and forget it, was Razor's advice. I've never known him wrong. Maybe I was aging. You don't have the same reflexes at twenty-one. I had just one thing in common with Mallore. I'd have liked to see tonight over.

I'd fixed to meet my mercs at the Arches of Paradise at Meadowlands Terminus. It's about the only place there you're not only allowed to arrive looking rough trade, you're liable to get slung out if you don't.

It's a big fast-food patronized by the local juves, where the decor's plastic sawdust and fake candles on fake wagon-wheels and the patrons have steel-toed boots and pants tied up at the ankles. A breeze redolent of whispering sage blows through with the help of wall-fans and never quite licks the smell of stale grease. The boys who're old enough have designer stubble, except for the ones who believe they can make a beard. Most of them are mistaken. They look as macho as cotton candy.

They give cover to real machos if a few want to hang out without attracting attention. The rich kids fancy de-clawed tomcats and aren't too smart about telling designer whores from the real thing. There are girls, but I wouldn't accept a light from one unless it'd been disinfected, and then I'd rather not smoke.

My guys were the ones with their feet on the floor. A good merc doesn't attract attention by getting thrown out before an operation. They looked cleaner than the local boys. I picked out a medium-sized guy with a cold eye, a sensitively shaved beard and muscle tattoos and strolled up to sit by him. There was an empty seat, which could mean we were going to understand each other.

"Cass Blaine. These guys are with me. You're mostly protecting them. You had Sword's instructions?"

The cold eye looked me up and down, then flickered over my escort. "Coffee, Toots?"

"Not before I work. I don't have guy equipment."

"Have one anyhow," he said low. "You don't hafta drink it, it's disgusting. Yeah, had a list from Sword. Says you're a tough lady."

"This would be an inconvenient time to doubt it. I'd have to carve my name on your cute little cheek and people would look at us. Are you going on my terms or not?"

He signaled the table robot. "You're paying, I'm told."

"You should have the money in your accounts as of this afternoon."

"Check." He moved his shaven chin around the tables. "Raven. Plus twenty guys, all known to me."

"Meaning what?"

"If they fuck up I kill them myself."

"Satisfactory. They're briefed?"

"Uh-huh."

"Stun unless I order otherwise or you find you're under real fire, minimum-loss both sides. If the cops show, you can leave by the nearest exit and you needn't ask the teacher."

"We got Sword's directions." The cold eye fixed me. "He'd like your butt out whole."

"Not part of my orders. I told Sword, my butt's my problem. Hanging in when I say go'll only complicate things. You answer to me or you don't answer."

A narrow smile. "He also said you'd say that. Ditch the coffee any time, it's not worth saving."

Dosh led the way up the moonlit roads through pine-smelling darkness and drifts of magnolia and jasmine. The only sounds in the leaf-rustling night were his padded steps, the sharper click of Mallore's kid heels and an occasional clink from some guy's equipment.

Dosh, Moke and Mallore walked side by side with me loitering behind like a tart looking for her party. Raven and his group had vanished in the shadows, their feet silent. Moke always moves like a cat, even in sneakers. My profession depends on having the kind of soles that neither skid nor clack.

We turned at the junction and around into the looping hairpins of the drive up to the crest. Dosh looked over his shoulder to check we had our escort. I didn't bother. If Raven knew his job he was right behind.

Moke dropped back to whisper, "Not Swordfish?"

"Hope we don't need him. He comes expensive."

A slander. Sword's expensive but if you need help you need his. Mokey gave me an odd look, but went on.

A withered wreath was hanging on the bars of the gate where the dog had barked. Kids, probably. That's show business. At the top of the street I stopped at the decorative iron that had bothered Wings fifteen seconds and waited for

our support group. Raven materialized from the shrubbery
and joined us.

"This it?"

"Yeah. Watch it. We went in like butter last time, neither
man nor beast. Tonight I'm expecting the full show. Dogs,
guards, mutated goddalls, you name it. Do what you have to
with the beasts, they're liable to be insane. Don't kill guys
unless you have to, they may not be what they seem."

He nodded and spent some passes on the gate. He wasn't
as good as Wings. It must have taken him twenty seconds.
It swung back.

"Let me and a couple of guys go ahead, you come up
with the group." He gestured at Mallore. "She safe?"

The answer was she was probably the only person who
was, but I wasn't telling him that.

"You kidding? Watch her silky little ass, it's what Dosh
wants you for."

"What do you want us for?"

"To watch his. Don't worry if I drop out of sight. Got a
couple things to do. Protect my guys, and apart from that
follow orders."

"Get in, take out the opposition, find the big guy and give
it to him," he translated.

"It could come to that. Follow the script until you see it's
come apart. Be clever, guy, I'm relying on you."

Another thin smile. "We're gone."

They were. A file of shapes slipped like shadows through
the gateway and vanished. I gestured to Dosh, Moke and
Mallore.

"Stay in the middle. The advance group's taking out the
fauna and scouting for mantraps. There are at least two other
groups behind set for assault. One of their aims is protecting
you, don't shoot anyone by mistake. Hold your fire until
you're in the house, let these guys shoot for you here."

I figured that's what I'd do in Raven's place, divide my

forces in three and approach the house from different
angles. I'd counted seven including him disappearing up the
path and a faint rustling in the shrubbery said the mercs
were spreading out in both directions from the gate. We
went straight up the palely gleaming drive, the bushes
closing in on both sides.

Mallore shivered. "When do we get our guns?"

"Now." I had my own in my hand, the tracking laser
socketed. It was an automatic disruptor pistol this time,
lacking the elegant line of the rifle but better at close range
and good for general-purpose damage. I handed the bag to
Moke. "Give them, Mokey, and don't stand still too long.
My thumbs are pricking."

They were right.

The mutated hound came at us out of the shrubbery while
Moke was still digging in the depths of the bag. It was big,
dark, low-slung and as fast as a cheetah. Automatic targeting's faster. The disruptor burped and its wet remains
splatted across the crushed stone in front of us, leaving
sinister dapplings in the moonlight and a few shapeless
chunks gleaming among the shadows.

"Move!" I hissed. "These bastards hunt in pairs and I'd
rather not have one of you between me and it when its mate
comes through. The blood-smell could attract something
else, too. Don't know what they've got. Stay on the path and
watch your feet."

Moke's glance as he returned the bag was sober.

"Not kidding this time."

"Only a little." I pushed him forward to keep up with
Dosh, leading off boldly with his darter, and Mallore,
waving her nasty skeleton killing-machine. Looked to me
the person likeliest to get killed was Dosh and I was happy
the damned thing wasn't fully charged. But the hound was

nastier than anything I'd quite expected and I was sorry now I hadn't armed at least Moke thoroughly.

If one of them was in the way when the next hound came out, somebody really could get hurt. I was surprised they'd expose Mallore to that kind of danger, until it came to me all they needed was either a good deterrent transmitter under her clothes or an effective blocker in the beasts. I still thought the film business wasn't very tasty. I wouldn't rely on a blocker with a mute hound myself. I had what I preferred right in my hand.

I'd relied on Raven and his gang to clear the path and I hadn't expected quite such wild game in the woods. I followed close behind, tense. A stunner would knock even a hound sideways, but some of these big bastards have next to no nervous system and you can have quite a time convincing them they're dead. I seriously hoped Dosh or Moke, or both, had fast reactions. The stunner would slow the beast for the second it might take me to range it.

We followed around the curves of the path, Dosh alert at the front, Moke covering the rear, me trying to look all ways. There was more dark splashing a few yards ahead, I hoped animal. Dosh halted for the briefest moment at it, and the second hound came off the branch above at exactly the same instant. Did I say the fuckers climb trees?

It wasn't the mate of the original. Different breed. The huge head with slavering fangs was like Hans Christian Andersen's nightmare with eyes as big as the round tower at Copenhagen. The reinforced hind legs were made for grasping branches and furnished with claws like carving knives. Probably the blood on the path belonged to its partner and one of Raven's clan had already taken care of it.

Dosh's start saved him. I sighted the monster in mid-air and got a line over his head to blow it apart before it hit the ground. The remains struck with a wet thunk and Mallore jumped back with a squeak that for once was justified.

I shoved forward and took Dosh's arm. He was shaking.

"You okay, Doshky?"

"Yeah," he said, his voice husky. "Just splattered. You think they've got many of those?"

"We're short of one. I'd like to know what happened to it. Don't relax yet, but keep moving. We'll be better out of the shrubbery. Once we're in the open we'll see them coming."

"And they'll see us," Moke observed softly.

"That's why we have mercs, Mokey. They're supposed to be clearing the ground. Don't blame 'em, the woods seem full of the bastards. If they haven't got around to dismantling the mantraps we're in trouble.

"Oh. So long as we aren't in trouble now."

I gave him back his tight grin and fell to the rear again. I calculated if my missing hound was alive and trailing us, and they make up for lack of nervous system with a set of sensors can follow human sweat ten hours old over wet country, it was probably coming from that way. They're not intelligent but they're hellish well-programmed. The result can sometimes look like natural low cunning.

We'd got to the edge of the bushes and started out across the open ground when my enhanced senses registered a movement behind. I turned and fired in one motion. That took half a second. My brain caught up with my targeting program late enough to reflect if it was Raven I was going to be sorry.

"Jesus," Moke said.

It wasn't Raven. I guess my first hound had been the female. This one, which was fairly intact except for being short of a head, was as big as a pony and had paws the size of manhole-covers decorated with full sets of hunting knives. It was still twitching, as if it meant to get back up and savage us with the gap where its head used to be.

"Better. I was waiting for that. Let's go," I said, trying to sound confident.

I was thinking Sword had done too good a job. They'd expected, right, two ordinary guys and a wetwad. They'd got Swordfish. This time they were tooled for bear. I hoped Raven and his crew weren't paying. I'd asked them not to hurt people. I hadn't told them they were likely to be eaten alive by the inmates.

It's true you have a paying contract with a merc, but it's a good idea to remember they're human. It not only makes them easier to work with, it gives them a chance to do their job and save your life.

Raven and his group had been doing aces. The stretch of turf between the shrubbery and the house was dotted not only with flowering brush and specimen trees but with the charred carcasses of more hounds, a couple nearly as big as elephants, and the wreckage of three or four downed surveillance robots. One of them lay buzzing dismally close to us, its long laser-arm twitching in spasms as it tried to lift it and fry us where we stood.

A little flying-eye camera unit was crashed by the steps, making mournful clockwork noises. It looked pathetic, like a wounded Mickey Mouse, but I know those little suckers. They not only let the garrison know you're coming, they have a sulfuric-acid spray designed to go off in your face and make sure you don't get there. This house had security in spades and whoever downed it had done us a favor.

Raven was waiting by the steps masked by an oleander in a terra-cotta jar. He stepped out as we got level.

"What the hell they got in here, military spy base? Never seen stuff like this at a private house."

"This is a private House house," Dosh whispered.

Raven wasn't impressed. "You're kidding. I took out the third downtown west sub-sheik on a private contract last year, he had two pairs of hounds, two big survey jobs and three cameras. And he was expecting us. This sucker's defended like Fort Knox. You sure this is limited-casualty?" To me.

"Yep. Don't be fooled, this stuff can kill you. But it's guarding nothing." I made sure Mallore wasn't in line of ear. "Once you're in, don't believe guys are what they look like, though you better believe they shoot real guns. Met any human resistance?"

"Dogs and mechanicals. We're ready to go in."

"Losses?"

"Not yet." He grinned, a gleam of enamel in the faint light. "We got tools."

Which meant they had effective detectors. I like competence. I glanced up at the house. It looked dead, but I could feel the internal buzz from here. It wasn't.

"As soon as you're ready. We'll wait for the door. Don't expect me right away, I got business. Hope to catch you before the major mayhem. Action was in the cellar last time, don't mean it will be again."

I looked at Mallore. She was standing tensely at the foot of the steps, Dosh looming protectively at her shoulder. The big gun looked murderous in her tiny hands. She knew where the triggers were. What she wasn't going to do was tell us. I'd thought of torture and decided it would be too much of a pleasure. Perhaps for us both. I went on keeping my voice low.

"Keep your eye on Mokey, guy in the overalls. I think he could be a target. Dosh may or mayn't, but I wouldn't like to lose either. Don't bother about the lady, I doubt if anyone's going to boo her seriously."

He raised a brow. "If you say so. Diverson's around the back. Give me fifteen seconds plus two-three minutes for the door. We'll try to keep their little behinds clean. Sure you want to go this way?"

I sighed. "I think it's expected."

Resigned shrug. I knew what he was thinking. If he thought something was expected, that's the last thing he'd do. Normally I'd agree. This time was different. Getting off the chalk-marks too early could throw the whole deal so far out I'd lose control. This way, if they knew where I was, at least I had a good idea of where to look for them.

"Fifteen seconds."

And he disappeared into the night.

"How are we going to get in?" Mallore whispered, raking the snout of her gun around as if she meant to take out the entire neighborhood.

The door Moke had efficiently destroyed had been replaced by a frank cero-steel plate looked as if they'd borrowed it from an armored ram-drone. The camera-unit above had been shot out but the door itself showed only soot from a surface flashburn.

I smiled nicely.

"Somebody's going to come and open the door and we're going to walk right into the hall. Don't shoot him, he's ours."

She gasped and took a harder grip on her cannon.

It looked to me as if she was truly hyped. The emotional reactions being recorded were hers, so anticipation and terror probably came high on the list of what switched the clients on. It maybe wasn't surprising she spent her life high.

The star used to carry a camera implanted in her eye and the audience got to share her reactions directly through her sensorium. The ladies of the epoch did a lot of cute things, running along Bondi beach under the spray, eating with the Arcadian Ambassador, like that. They were great times.

The bad news is, human sensoria can't be completely divorced from human mental and physical reactions. You got the spray, and the mosquito-bite on the lady's left leg. The Ambassador and the smell of his armpits. The joy of blue sky and the lady's sweaty panties. To stick to the cleaner variants. There were less clean.

For instance there was poor Angie Merton. Angie was doing her job interviewing a top spaceball star when the pickups picked an inclination in her little subconscious to see what it felt like to have the guy on top of her whopping. Ba-ad material. Which the studio dutifully suppressed in the interests of public morals and decency.

Nobody knows how the tape got liberated, but it did. It then sold a million copies in the black bazaars, the guy was inundated with ladies wanting a hard date and Angie got raped on the way home and disappeared into a clinic from which she didn't noticeably come out.

That was the up side. The down was, even that didn't touch the dark stuff. I mean the black urges of the human psyche that long for blood, screaming and death. Not you or me, naturally. The other guy. There are a lot of other guys. Their tastes vary from an innocent desire for interesting fantasy to a full-scale lust for everything a human can experience. Via the pains of another human.

Not to mention the crime wave. Personal interviews with the rich and great were the finest thing since the invention of Christmas for smash-and-grab artists. Nothing like getting to estimate the family jewelry really close up, especially with a freeze-frame facility practically made the reproductions for you, except being escorted around the apartment so you knew where all the hot spots were.

So that's when the industry reorganized and came up with Mallore. To take an example. The personal interviews went back to plain vid. The camera came out of the eye because people had stopped wanting to see what the heroine saw, they'd started wanting to see her and her co-stars suffer. She felt, the other guy suffered and the camera recorded it.

Now they make stories, and the stories are about people who hurt, and the star watches the hurting and feels for everyone. People like to cry, too. But what they register's the high spots, because nobody wants to be Heroine all the time. Catching cramps, getting fly-bitten, eating greasy soup. They want her clothes, her furnishings, her thrilly shivers, the session in bed in the middle, the feel of some big evil killing-device in her wet little palms like the one Mallore was handling now.

Big scenes.

We were in the middle of a big scene. So someone was around the place taping. The eye with the camera belonged to someone else now, probably several someones, and some smart Tech was out there managing it, picking shots, calculating angles.

I was there to calculate him.

I gestured my group to the two sides of the steps in case the door chose to blow out. Moke and me on one side, Dosh and Mallore on the other. We crouched behind a pillar each and waited. I figured having Miss Hot-Pants out of the way wouldn't make a blind bit of difference to the fight, but it might stop one of Raven's mercs getting his nervous system razzed by Honeybuns' itchy trigger-finger.

The two faces opposite shone pale in the darkness. Mallore was enjoying it in some weird way. I guess if she didn't get off on guys dying all around her she wouldn't do it. Dosh wasn't but he was hanging in. I know him. He loves acting hero; he's genuinely brave, tough and protective. But he hates the feel of a darter, he'd rather do almost anything than get into a fight if he doesn't have to and the idea of killing turns his stomach. Moke's the cooler. Dosh was there for one reason and she was called Mallore.

Moke touched my shoulder from his oleander and put his lips to my ear.

"What's going down, Cass? Not what's billed, I know you better. What are you pulling?"

"Don't ask. As soon as that door opens get inside and take shelter. And no fucking heroics, just keep your head down. Tinker Bell isn't in danger, take my word for it. If you get assassinated on her account I'll kill you myself."

He laughed, a soft snort of breath down the back of my neck, and withdrew behind his pot.

Raven's fifteen seconds were up and things were hanging.

Then there was an explosion from the back of the house, a blue-white magnesium flare that lit up the night and left us blinded. It was accompanied by noises of breaking glass, a lot of human shouts and screams and a single ululating wail like a wolf in its death-agonies. I could make out the sizzle of laser-fire and the soft plops of heavy disruptors.

Then the sounds faded and became muffled as the fight moved inside. I could feel a sort of hidden ebullition in there, noises more sensed than heard, a vibration of the air that said violence and destruction.

The front with its curtained windows stayed dark. We went on standing at the foot of the steps, shivering a little with tension and the chill of the night air.

Then the armored slab swung open and a guy with a laser-rifle that glowed dully around the muzzle waved to us. I gave Moke a push.

"Go on. Watch yourself and Doshky, let Madam look after herself. She will. I'll catch you up."

He gave me an exasperated look and went past me up the steps at a trot. Dosh followed two at a time, Mallore skittering at his heels like a ferret at a rabbit hole. They disappeared.

I stayed where I was, scrunched up in the shade of my oleander. They had to show soon. The fucking organizers.

I was going to be there for them.

The night was cold and damp. An orange-pink moon was setting over the dome and the garden was still. The grounded Mickey went on clicking and fizzing by the steps, leaking a drizzle of acid onto the marble. The oleander dripped down the back of my neck.

Then a shadow swung around the house at roof-level and came in to land on the grass. They'd been filming the fight, with maybe back-up on Heroine. Now the action was hers they'd come around front.

Raven's diversion had diverted everybody. Mallore's personal camera must have been on automatic while they'd taken in the mayhem behind.

I felt in my bag, found my number-one grenade and lobbed it. It was Hallway's double-action special. It hit the shield, clung, and glowed phosphorus-bright for the seconds it took to melt its way in. Then it dropped and blew. The canopy stayed intact.

There was a panic inside. I saw waving arms and someone had a try at getting the canopy open before the gas finished them. He almost made it. It cracked, letting out a tendril of mist, and dropped back. I was grateful. It saved me the trouble of cutting. Then his body slumped and the only movement was a lazy swirl of vapor like a boiling coffeepot.

I pulled down my face-mask. The canopy lifted releasing a dissolving gray cloud and thrust out a helpful step.

Three guys, two male, one female. They were all out for a three-hour count. We weren't going to take that long. One was lying against the side of the bubble but the others were still belted in front of their screens.

The screens, unlike the operators, were awake. If they'd been looking up front while my mercs took out the rear they'd have seen us. There was a clear shot of the door with platform, and me, small and bright, looking at the screen inside. Another showed the rear where Raven had vaporized a good bit of wall. The gap was big enough for a tank and the breaking glass had come from all the rear windows. I hoped he'd been scoping when he decided there was no one close enough to get killed. A couple of bodies lay about in picturesque poses. The action had moved away. The only movement was the shiver of the trees.

Other screens showed inside. A merc in tattoos was sacking a boudoir of Oriental ladies upstairs and guys in the cellar were exchanging laser-fire behind furniture. There were a lot of burn marks but body-wise I gave it to the mercs.

The main fight was in the hall, which had lost its drapes and was filled with smoke and artificial lightning. I was pleased to see someone had shot down the dragon. More ladies were trying to disappear into the wallpaper.

Mallore was in the middle swinging her laser like a garden-hose and I was God-all thankful I'd asked Hallway to see it only tickled or she'd have solved the world's population problem single-handed. Dosh was supporting her with the darter too much in the open for my taste, so it was lucky Raven was behind scientifically picking off anyone who looked close to hitting them.

Moke had vanished behind an angle of wall and was trying to disrupt a pack of armed goons without hurting anyone, which is a lot Moke but very little war. It looked fairly authentic, which was probably all the camera team asked. I did wonder what the guys involved thought they were doing. I suppose in adventures the shooting doesn't have to make sense so long as it happens.

It seemed to me we'd had enough and if this went on much longer someone was going to get hurt. I groped around the platform for a bullhorn, didn't find one, which seemed to me stupid, and was grateful Hallway'd told me what to look for.

I checked over the switches, relays and meters that crusted the instrument panel. If Hall had explained right, there was a main channel connecting with a central control board supervised by the director himself. He was the guy who decided what went through. He'd have an override to cut out scenes he didn't like and theoretically he could cut out the whole board if he didn't like what he saw. And I had to override his override.

I'd memorized the wiring diagrams but this wasn't the same. They never are. The layout was similar but I couldn't see a link relay among the lines of sound, color and tone controls that lay like whale's teeth under the screens. It had to be there.

The body of the woman, a well-tended brunette in a silk overall who'd disarranged her coiffure slumping over her panel, hid part of the array. I unbelted her and hooked my hands under her armpits. She was demonically heavy for a youngish bim. I ended by tipping her on the floor and she lost some more hairpins. She was going to be mad when she woke up.

Just under her elbow a switch-box had a stylized camera etched in gold. I flicked it open and found a single red switch. So-ho. The next bit was delicate. I didn't know how much inside detail the director could see but I didn't think he'd sit patiently to get disconnected. If I was too violent I could cut the link permanently and I didn't want that either.

I shielded the panel with my body while I worked fast on the switch-box. The outer cover came loose and I lifted the switch out in a snake's nest of wires. I chose carefully and snipped.

The platform lights dimmed and I thought for a moment I'd lost it. We seemed to be still recording but if I couldn't control the output I was wasting my time. Then they came back up, soft and clear. Right. Now the gizmo. And set.

All that left was the oration. I hoped they couldn't cut out because I had a yen to tell these punks what I thought. The microphone was hooked under the panel beneath the other Tech. I heaved him aside less daintily. He was a big baldish guy with a paunch who weighed easily twice what I did. That's hernia country.

I unhooked the micro, found the mike-on button and flicked it. I got an induction hum that sounded alive. I poised it and sought inspiration. It wasn't first steps on the moon but I wanted to make an impression.

"Hi, guys. This is Cassandra Blaine, live from your camera platform on the beautiful Meadowlands Development. It's not as beautiful as it was before we got here but I guess that's par. I want to tell you how much me and my guys appreciated the warmth of your welcome. We can't wait to pay you back."

I fiddled with the controls and one of the outside cameras swiveled. I swung it a bit and watched the sky making vertiginous circles.

"Hey, this is nice. It's unlucky I don't take to your story. I got two complaints. One is, you're about to get my nice friend Mokey taken out by a gang of goons to make pretty. I'm against that on account of the guy's a genius and he got a lot of work ahead dying's going to disrupt for him. And the second is, I don't like the heroine. You looked at her? You and I know she's old enough to be Dosh's grandma,

which makes her going to bed with him sort of distasteful.
And she's likewise higher than a kite which is a bad
example for the kiddies. If there ain't any it's a bad example
for the old guys.''

I worked the inside camera to get a close-up of Mallore's
right eyeball. I was getting the hang of the job. Mallore's
right eyeball was incredibly repulsive in closeup, huge,
staring and almost entirely black, the rim of periwinkle
almost invisible even enlarged. Broken red veins seamed the
white like the map of a delta. The thick makeup on her
eyelashes made them stand up like telegraph poles. I
swiveled a bit to get the left. It wasn't any better. Her
makeup was smeared. At that range you could see the scars
at the corners where a surgeon had lopped thirty years off
her.

"In addition to which, she's visibly certifiable. If I hadn't
jinxed that cannon you'd be short roughly fifteen extras,
which got to be unlegal. It likewise distresses their families,
which even Umps often got. You want my opinion, she
ought to be fucking locked up. Consequent to which, I'm
changing your story. Your heroine's shooting nobody which
is dumb in a heroine and the rest of us are about to go home
where we got things to do. If you got our pay, send the
money posthaste in a plain envelope. This is the story of
the film cast that left. Have a nice evening, guys, and don't
let the reviews get you down. This is Cassandra Blaine,
signing off from the once beautiful Meadowlands Development.''

I started to lower the mike, had a thought and picked it
back up.

"Oh. If you want to know how the Strip shifts things,
look. It's a hound-roast.''

I hooked the micro back, hoisted myself out of the
platform and dropped on the lawn. Monstrous carcasses lay
between me and the trees. I estimated distance and gave the

platform a shove. As I'd expected, the grav units were still taking most of the weight and it was barely resting on the ground.

It slid away, skating over the grass. When it looked far enough away I fished in my bag some more. This was the other grenade, the business one. I slung it at our fur-clad friends. It hit the biggest roughly amidships, clinked on something metallic in the cybernetic reinforcement, stuck and began to spit white light that ate up the darkness.

The flare lit the sky violently enough to throw back a reflection from the dome above us and start an auroral display across the western horizon as the field interacted with gouts of chemical smoke. The carcass splattered and its plastic bits began to melt, crackling. The nearer bushes sizzled, smoked and caught fire.

By the time I left they were roaring merrily. I hoped the Techs were okay but I didn't think they'd wait too long for rescue. The scene was getting showy.

It was one of Hallway's smallest bombs, at that.

I picked up my shouter and made for the house.

Smoke and flame met me as I stepped through the door and I added two cents' worth of tranquilizer by laying out a couple of marksmen (if they deserved the name—none of them came within two inches, which is damned bad sighting for a laser) by way of getting attention. Then I raised the shouter.

Hallway'd said if there were metal connections between floors everybody in the place would hear it. He was right.

"Cut!" I yelled.

The house rang like a gong and everybody in sight stopped dead and stared, their mouths hanging.

Raven halted with his disruptor raised, flipped me a cool salute and gave me an eyeful of white enamel.

"Not before time. Some of these guys were getting excited."

Mallore turned with her gun flailing and I thought she was about to scramble me along with the other half of the population. I put my gun-muzzle in her face and gave her my own enamel.

"Cool it, sweetheart. They aren't filming any more, I just bitched their saucer and laid on a pup-fry. It's outside, if you want to check."

"Oh, that's where the light's from," Raven said. "Thought sunrise was early. Guess you fried it righteously, princess."

"My teacher whopped me for carelessness."

I glanced around at gorillas peeping from doorways, mercs behind battleshields—a real merc isn't fool enough to rely on the armchairs—and Eastern ladies timidly lifting jeweled heads from slave-braceleted arms. Bodies lay sprawled among cushions, drapes and overturned furniture. They all looked like defenders.

"Any losses?" I asked Raven.

"Two guys hurt in the rumble out back, neither of them badly. We had to damage the house a bit."

"So I saw. You did fine. I'll ask Hallway to cover your bills."

"It's in the price," he said. "Stupid bastards."

None of the mercs near me seemed surprised. Discipline's a wonderful thing.

I raised the shouter again, for those above and below stairs.

"Okay, listen up, guys. I'm not sure what you think you're doing here, but I know what I am. This is, or was, a film. Production is terminated. The camera crew's no longer filming anything except you filing quietly home, so what you do now's your own business. I've a piece of advice."

Mallore had let the muzzle of her gun fall. She was

looking wildly around, her face screwed in an effort to grab what was happening. Her dandelion hair looked ready to give off sparks like Elsa Lanchester. A snail-trail of drool led from the corner of her mouth down towards her chin.

''Who do you think you are?'' she shredded at me in a voice like fingernails on slate. ''What right have you to give orders? She's lying,'' she shrieked.

''Look outside,'' I invited. ''I'm a guy ain't going to die so this pack of shitrats can make a fortune. My right is, I got the drop on you. And my advice is, get clever. The types you're fighting aren't House, or a rival gang, or the Sons of the Space Cadets. They're professionals and they're doing what they're paid for. They aren't here to kill, but they can if you make them. The door's over there and anyone who wants can go through it. I recommend it. We're getting law any minute and I don't think you want to be around.''

Mallore's knuckles were white, her eyes flat and glassy, her raised voice like shapes in tin sheet.

''Law's what we need. I order you to stay where you are. You all have contracts. Any man or woman who leaves will not only forfeit their salary, they'll be blackballed from the profession and face a civil liability suit for our losses. These so-called soldiers are nothing but a gang of street thugs and the police will take care of them in seconds. This person''—me—''is not only without authority, she's a madwoman.''

I laughed and hefted my disruptor. Raven's dry chuckle suggested a certain lack of appreciation of her assessment of his past and future.

''My authority's here. Be intelligent. Money's no use if you're dead, and you're going to be if you put up a fight. You think these finks'll sue any of us in public court for refusing to commit murder? And I can't think of a better profession to be blackballed from. Judging from the specimens on view.''

Dosh had lowered his gun. He was staring at me as if I'd pistol-whipped him, blank with dismay.

"Cass, it's true? This is the film?"

"Sorry, Doshky. It is. It was. We're the fall-guys. Take a good look at your dame. She's old enough to be your mother and she's wired to the frontal lobes with enough high to run a power-station. Did you think it was to meet the bad doggies? She's running the show. She's made puppets of us all. Get reasonable, guy. It's a set-up, and we're set."

He turned slowly.

"Lorey?"

She ignored him with the expression she might have used on a bluebottle.

"Do as you're told and get into position, now!"

She wasn't too wrong. If she didn't hold them now she'd lose them. But I could see Dosh's face and I didn't forgive her.

"I advise against."

The cast hesitated, looking from one of us to the other. More had come in herded by Raven's mercs, their faces flat. The guy from upstairs strolled down with a frothing of gauze on his heels, the girls clutching each other. The harem was ready to take to its heels and toes just as soon as someone cleared the guns from the line of flight.

Mallore ran a steely eye around and raised the muzzle of her laser. "The first person who moves, dies. Back to your places."

That decided one. A velvet-suited orangutan raised his blaster with the nose pointed at Raven's head.

Raven shot him where he stood with a shift of his gun so lazy and slight he scarcely seemed to have moved. The body hit the floor with a thump. His cold thin smile was unchanged.

"Any more smart guys?"

The orang was bleeding from the nose and ears. Raven

was following instructions. It's a common result of a stun-charge at close range. The goons didn't know that. They'd seen someone die.

"Right now you aren't getting dead," I told them. "Or not from her. That chunk of tin's stun only. But don't think too long, our offer's limited."

Raven smiled whitely around, his disruptor barrel tipped. He looked very dashing and as safe as a snake. It was a class act.

Everything depended on what they did next. If they started shooting, he wasn't going to be able to hold his men. I'd given permission for them to shoot for real if they met live ammunition. You can't expect even mercs to play clay duck all night. They'd been pretty controlled.

The two sides eyed each other, each waiting for the other to make the first move.

Then a big goon near the staircase swore and pitched his gun to the ground.

"I'm gone. Who's coming?"

It was what half a dozen had been waiting for. They dropped their artillery and made for the door at a run. Rainbow gauzes fluttered after.

Mallore stooped like a raptor and scooped up a fallen blaster.

"Stop!" she shrilled. "This one's loaded."

Her finger was tightening on the trigger and the fucker was on wide beam, straight on the backs of the fleeing peahens. I got to her level and knocked the muzzle up with the barrel of my disruptor a fraction of a second before Raven got to the same place. The beam cut a shaft a yard wide the breadth of the ceiling and showered us all with hot plaster.

Raven shook his head in sorrow and anger. He let her have the cross of his own gun across the side of the skull and she tottered and slumped. He was going easy. Some people have these eggshell bones. But she wasn't shooting anyone for a few minutes.

"No!" Dosh said wildly.

I felt bad for him. He was seeing his fragile victim-child and his dream of fame fading into gray daylight in the same moment. For him it was a real betrayal. He'd wanted so much to be Hero. I consoled myself we were saving Mokey's life and stood on tiptoe to pull his earlobe.

"Sorry, guy."

He ignored me. He dropped to his knees and tenderly lifted Mallore's body. He was searching her face, looking for the proof I was wrong. I kicked the blaster out of her reach and turned back to our audience.

"Well? The door's open. Go through it."

That settled them. They made for it in a bunch. The fluttering gauzes were already out of sight. We listened to the pound of their feet down the path and saw their wavering shadows in the light of burning shrubbery. The place stank. They vanished in the smoke and were gone.

We had the house to ourselves except for a few bodies here and there and the ruins of war.

Raven lowered his gun and lifted an eyebrow.

"Not much fighting spirit. But I guess you got your minimum losses. Want us to take you home?"

"No, thanks. I want you guys out before the cops arrive. After which, since I don't want Sister Cloud with us and I don't like to leave her alone with the wounded in case she robs graves, we see her arrested and use our own arrangements. You've done what you were paid for. Thanks. See you around. Go easy leaving, I didn't contract for you landing in jail."

"Don't worry."

They left, grinning, not by the door and not in a bunch. They filtered into the smoke like more smoke and evaporated into other dimensions. Or gardens. Anyhow, they got invisible fast.

Raven stayed to say, "Sword would rather I took you home."

"My compliments to you both, but I'll see this out. Give Sword my love and watch out crossing the road."

He grinned slightly. "He's going to be real grateful. Do the same."

"Right."

"And watch that. She's poisonous." This was Mallore, groaning in Dosh's arms.

"She's higher than Mount Goldberg. Don't worry, I got the gun."

He tipped me a salute with his and went.

Moke had come out slowly from his doorway and stood at my shoulder with his disruptor hanging.

"Staying around could be a bad idea, Cass. I think we better leave damned soon. Don't like the sound of those copts."

"Sure, mec. Just as soon as Sissie's gone the other way."

Mallore was struggling woozily to her feet with a worried Dosh supporting her.

"Come on, kiddo," he said, laying that kind healing arm around her shoulders he'd given each of us in turn. "You'll be all right. They've gone. There's only us. It's over."

The wailing of sirens and the whirling flash of blue and yellow lights filled the garden. Rotors hissed outside, blowing clouds of grit in through the smashed windows. Boots crunched on the path. Loud voices were shouting orders.

"Where's my gun?" Mallore asked, gummily. She sounded as if she was in the throes of landing maneuvers, coming down fast from her big high with a hard pad ahead.

"Here," Dosh said, handing her the laser. "Feel safer now? But you're okay, we're here."

She turned her head, her fluffy hair flattened at one side with dark blood.

"Why, so you are. The bitch, the wimp and the fairy. Lucky me."

She jerked her arm loose from Dosh's hand. "Let me go, you weak-wristed son of a whore. No, it's you and your mother both, isn't it? Where's the fucking law?"

She dragged towards the door, her feet uncertain on the burned fur. Outside someone was organizing a bullhorn. I could hear the feedback whine of a badly adjusted mike.

"Hey, Lorey, wait," Dosh called, starting after her.

"Dosh! Come on, the back way, man. We've done too much here. Dosh!"

He kept going. I started forward and Moke caught my arm. He shook his head.

"Dosh, come on." He was urgent. "Cassie's right. This is film stuff and Mallore led us into it. Didn't you hear what she said? Let's go, fast."

He took several urgent steps after them. Dosh's being was so focused on Mallore he barely bothered to look around. He felt Moke within a step and stiff-armed him away hard enough to throw him off balance. Mokey caught his feet in the twisted drapes that cluttered the floor and fell awkwardly. I ran to offer a hand. He was looking after Dosh, his face blank.

"Doshky! Wait!" I yelled. He kept going, without looking back.

"Fucking dreams of fame. Doshky!"

Mallore was in the doorway now, her frail figure outlined in the glare of the police beacons. She stretched out her arms, hurt and pathetic.

"Help me! Save me!"

It was the old fragile Bo-Peep voice we hadn't heard for

a quarter of an hour. Her head seemed to loll, her trembling
knees to buckle as if she was falling. Dosh sprang forward
to catch her.

She let him get close enough for his fingers to brush the
velvet of her sleeve, and swung like a spitting cobra. I saw
the laser come up, and had no time to do more than open my
mouth to scream. My own gun was slung on my back, both
my hands around Mokey and his body prevented me from
getting it into line.

"Lorey, we love you!" Dosh yelled.

The laser-beam caught him in the chest and we saw him
burn.

His mouth was still open as he fell, his blue eyes wide,
disbelieving. It came to me she'd spoiled his new soft-
leather jacket, the one he liked. He'd paid for every stitch
she had on before he bought anything for himself, then he'd
picked it specially. I could see him strapping it up, hard over
his darter, the warm firm-lipped hero on his way to save the
future of the poor little kid with the bad, bad dreams.

"Dosh." The scream came out as a strangled whimper. I
tried to get to my feet, wrestling the gun around.

Moke caught me by the wrist and whipped me towards
him with more strength than I knew he had.

"He's dead, Cassie. Come on, or it's us next. Back way."

"Dosh," I repeated, pulling against his hand. "We got to
go back, Moke. He's hurt, he needs an ambulance. There's
got to be a phone . . ."

I knew better, of course. Nobody gets a laser-charge full
in the chest and walks away. I knew the truth as well as
Moke did. I just wanted it not to be true so badly I felt I
could reach out and twist time in my hands, wring it around
until it went into reverse and gave us the last few minutes
back again. It just didn't have any right to be like that. It had
to be not so.

"It can't," I said patiently to Moke.

''Come on, girl,'' he said, pulling me away. ''Where's the back door?''

I think I cried and kicked at him all the way out. I don't exactly remember.

The next thing I do remember we were out in the cold air on a damp hillside, with the voices of police microphones booming on the other side of the house. There was coarse grass under our feet and the last fragment of a setting moon on the skyline, and Dosh was behind us, dead.

Behind the house the land sloped away towards the deep narrow valley, almost a ravine, that backed on the Meadowlands property and separated it from the wild country beyond. Clumps of rhododendrons hid the sharpness of the drop and Moke and I thrust ourselves into one as the whistle of a police copt loudened above the roof.

Its searchlight was turned down on the garden and the brightness of the beam threw everything into a brilliant glare that left patches of shadow like gaps in the surface of reality wherever it was interrupted. If it had caught us in the open we'd have been done for. We crouched against each other under the leaves and tried to make invisible.

We could see two more copts patrolling the hillside across the valley, their searchlights cutting white swathes in the darkness and showing a moving panorama of wild scrub, thorn-brush and long yellowed grass. The wandering flashes of helmet-lamps moved below intermittently into and out of the bushes.

I scrubbed my hands over my eyes. "Oh, God, Moke."

He gave me a shake. "Pull yourself together, Cass. We'll cry later. What did you mean to do?"

I was shuddering in my satin pants. It had been stupid to be showy, but I'd really wanted to look equal to their cheapie heroine. Now I was chilled to the bone and if a spotlight caught me I was going to blaze like a neon sign.

"I've stuff planted. Down behind. But we've got to get there. Things went too wrong. I'm not sure I can stand, Moke."

"You can stand," he whispered, catching my hands. His were cold, but not as cold as mine. He squeezed. "Come on, soldier. We're depending on you."

"We?"

"Me and Dosh. You think he wanted you in jail? Come on, girl. What?"

I nodded to the slope. "Down there."

He poked out his nose. The copt was still circling over the roof but there was nobody in sight on the ground. Behind us a hundred yards of turf greened and watered like baize glowed in the half-light beyond the spot. Beyond the garden fell away into a precipice of darkness.

"Clear, if we can get over the brow. What's down there?"

"Something to keep the mutes in. Force-field, trench, electrified wire, any combination. We got to get across. Then the valley. They're not likely to follow us out of the dome."

"We better move. As soon as they come around we're cooked."

"Wait. They're in the house. Full of unconscious guys. We need shadow. Sister Mallore's got explaining to do, I don't think a plain Art card's getting her out of this. Give the copt a chance."

We clung together, trying to control our shivers.

"I worked as houseboy for an Ari couple as a kid," Mokey whispered. "Exclusive. Don't like neighbors. Bet they've sharks in the moat."

"If sharks is all."

"Anybody'd think you didn't like animals." He stiffened. "This is it. Come on, they're buzzing next door."

The searchlight had moved on and was doing its stuff on

the other side of the wall. The garden was backlit by the glare, but with luck their own spot would blind them. They'd have an infrared scope. Question was which way it was facing.

Mokey grabbed my hand and yanked me out to breaking stems and tearing skin. I lost my scarf on a spur and jerked back to snatch it. No proofs. The bushes covered us the first few yards, then a nervy interval of exposure. If they were scoping they were going to shoot.

Moke ran like a deer, bent double and dragging me after. The first few steps I really thought my legs would fold, then some automatic reflex took over and I caught up. The turf lasted over the crest and part of the way down as we dived into the protection of shadow. Then we were knee-deep in tussocky grass.

I dropped to my belly. My clothes were too bright, too light, too thin. I was cold and wet. Moke's dark jump blended. My slick boots skidded on the bank.

The last pink horn of moon disappeared behind the ridge and left the countryside black apart from the crisscrossing beams of the copts on the opposite hillside. They were running search patterns, weaving methodically back and forth. We could hear the shouts of the foot patrols below filling the gaps. Moke lifted his head.

"There's a lot."

"Looking for mercs. If I'd been Raven I'd've gone over some walls."

"Let 'em keep looking. I don't mean Raven any harm, but he's better armed than we are."

"He's long gone."

"Fine. Where's the drawbridge?"

"Optimist. If you see a bog-hole, tell me. I want to roll."

He glanced back with concern. "You all right?"

"Just need to get dirty." I was trying to control the

clacking of my teeth. Poor Moke. He trusted me. I didn't know how to tell him I wasn't up to the job any more.

"You are dirty. What's that?"

The stone wall that guarded the lot petered out in a long measured slope just below us. A dark smudge barred the bank.

"Watch your feet. That's the pit, and God knows what's in it."

We edged down. Mokey's soles were better than mine but the grass was slippery and neither of us wanted to imitate the bobsled run at St. Moritz.

The grass gave out and a ledge of gray-white concrete shone faintly. A nasty place, but safe so long as the copt didn't come over. If it did it would catch us in the open. The slope was a plane of black shadow.

I caught Moke's hand and leaned out. My socketed gun still gave me night vision. I saw a cut twenty yards wide and ten deep furred with spikes. A secondary trench ran the length of the first. I couldn't see into it but it didn't look like a pedestrian underpass.

"Careful people. Their mutes were safe. Bet those suckers are electrified."

"No good?" Moke asked.

He lay on his belly, grubbed a handful of earth and threw it gently towards the spikes. A flash of fire swallowed it before it touched and for a moment the whole array quivered in a marshy blue glow. The same glow shimmered off the screen that rose from the central trench. It went fifty feet up and a trill of electrical discharge quivered over it.

"Uh-huh. Those copts are working upwards."

"So long as they aren't too fast. Got things to do." I dug in the bottom of my bag. "Interference resonator, for boarding. Plus stiff-jack."

He looked over. "Elegant. What's it do?"

"They. Not nice, but possible. How's your head for heights?"

"Seen me fall?"

"You haven't seen this."

I was trying to set the resonator straight to make a good hole. I switched it in. The screen snapped and crackled and began to throw off a spiral of sparks. It slowly irised outward. The gap was black, edged with flashes of fire and crossed by minor lightning bolts like a stormy sky. It wasn't more than three feet in diameter.

"Damn. Hallway told me this was a hand job but I'd a weight problem. It's meant to be up against the screen. It won't hold long, it's on full stretch and the battery's small. When I snap the jack, get on and run, Moke, and don't look down. If you touch the edges of that hole you'll be fried like a gnat."

My stomach clenched. I swallowed something that hurt and took the end of the jack in my hand. It felt like wide gauze bandage. The throwing edge was weighted and as soon as it was stretched it would firm like a plank. A plank twenty-five yards long and ten inches wide. Not much spared at the ends. I hoped I'd judged right. And that I could throw without a twist.

I flicked my wrist and it unrolled, through the hole and out. It looked as wide as a shoelace. Stiff-jack works on inertia. Start with enough momentum and it keeps going. When it reached the other side it gave a spastic twitch and went rigid. I laid my end down. It was anchored, for the moment.

"Get going, mec. Avoid the discharges, I don't want you over the edge. Move."

He glanced at me, and went. The little resonator was flickering already. He moved swiftly and surely as walking the edge of a pavement. As he got to the hole a flash moved

across it, and he paused a second before he ducked through
and vanished.

I waited for the jack to stop vibrating, and launched out
myself. I've the habit of high narrow places. I've never done
it shaking so bad. My damned bootsoles were as slick as
glass. The jack was solid but it was like walking a tightrope
in ice skates.

I tried to do as I'd advised Moke, look straight ahead and
put my feet one in front of the other, fast and smooth. I
could see his outline tensed, his face lit by sheaves of
sparks.

The resonator was running out of charge. The hole irised
in for a moment, flickered and drew slowly back out. Harsh
flashing discharges moved across it. I waited, wishing I had
a pole. Then the clear sky showed on the other side and I
ducked through. The tail of the next flash flicked me and
static lifted my hair. Then I was away.

I grabbed Moke's hands and a terminal flare from behind
brought darkness. The jack, sectioned, fell away and vanished. Hungry lightnings ate it. Mokey hauled me forward
and we fell on the concrete.

"So far so good. As the guy said when."

"Yeah. Let's hope the fireworks haven't brought the
cavalry."

He looked nervously back. Nothing, except circulating
lights, distant shouts and the flat yammer of radios. The
cops were probably looking for Raven in a haystack. I
would have taken bets on their chances of not finding him.

"We're in luck, guess they get small-beast trouble.
Move, before they come down anyway. Into the briars,
Brer."

We skidded and thumped down the slope. Below the
chains of helmet-lamps still moved in overlapping lines
across the valley bottom and the two copts wove their
search patterns nearer and nearer.

"If they've a scanner they'll see us like daylight," Moke whispered.

"Not if I get to my stash. Hallway laid this on for me. It better be good."

There ought to be an emitter, frequencied on me. A high thin gnat-whine in the farthest corners of my ears. The difficulty was locating it. I turned my head slowly, trying to range.

"That way, I think. It'll have a visual signal, but nothing we'll see until we're on top. Try bushes and long grass."

We flattened ourselves and scurried like weasels. The whine was getting louder. Moke turned a pale blur of face. "You sure?"

"Yes. Left, not too fast. We've got to be on top of it."

"Here!" A soft red ember in a clump of rushes. It brightened to a warm glow as I got up.

"Nice Hallway. Pull it out, Moke."

A long soft bundle wrapped in camouflage repeller.

"What's in it?"

"Coolsuits." I bit on it. "Three. And a couple gadgets. Get suited fast, guy, those copts are moving."

He shucked clothes without speaking. So did I. It felt good to wear something warm with non-slip soles.

"Gear. All of it. Keep the gun, you'll need it. Okay, we were never here."

I turned the disruptor on the pile and watched it blow to dust. "Can't leave anything behind. Now we move. If you meet a cop try not to trip over it. You aren't inaudible so if you sneeze you're a bird. Let's make country."

The valley bottom was clumped with briars, knee-deep in bracken and wet grass. Moke kept a hand on my shoulder and I held the disruptor. We passed close enough to a couple of cops to hear the crackle of their radios, and once the nearer of the two copts passed directly over and pinned us with its beam like dead moths.

It takes sand to stand still while a full-beam searchlight plays around you, but Mokey got the idea fast and I just had time to ground the gun before the light caught us. A good scope shows detail.

We stood in the middle of the goldfish bowl of glare for half the length of the universe before the copt moved on. I shouldered the disruptor and felt for Moke's hand. "Let's keep moving."

The dome edge was over the crest. It took a strenuous scramble in the dark, falling over humps and into holes.

"Impressive," Mokey said. "What's the miracle this time, Cass?"

The force-field's invisible, but a ten-foot band of bare earth where nothing grew lay beneath it and a sharp warping of the constellations over our heads showed where it curved the space above.

"No miracle. They have to let birds out. It's adjusted for life forms and aircraft, only it's electrified at ground level. How far can you jump?"

"Ten feet. What happens if I make nine-and-a-half?"

"You get unconscious and it yells for help. Run, and pick your feet up."

"What about you?"

"The same. You first, you're stronger."

I heard him crunch away across the grass. I wished bitterly for Dosh, our strong athletic other third. No use. We were on our own.

Moke came past me hard and fast and the wind of his passage blew in my eyes. A pause, and a thud from the other side. He gasped. I hadn't told him about the nasty shiver you get as you go through the warp. The grass bent under weight and I guessed he'd fallen forward. But he was over.

"Cass? Peel your mask."

"Why?"

"I'll catch you. Throw me your gear."

I slung the disruptor, then the bag. They were snatched out of the air.

"Now you."

I peeled back the hood, feeling the wind cold and sudden. I walked back. Ten feet isn't so great. Nothing for a moderate long-jumper. It just seems far when you have to.

I braced myself, reminded myself I'd jumped this on roofs without thinking, and gave it the fastest run I had. I'm often stressed on roofs but rarely physically tired. I thrust off as close to the edge as I dared, scissor-kicked—and saw I was falling short.

Moke grabbed my waist so hard I thought he'd sprung my ribs and lifted me out onto the grass. I brought him down with me and we sprawled, sobbing.

"That's twice, Moke. I'm off form."

"So'm I. You fit for a hike?"

"No. But we got no choice. We make as much country as we can. If we get tired we stay and wait for them to leave. Got a survival sheet. We walk around, until we can get back in other side of town. Then we make for Hallway's."

"That's one hell of a walk."

"It ain't getting shorter. Let's go."

We set off east, the lumpy yellowed grass catching at our shoes. The air was truly cold, with a raw biting dampness you never get inside. The trees and bushes were low and stunted, flattened by wind and centuries of acid rain. The old tough things, brambles and spiky weeds, snagged our suits. The air was acrid, itching our eyes and noses like smoke. The dull stars were crossed by bars of cloud underlit by the sick yellow glare of the city. Mokey silently took over the bag and disruptor and kept a grip on my arm.

I was having knee trouble. My legs refused to straighten between steps and I lurched like I was stoned. The ground

heaved uncertainly, trying to come to meet me. The tus-
socks were breaking the soles of my feet. I stumbled several
times and finally landed on all fours in a patch of mud.

Moke took my elbows and pulled me up.

"We're not going to make it. You're finished. And don't
talk survival sheets, this is exposure country. And, you're
getting mud on your suit and it shows. We got to do
something serious."

"Fly? I've done worse things than this. I'll get there."

"Not in shock you haven't. I think flying's a damned
good idea. See that copt?"

One of the two searchers had woven its path up one
direction and was returning in the other. It was below us and
maybe half a kay to the right.

"Uh-huh," I said, uneasily.

"I'm going to hitch a lift. Let's walk that way. We need
some brush for cover or they aren't going to believe us."

"What are they going to believe, Mokey?"

"That I'm a naked guy, all alone up here, who got
attacked by mercs. Got a way of attracting attention, like a
flashlight maybe?"

"I got a disruptor starts fires. But I don't know they'll
come for a guy, however naked. I'm the villain. How about
they find me in the bushes? Let me do the stripping. I won't
have to fake much."

He grunted. He'd started to peel his suit, but he pulled the
hood back while I shucked mine.

"Okay, adjust this."

I narrowed the aperture and set the register high.

"Don't spray it around or we'll roast if they don't see us
fast. A little fire, like this spiky bush here? Keep close, but
watch the light. Suits show in silhouette with a strong light
behind."

The bush flared with a startling whoosh and a sappy

smell. Smoke and flame rushed into the sky. The grass
began to crackle and blacken.

I got between the fire and the circling copt and waved my
arms like a drowning swimmer. I was as naked as a fish and
I didn't need to try to look weak. I didn't want the boys and
girls to think I was the kind of guy they burned on sight.

For a moment I thought they were too occupied, or
stupid, to see. Then the copt broke pattern and came
whirring out towards the fire. An enveloping halo filmed its
outline as it broke the field. I glanced back to check Moke
wasn't in sight. The stun-pistol showed, but I thought only
I would see it. Naked bims aren't so common out there.

I lifted my hands, remembering Mallore.

Murderess.

"Help! Please help me!"

The copt was coming down, its whistle moving down the
scale as it cut rotors. There was a space near us, rough and
marshy but wide enough to let it come close so they could
step off. I watched hungrily, waving my arms.

"Help!"

It glided in and hovered just above ground. The crew was
being careful. They hadn't cracked the hatch. If they were
scoping they'd find one life and a brush-fire. They were
maybe asking themselves how it started. They were going to
have to come and ask.

I made like September Morn, one fluttery hand over my
breasts and the other lower down, and staggered towards
them. I'd no difficulty tripping about.

"Help." The next tussock tripped me completely and I
went sprawling. That brought the fly-boys out. The hatch
lifted and they came tumbling, two, one of each.

Moke laid them out with a couple of brief plops. They
dropped and lay crisscrossed in the marsh.

If there was a third guy we were in trouble. There wasn't.
It was an observation craft. I staggered to the step.

"Can you fly, Moke?"

"Yeah. Learned with my Aris. I was houseboy, did the groceries."

"Great. Think I'll sit and shake a bit."

"Okay. Hang on. Don't want them two to die of exposure."

He laid them out on my survival sheet and tucked them in. They wouldn't have done it for him.

"Okay, Albert Schweitzer. Can we go?"

"Sure. Give me advice." He boosted me up. "Which way?"

"Ashton, mec. We just picked up dangerous prisoners. Swing this crate before somebody comes to congratulate us."

We hadn't got half a klick before there was an anxious voice on the radio.

"Parradine? What's going on?"

Moke gave me a panicky look. I picked up the mike. Acting was getting to be home ground.

"Pair of mercs in trouble in a bog-hole, stupid bastards. We pulled 'em out. Taking them to headquarters. How's your end?"

I thought crisp delivery with a gruffness that could be the radio would do for she-cop. It passed.

The guy sounded mad. "Fucking film-crew back there. Ought to be locked up. See you for a beer."

"Any time," I said. "Over and out."

I glanced at Moke. "And we're out, too."

He didn't answer. In the light from the panel his narrow face was gray, glazed with silent tears that ran down his cheeks and dripped off his chin into his suit. He stared straight ahead, concentrating on navigating, and the tears flowed down and down.

I felt as if I'd never cry again.

By the time Moke got us into Ashton and dumped the copt in the city center I felt like a used handkerchief. The old-fashioned linen kind, and used by someone with a cold in the head. I was soaked, muddy and had an irrepressible shiver in my solar plexus. Mokey had to catch my arm to stop me folding like a deck-chair.

He wasn't much better himself. We looked like the rag end of a bout of mud-wrestling.

"Where to?" I croaked.

"Not the Dog, it's the first place they'll look. And we've bought Eustace enough trouble. We need Swordfish."

"We won't get him. Sword doesn't stand still to be refused. It's more than his reputation's worth. And I've done it twice, once myself and once by Raven. He might let mine past because only he heard, but Raven's public. He may say no, he may cut your tongue out to make the point. Stay away, he's dangerous."

Moke looked at me. "You know, Cass, sometimes you don't understand people."

"I understand Sword."

"Do you?" He reached into the copt and pulled out a dark-green police poncho, thin, chilly and long enough to reach my heels. "Shed the suit and get into this. I know exactly where to dump you."

"Where's that?"

"Opera Square bath-house. Just the place for cold ladies with no clothes. Hot, crowded and everybody in their skin. Exactly what you need."

"How're we going to pay? I left my card at the Dog with the rest of my gear."

"That's okay, we'll get it. Dribble can go if we can't."

"Big deal. It'll need disinfecting. But you forgot. Dribble works for Sword. If you don't find one you won't find the other. And the guys here want cash up-front. It's difficult to repossess two hours of hot-room."

He smiled faintly, his narrow gray face opening like a break in the rain. He fished in his pocket with dirty fingers. "So I've got mine. Ordinary Ump allotment card such as big guys like you pick up with tongs, but it's got a week's cred and that'll buy you in, get you a soak and some food and something to wear for both of us. It won't be Adelaide, but it'll cover you. You'll be better without Adelaide anyhow, she stands out a mile."

"I bet our faces are over every vid in town by now. Especially mine. We're up for grabs in any public place at all."

"You haven't seen yourself. You look like the cat dragged you in and spat you out. In fact, no self-respecting cat would lay a claw on you in that state. A really public, public place is exactly where nobody's going to look. And me, nobody sees me if I stand at the crossroads and make like a windmill. Let me dispose of the artillery. A naked lady in a bath-house is like every other guy in the world but a naked lady plugged into a disruptor's apt to attract attention."

"There's a laser-artist on my tail," I said feebly.

"Not here and now there isn't. If he's any sense he's home in bed. Come on, strip and get into this and I'll see if I can get us off hooks."

"You can't stand Sword."

"Correct. It's mutual. If he doesn't like it he can say no, in which case we'll manage without him. Come on, kid, you're the poor lady got mugged and I'm the big cop delivering you to a place of safety. It'll explain everything, including why you're in shock. Remember to snivel, they'll expect it."

"I don't snivel."

"Cassandra doesn't snivel. Little Annie who got beaten up and rolled in a puddle by five hoodlums with razors snivels like a mountain brook. It's the world's most perfect disguise and it'll do you good. Get moving before you set."

It was four in the morning and the parking lot was as empty as the far side of Mercury. Moke zipped off my soiled suit like shelling shrimp and threw the poncho over me. Then he rolled up his own, except the legs which were so muddy they weren't invisible any more. He slung the second poncho over himself, fastened it to the neck and finished the effect with a regulation cap someone had left behind. Probably the lady, since it was too small. In the dark he looked slightly authentic.

He shouldered the bag with one arm and gathered me with the other. "Come on, kid. Hot steam down the road."

The Opera Square bath-house does business even at four A.M. At that hour the clientele's evenly divided between tarts coming off-shift and party-goers working off their first-half hangovers before they start the third quarter. Bare, it's hard to tell them apart. Maybe the tarts have better figures.

Moke was right about it being anonymous. I got perfunctory sympathy at the door. I guess the cops have to dump half the mugging cases in town there, they sure as hell don't bother to log them, it's not worth the effort. It went with a couple of clean towels and the offer of sandwiches and coffee. I took it, had a long shower, ate, sprawled in the steam room and accepted a massage that left me short of skin but with the beginnings of sensation in my legs and back. Then I showered some more and went back to the hot room to sprawl on a slab and snivel.

Only because I'd been told to. Actually it came with dismaying ease and I had to put a hard brake on before it became a full-scale bawl and got everyone in the place looking. I guess a lot of people snivel in there. It got me a couple of politely turned shoulders and another coffee from the attendant, who looked like a refugee from the screws' department of a women's prison. Her slab face said this was the end of the sympathy and if I made any more trouble I caught the street.

Being limited to two damp towels and a police poncho, I took the hint and snuffled into my coffee cup like my name was Annie.

A cold nose under the edge of my towel brought me around in a hurry. I slapped out reflexively, opened pink gummy eyes and saw Dribble squatting on his hind legs snout-to-nose with me and looking particularly self-satisfied. He was dribbling, of course. I was revolted to see whatever he'd found under the towel had excited him because he was showing two inches of infantile erection.

My neighbors, those who'd seen him, were making lemon-juice faces and drawing fastidiously away. The only thing to be said for the horrible creature is he moves quietly or we'd probably have had a riot. When they got the idea he was with me they gave me the same treatment. I didn't blame them. I wasn't sure how long I was keeping my coffee myself.

"Whaddya want?" I snarled, despising my lack of real venom. I was clean out of poison, though it's the only way I know of dealing with Dribble.

He dropped the bulging sack he had wedged between his teeth on the slab near my left ear and bared his eight inches of razored ivory. He probably thought it was a winning smile.

"You put on and come out, or Sword come in and getcha," he whistled smugly.

I poked open the edge of the bag. Navy-blue lace, red jump, silver boots. Not Adelaide. Something further uptown with Ari customers and gold-plated cred-cards. Two plastic bracelets with fiberoptic light-shows in different colors and a red and a silver scarf to twist into a headband. Not Moke's taste, unless I'd turned into a ring-tailed monkey.

"Pretty frillies," Dribble trilled with a libidinous giggle, leaning to peer in. "You put on now?"

"You pick these?" I asked aggressively.

"Not got card," he whimpered, putting on one of his pathetic acts. "Sword send, me carry." He brightened. "Put on?"

"If you've had your nose in 'em, short stuff, I'd rather come out naked."

He cringed. "Please not. No nose. Sword very bad temper."

He could say that again, though his amputated grammar left a doubt whether he was discussing Sword's normal state or the weather tonight. My experience of Sword's been he only loses his temper for a reason, and when he does you better take to the high ground. In this case it probably wasn't going to matter. If Moke was there we needed the mountains anyhow.

"Okay. Clear off, I'm not doing a dress-tease for you, dog-meat."

He whined on a note of injured suffering, lolled his horrible tongue at me and lolloped off four-legged. He left a trail of shrieks as he twitched towels on his way past.

The slab-faced attendant approached me looking like a prison matron handing out punishment detail.

"If that thing's yours I gotta ask you to leave."

"Nothing to do with me," I said. "Damn thing thinks it's Puck. But don't get uptight, I'm going."

A traxie was waiting in the street with an anxious Moke in front and Dribble bouncing energetically in the back. Mokey leaned to hold open the door and I fell on the cushions, throwing shiny scarlet arms around his kind neck.

"Sorry, Cass. Kept you waiting," he said. "Took longer than I thought."

He was wearing a knit sweater and velvet jeans that made him almost handsome. I saw for a moment if he ever got successful he was going to be distinguished. It wasn't a thought I'd ever had about Moke.

"Sword's mad, huh?" I said, jerking the door to.

Dribble giggled, on a knifing scale like little silver scalpels. "Why'n't ask?"

I turned and caught a ripple in the fabric of things at the edge of my eye. Back seat, one guy in coolsuit. Swordfish, if it was him, had his filters down. Nothing showed at all.

"Sword?" My voice quavered. "You came?"

"As you see." His tone was so neutral it left shapes in the air.

"You were right and I was wrong." I bit the inside of my cheek. You don't cry in front of Swordfish. "I killed Doshky."

"I've had this conversation already." The atmosphere shed ice-flakes like the South Pole in July. "Oddly enough the genius wants the credit himself."

Moke shuddered, his face going a shade grayer. "If I'd taken Dosh seriously, if I'd gone after him faster, if I hadn't been in Cass's way when she needed to get her gun out, this wouldn't have happened."

"And if I'd understood my responsibilities to you three rejects from the nursery class, particularly if I'd had the common good sense to put Cassandra across my knee and whale the tar out of her starting seven years ago when we first met, we could all be home in bed."

Sword hadn't warmed but there was a dry irony in his tone. "She's been trying to convince me she was grown up since she was fourteen and the day before yesterday I was fool enough to believe her. I think the honors are even. I don't feel like arguing. I'd rather get some sleep."

The traxie whined softly, slid a little way on its skids and rose into the air. Which meant Sword had the controls. The corridor of light sucked it up and catapulted it across the cliffs and spires of Lower Ashton.

"You despised Dosh," Moke said. His voice was bitter. "Because he was a tart. You couldn't see he was honest. At least as honest as you."

"I doubt it," Swordfish retorted. "I've yet to go soggy over a re-surged bitch with a baby voice and no tits when I've a woman in the house. His profession wasn't my business. My reasons for disliking him were entirely personal. I don't deny I did. For Cassandra's sake, since she valued him, I'd have saved him if I could. If I'd had the nous to ignore you all, do what I knew was right and be there. Since I didn't I take some blame. That doesn't oblige me to admire him. It doesn't oblige me to let off firecrackers either."

"I thought I could save us," I said miserably. "Hallway'd worked out how to get money. Enough to take us off-planet. It was fixed. I meant to show up the film company, sabotage their game and come back, collect and leave. The three of us. I knew we'd be on film and I thought they'd be scoping. They could have seen through your suit, Sword. They've got the equipment. That's why I didn't want you. I thought I could handle it. I was wrong. I never thought Dosh would stick to Mallore rather than Moke and me. Moke says I'm bad at understanding people. I must be. I hadn't understood how badly he needed to be in films.''

"Anyone who wants to see my face has only to ask," Swordfish said. He sounded dangerous. "I could have told you that. Quite a number of people have seen it. None of them's asked for a second look. I'm going to tell you the truth once and once only. Doshchenko was a trusting guy of twenty-six with the mentality of a sixteen-year-old, he was killed by Nimbus and the sooner you get that into your heads the better. I warned you she ate her mates. Christ,'' he added, on a tone of rising derision. "How did I get stuck with the Babes in the Wood? Stay quiet, children, I'll cover you with leaves. I'm going to start advertising as nursemaid. Now shut up."

We did. I leaked tears into Mokey's shoulder. It surprised me how much Sword's contempt hurt. He isn't even human.

"I told you," I whispered. "He despises us."

"Hush, Cass." Moke hugged me. "I'm what's making him mad. You don't understand how we are."

That made two of them. I folded like an oyster, pulled my knees up to my chin and wept into my thighs. After a while a hand massaged the back of my neck, then the rest of the arm slid down the front, prized my shell open and gave me a shoulder to cry on. I cried on it. I thought it was Moke's. Only when we got up to get out he was hunched at the other side of the seat with a closed face.

I find guys hard to understand.

"Mallore," Swordfish said. "Alias Nimbus."

His eyes were on view today, turned down to a printout in his hands. They were still cold. The rest was invisible though from the scenery he had a leg cocked up on the coffee-table.

The apartment was on the upper floor of an uptown slab with foreign names on the furniture. It had as much character as a Homes-and-Gardens window display. Mokey was full-length on a blue-gray leather couch twice his own length and I had a pink chair deep enough to go skin-diving in. Sword had the other. The coffee table was glass, free-form and unsupported. It had a coffee maker made out of a lot of glass globes and twisty tubes and two porcelain cups on it. One mine, one Moke's. Sword has to eat and drink sometime but nobody's seen him. For all I know he puts down roots.

Outside the wraparound double-wall window you could see the upper floors of a couple of similar slabs with sun-umbrellas and jolly flower-boxes on the balconies and a hazed sky cut by contrails. If they're looking for you in the lower depths come up for air, was Sword's reasoning.

Moke and me'd had a night and half a day of scary comfort in a bed the size of the Loop where we'd been afraid to sleep in case we fell through, and our own kitchen. It looked like the flight deck of an interstellar cruiser and we hadn't liked to touch anything in case it exploded. Mokey'd finally solved the coffee-machine and we'd breakfasted on bread and caviar out of the icebox. Right afterwards the dumb-waiter whirred and spat out a four-course something we hadn't room for.

I thought if we got rich we were going to have to go to night-school to learn what buttons to press.

Swordfish straightened his printout with a flat snap to get our attention.

"Did a few minor epics. *Ruby of the Jungle,* stuff like that, which incidentally got a complaint from the Amazon Basin Conservancy Council. First serious film was *Desert Dust* sixteen years ago. She was young enough to have a lot of her own skeleton and look her age. Second male and female leads died, along with thirteen extras and half a dozen horses. The hero was supposed to survive to claim her but he had a rotor failure as he brought his microlite down in the last scene and his backup zonked. She played it herself with tears in her eyes, cradling his body. It could have been an accident. An animal protection society complained about the horses.

"Following year she played in two movies, one a comedy that flopped. Only casualties were the butler and second female when the house went up in a lot fire. Hilarious scenes of Nimbus and the male lead, a well-known romantic star, escaping by the roof and falling in the pool. The guy had to be resuscitated but made it. Film didn't. Studio concluded she hadn't comedy potential. Second was a historical drama where two complete armies slaughtered each other, plus several torture scenes and a public execution. She was the Eurasian whore who saved the hero's life. He lived, but word was he had to be dragged off by the techs after the last kiss before he got through strangling her. His contract was annulled."

He glanced up, a cold flash. "She hasn't looked back. She had surgery after the war epic to emphasize her youth and fragility and she's been getting younger and more fragile every couple of years since. Her record's impressive. Hero number four, in the jungle again. Bitten in the foot by something unidentified and died in agony. She reached civilization alone. Five: Antarctic adventure, somebody closed the door with the guy outside, they found the stiff in the morning. Six fell off his horse in the middle of a Cossack charge and ended as steak tartare. Seven's a dilly, they were doing a spaceship-downed-in-alien-jungle sequence where the crew eat each other. Ended with him and her. She ate him. Rescue flight was late. Eight: Ancient Egypt and sacred crocodiles. He fell in."

He raised expressionless eyes. "You want more? She's made twenty-three films. None of her co-stars has survived since the guy tried to strangle her. Company's racked up fifteen complaints from Animal Rights, seven from Native

Affairs, four from Alien Protection and one from the International Court. Her filming since has been local. They've made enough millions to run half the Solar System and she's still a number one pull.''

"She's a mass murderess," Mokey said. He was pale. "I backed Dosh to take the contract."

A ripple across the pink chair could have been a shrug.

"Impossible to say how many deaths were hers, how many were rigged by the studio and how many were fight-offs she happened to win. Cassandra, stop biting your nails."

"I'm not." I looked down and saw ragged edges along both thumbs.

"You're biting your nails, Cass," Mokey told me.

I sat on my hands and stared earnestly at Sword. He looked grimly back.

"Let's just say Nimbus's films end on a note of pathos with the lorn heroine coming through single-handed, and she's one tough lady." The gray gaze took in Moke's pallor. "No use blaming yourself, you were hustled. Nimbus is unique. Most films have casualties but only hers sweep the board. Naturally they didn't tell you. Cassandra, I won't warn you again."

I put my hands back under my thighs. "Don't nag, Sword. You're not my brother."

"I know that better than you. You want to see her?"

Mokey glanced across. "How do you feel, Cass?"

"Sick. Let's do it."

Sword's invisible hand played over a pad and the wall-screen lit.

Jungle. Hot greenery, wet smells, steaming earth and vegetable rot. Things that rustled and other things that zinged and whistled. A blue enameled butterfly the size of a sparrow flew slowly across the room from right to left.

''If you want to feel this you better plug in. Jacks in the chair-arms.''

Moke and I did. Sword didn't. Maybe he'd been there.

Terror, underlaid with heat, sweat, weariness. There was numbed pain, a muted itch from a dozen festering sores. Everything ached. Loss, loneliness, despair. And backing it a desperate resolution.

A woman came out of the vegetation towards us. She was young and slender with a firm roundness under her torn sweat-stained shirt and the muddy jeans that clung to her hips. Golden-brown strands of hair were plastered to her face, the heavy silk rope bundled at the back of her neck.

Sweat ran from under it, from under her arms, her small breasts, down her jean-covered thighs. Her eyes, large, wide and green-gray, stared straight ahead, glazed with fatigue. She strained for movement in the leafy masses.

She'd lost everything, she'd nothing more to hope for. She went on putting one foot in front of the other for want of anything else to do. In spite of her folding knees and aching calves. Because she was there. She lifted a wrist to brush sweat out of her eyes and I saw the welling pit of a huge ulcerous bite on the back of her hand.

Something stirred in the rustling leaves to her right. Something dangerous, unnatural. She forced her exhausted muscles to react, snatching at the gun at her belt . . .

Sudden blankness, sight and feeling cut off as if I'd gone numb and blind, left me choking, suspended in mid-air. I was dazed, eyes filled with tears.

I blinked. She'd been so brave, indomitable, small . . .

Sword looked at me with something like compassion. He'd jerked the film and pulled my jack in the same instant. On the couch Mokey pinched his nose. There was pain in his face.

"Good, isn't she? I thought I'd spare you the bit upset the Nature Conservancy. You okay, Genius?"

Moke slowly drew out his jack. "Yes, she's good. Very good. How does she make you feel so sorry?"

"Talent." Sword was dry. "I didn't say she wasn't an actress. She feels her parts. It's a pity so few of her co-stars survive. That's *Ruby of the Jungle* just before she turned major. She was under thirty and had her own eyes."

I scrubbed my face angrily. Yes, she was good. Damnably. And she had a good body and an intelligent face in those days. Not the fragile scarecrow with the hyped-out stare we'd found in the street. I discovered my thumb in my mouth again and hastily pulled it out. For a moment back there I'd been sorry for her. I wondered what pressures she'd had on her, what off-screen fights had gone down to turn her from what she'd been into what she was.

Yet she'd been acting. What did she feel when she was herself? Did she have a self to feel?

I bit at my nail and pain brought me to reality. Yes, she did. Enough to know when her film had been sabotaged and she wasn't winning any more. Enough to turn and shoot Dosh as he stretched his hand to help her, to make it look like he was attacking her, to explain the mayhem. Like a striking snake. As she'd reached for her gun back in the jungle. Just before Swordfish pulled my jack so I needn't see someone else die.

Sixteen years of killing. Becoming less human every year and killing more and more as she went. The girl on the screen was already dead. Maybe there'd once been an actress named Nimbus who had a great future and wanted to grab it with both hands. Now there was only Mallore.

Murderess.

"So?" Sword asked calmly.

Moke said nothing. His green eyes were blank.

I pulled my thumb out of my mouth. "I want her."

"Uh-uh. Not twice." Swordfish sounded so exactly like Razor in a tough mood he caught me short. Then I hauled my act together and met his eyes.

"No, listen. So long as what's going down is guy stuff I use guys. I've asked you and I've asked Raven. I'm not stupid enough to think I can do strong bits myself. Last time I got it wrong because I didn't know Nimbus. After all, it was three to one. I was like Moke, I didn't think she'd kill. I kept Raven around till the house was under control, ask him. I'm not a fighter, I'm a thief. I can use tools but when I need help I ask. I do and I will. But I have to finish the job. It's between her and me and I want her."

"And how," Sword asked with disapproving delicacy, "do you intend to get her?"

"I want her looking the filth she is. Not just because of Dosh, though it's Dosh she's done to Moke and me. For everything."

"And how do you mean to do it?" He still sounded like the cat that walks by itself and lifts its paws at every step.

"You know how it's done. You've done it. Nimbus is a big star. She's a beauty, a rich arrogant woman who thinks she has the right to do anything to anybody and she uses people like toilet paper. She enjoys power. I've watched her pull Dosh's strings. And mine. She even had to have a go at Moke because she needs 'em all. She's got to have everything, all the attention, the sympathy, the suffering. Exposure. On the big screen where everyone can see her. Well, I want the same. In spades."

"You want a public confession."

"If we can cut it. Or just show her as she is. In public. On screen. She's still heroine, still getting away with murder. I want her to lose so everyone will know it. I want people to understand what she's done."

Moke was looking hard at the wall. I could hear him cutting back his breath.

At last he said, "Let her go, Cass. You won already. You spoiled her part. She's got to be mad as hell. She may have saved her face if the cops bought the story, but she hasn't shined up her career. Facing her again won't bring anyone back. Not Dosh, not anyone. She's a poisonous woman and she can only hurt you. You'll hurt yourself. Let her rot."

"But she isn't going to rot, Mokey. She's going to make more films and kill more people and get richer and more famous every day. She'll kill us if she can. I owe her, and I pay."

Sword's hard steady eyes were on my face. "It's going to cost."

"I'll get what it takes. Name your price."

"Nobody pays me to bury my friends. I'm talking venue, cameras, equipment. If you want this to go out where it'll be seen a tape that can be suppressed or edited is no good. We've got to patch it into the public vid programs and make people watch. It's got to be a general broadcast, and it's got to parasite the public waves. That's big bucks."

I laughed. "We got big bucks. You've no idea how big." I took another bite of nail. There seemed to be red stuff running down my finger. I licked it. "Let me talk to Hallway."

His hand fastened brutally on my wrist. "Get me the nuskin from the bathroom, will you, Genius? Okay, you want a show. I think your intellectual friend could be right and you aren't going to enjoy it. You haven't the temperament. But I won't watch you eat yourself. I'll see Hallway. We'll get gear and we'll discuss money. And I'll stage it for you. But understand me, Cass. What I start I finish. Be sure it's what you want. If I begin you aren't going to switch me off."

"I want a show. Go ahead. I'll do the talking, but I need

your help for technics and scenery. Do it. I won't change my mind.''

He went on looking at me until Moke came back with the spray. Then I saw the ripple of a shrug.

''Okay, but I hope you've a good script. She strikes me as a lady who won't haze easily. Maybe you could use a couple of hands.''

''No, Sword. I don't like her enough to want to be twins. I want her reputation demolished, not her skeleton. That's her trick. No bloodline specials.''

He snorted. ''Which I do every morning before breakfast. They lay on a truck for my personal corpses. Let's keep our private quarrels for later. We're now going to forget it until tomorrow. I got planning to do. Give me your hand and hold still.''

He was neat, quick and competent. Sword the nursemaid. I'd seen everything.

I loped down the street trying to look alone in a green catsuit contrasted nicely with my scarlet wig, over black gauze nothings said specialist catalogue, and silver boots. And gloves. Swordfish refused to go anywhere with me unless I wore them and kept them on.

"You're getting into a rut, guy. Sexy underwear. If I didn't know you I'd say you had fantasies."

"I'll indent for pink cotton bloomers," the air retorted. He was back to his warm easy tone. Action agrees with him. "Stay quiet to the next intersection and I'll give you a present."

"Like what?"

Swordfish's presents have a habit of blowing up in your face.

"The head of Alfredo Garcia. Shut up."

The next intersection was only exceptional in having a newsvendor. The air gave me a card.

"This is illegal," I said, shocked. The air snarled.

The machine burped, whirred and ran headlines.

"What am I looking for?"

"Page One. I only use small ads in emergencies."

I smiled sweetly at a runty guy in a business suit who was looking at me with gooseberry eyes.

"I'm practicing to be a ventriloquist," I told him.

He blinked twice, flushed and scurried away. I guess he thought I was about to do something dangerous with a zip-gun.

Page One was the story with pictures of some top-grade head of a big Ari combine who'd come unstuck and left his fortune all over the Stock Exchange in the form of nose-wipes. It's the sort of deal I contribute to myself. This one was also currently in jail on a list of vice charges would have nauseated a buffalo.

That's not usual. They almost always get away with it. Somebody disliked him a lot. I'd never heard of the guy considering the noise but the Social Register ain't my thing. I only use it to get addresses for my heists.

"Who is he?"

"Your ex-employer. The one who wanted a contract."

I contemplated Sword, or where I thought he might be. Someone had pulled strings. As thick as the Atlantic cable.

"Where's the money?"

A low laugh, of the sort keeps respectable virgins awake nights. The one you hear in the bed-curtains after they've locked the door and gone away.

"Some of his friends are richer than yesterday. He bought you an apartment and a pile of exclusive underwear. Try thinking of him with gratitude when you open the next can of caviar."

"You didn't dirty your own hands with it, of course."

The laugh dropped a couple of tones, to the sort keeps great white sharks awake nights.

"Me? I've an army to run. They march on their bellies."

Literally, in some cases.

"Remind me not to offend you."

"You offend me every time we meet, usually on purpose. Let's go see Hallway."

Hallway's got to use his own technology. He sees too well. He put down his operating tools and came across stripping gloves.

"Cassandra. Heard about Doschenko. I'm sorry. He was a nice kid." Hall's always sincere. He gave me a hug and shake as proof. "Hi, Sword. You guys together again?"

He offered his hand and seemed to get it shaken. I've a fantasy Sword and Hall are twins. They're both skinny and over-tall. But I can't outfit Swordfish with kind pale eyes, boyish smile and red hair. And nobody could call him pacifist. But Hall's a Luney. They're all odd. Maybe they're cousins.

"Cass tells me you've found the way to the wishing-well."

"And how. It's the golden ass. You spread your cloth and hang on its tail. But Cass has moral reservations. She wants her exact pound."

"Hall's tapped into the film company accounts," I explained. "We figured they didn't mean to pay us. 'Specially after what you read last night. Cheaper to waste people than money, right? So I'm claiming what they owe. For three. Should cover costs. It bribed us."

"Poetic justice," Hallway said. "Cass wants to use their bribe-money to pay them."

"That sounds like the Babes. Okay, let's do business. I don't give a fuck for poetry or penny-counting, let's calculate necessities. I got a list of supplies and if the film company's paying that's fine by me. They'll get their money's worth. I rate star billing so I'm taking the salary. In advance. How long will it take to get this stuff and rig it?"

The list, like most of Sword's gear, came out of the air and into Hallway's hand. Hallway glanced over it and raised pale brows.

"What I like about you is nobody can say you think small. Where's this going?"

"You know the old rink on Fourth and Ninety-Second?"

"Isn't it a ruin?"

"On the outside. I've used it for a couple of productions

so I can vouch the interior's sound. Nothing quite this scale but it'll do. I got labor, get me material.''

''And who's getting you out of the country?'' Hallway murmured politely. ''Don't answer that.''

''You think there isn't an answer?''

''I'm sure there is. I'd rather not know about it before I have to.'' Another white smile. ''I value such health as I have. Some of this stuff's specialized. Take me a couple of days.''

''Not too long, Hall. The city's getting hottish. Someone wants Cass's tail, and badly. If I'm going to tie a knot in theirs we can't give them time to sniff around. Ain't as if we were dealing with adults here.''

''Sword's sore because he wanted to stop this and I got in his way.''

''I know why Sword's sore,'' Hallway said. ''You holding his hand, Cass, or you want something too?''

''You bet there is. I got my own list. It's shorter than his and easier to get. Only I need it. And information.''

''Just ask,'' Hallway said. ''When did I let you down?''

''I could give exact dates,'' Swordfish said. ''But I already admitted it wasn't your fault.''

They looked at each other, eye to eye. They had to be twins. Or Luneys.

''We've a difference of opinion on that,'' Hallway said quietly after a moment. ''But I'm not going to argue again. I'll get your stuff. You've never needed to blackmail me, Sword.''

''I know. It's why I never do.''

Hallway turned away to his deck. It's the first time I've seen him with his head bowed.

''I wish you wouldn't,'' Moke said miserably. He'd got a bag of plaster someplace and the free-form coffee table was in the state as comes with Moke. It had an erection that looked something like a rock and something like a cave and something like a guy with a bellyache. It had bits of wire and sacking sticking out where he hadn't got around to the details. The place had stopped looking like any sort of shop window if you don't count the lower-class kind of junk shop. It's called the creative process. "Sword was spitting fire after the last time."

"Not with me."

"With me. For letting you. He's right, I'm older and I ought to know better. I'm trying to."

"I damn well wish he'd stop treating me like I was fourteen still."

"I think he wishes you were. Then he'd have a chance of sitting on you and making it stick."

"I thought he was sitting pretty good. You never told me how you found him."

"He found me. I wandered around a bit looking out for Dribble and Swordfish landed on my neck like a ton of steel girders. Jet-propelled. He knew the whole thing before I told him. He tore me off so many strips I nearly needed a new skeleton and the only reason he didn't lock me in the cellar and leave me was I wouldn't tell him where you were until I got to come. You'll have noticed we weren't exactly speaking."

"It's the jungle drums. Boom-a-boom. They call it sources but it's a little guy sitting someplace with a tom-tom. I'm getting escorted everywhere. Like you, under surveillance. Only reason he doesn't lock me in a cellar and leave me is I'd bite his ankles. It's my business, Moke. Like that mess is yours."

He smiled sadly. "This mess is what I was going to make for Eklund, for the show that didn't exist. I got to do something to stop myself going crazy. Or I'd be eating my fingers off like you."

"I got to do this to stop myself eating my fingers off. I

keep turning over in bed and thinking how badly Dosh is going to like it here.''

He rubbed a cheek lightly frosted with plaster-dust against mine. ''I think the same every time I look at the collection of sweaters in the closet. Doshky would've known how to light up the town on unlimited credit. It ain't fair, girl.''

''Well, it's going to get a bit fairer. Trust me, Mokey.'' It came to me I'd said some of the same thing to Sword before I fucked up last. ''Or at least trust Swordfish. You build things, I break 'em. Why does that guy have a hole in his guts?''

Next time I looked in on him he'd finished removing his guy's guts and was starting in on his heart.

I thought that was going too far. I told him so.

You got to have one or the other.

Hallway was taking trouble over this deal. We spent an itchy forty-eight hours sitting around the apartment while Moke perfected his gutless rockman and I had about seventeen baths. That let me try all the colored glass bottles in the bathroom before Sword appeared and gave us the high sign.

"Tonight," he said.

Appeared is never right for Swordfish. He manifests. He did it this time as the usual eyes too high up, a package, and a rectangle of white plastic. Engraved in gilt. Tall snob country. Most people choose little holos that pop out and sing at you.

This one just sat there. If you could read and write you got to know the Countess Cara Adair requested the presence of the Honorable Jocelyn Reeves-Baker at the cocktail party which was going down at her place starting eight-thirty.

"That's you," Sword said. "You're in the parcel. You need help with Face?"

That got an unhappy exchange of looks between Mokey and me. Face is the ultimate makeup form and Dosh is an expert. Had been. I've never got further than wigs and dresses and Moke thinks he's overdone if he has shoes on.

"Yes," Sword translated. "Okay, I'm lady's maid. Nimbus will be there. We've been waiting for that. The lady likes amusement. Right now she's sulking because you busted her film. Her producer isn't pleased either. So she'll be looking for entertainment. Entertain her, Cassandra. And get her to go for a walk in the garden at midnight. We'll do the rest. You had a shower lately?''

He had to be joking.

The Face was a pig. I spent the first five minutes convinced I was going to suffocate and the next half-hour trying to hold off tic douloureux. It felt tight and clinging against my face like having a plastic bag over your head. It is having a plastic bag over your head.

"What happens if I sneeze?" I lisped from behind the Honorable Jocelyn's over-full lips, watching her fake lashes bat in the mirror like briar bushes.

"Don't be infantile," Sword said. This Face came down to my waist and up to my hips so it seemed to me it would have been simpler to complete the shape, inflate it and send it by itself. There was a gap maybe ten inches around the middle was me. Truth is, it wasn't sneezing I was worried about.

"It's like a coolsuit only it can block your sweat glands, so we need to leave skin free. If you want to do anything, do it. Quit wriggling, I'm trying to get your nails right."

I've known Sword since my mama locked the door and he and Razor got me between them. It's as well. He's the only guy besides Mokey I'd trust to plastic skin my bulges without heavy breathing and I don't always trust Mokey. Even with Sword I wondered if the journey was really necessary. Until I saw the dress. I'll tell you something. Rich ladies call themselves prettier names but I'd say the Honorable Josh was a whore. It's the only kind of mammal I know shows that much of herself in public. The reason I was me around the waist was it was the only bit actually covered.

"Right," Swordfish said brutally when he'd finished hauling and grinding the tenderer bits of my figure into the crevices. "You can paint your nipples yourself. I draw the line right there."

I was glad he drew it somewhere. We'd got close for a minute or two. Like space-wrestlers exchanging bearhugs. I stretched Josh's hand, toad-white and longer than mine, and tried to pick up a paint-stick. Her inch-and-a-half of pink glitter nail didn't help.

"Who is this bim?"

"Lady Jocelyn comes from Dis, which is useful because nobody's met her. What's even more useful is nobody comes from Dis so you aren't going to meet anyone you ought to know. Her daddy owns half the world's hydroponics farms which lets you faint if anyone's ill-mannered enough to mention algae. They will, Aris specialize in bad manners. Hit the deck. They also specialize in high-fidelity fusses. Pout at Nimbus, she adores pale young things who pass out. Don't stay passed out long or you'll get assaulted and I know you too well to think you'll stand still for it. For Christ's sake, it's your nipples you're gilding, not your entire upper half. Sit still and I'll wipe it."

"No, you won't. I bet Josh has three fawning slave-girls to do this. It's like working at five yards with pincers. Did you have to get a dame descended from a line of Chinese perverts?"

"It happens to be the style on Dis. You're stuck with it because it's the only place you can come from I can guarantee you won't meet the neighbors." He snatched the wipe impatiently and cleaned around the edges. "Better. Now don't move or you could end up wearing this for real."

The Honorable Jocelyn among her other filthy habits wore breast-jewelry. The sight of bims with heavy chains trailing from their pierced nipples has always made me queasy. I sat like a statue while Sword's hard fingers slotted a hook through the layer of plastic, trying to shrink my skin inside. The other nipple had a platinum ring the size of a wheel-disk with little diamond tears all the way around.

"If she wears this kind of stuff on her pubes . . ." I whined.

"She does. Sit still or I'll do you an injury."

"Can I be sick now?"

"Sure. Come back when you've finished and I'll fix the rest of the ice."

What I like about Sword is he's all heart. Carved out of flint. I sighed and sat.

"Doesn't this give her lovers a hard time?"

"Be grateful. It's her daddy's idea, it holds 'em back. With any luck you may leave without getting raped."

"You sure this is daddy's idea?"

"Yes. Who else's would it be?"

"I had this thought it might be yours."

"In that case say thanks."

"Thanks. Why is it bims always get the remnants of the feudal system? Catch me a guy who'd do this to his prick."

"Stay around," he said with irony.

"I'd rather not. I can see who gets to suffer in the end."

He straightened, or at least the eyes got to their usual level. "Not bad. She sticks out in places you don't."

"I'd noticed," I snarled. "Remind me not to sit down. I got a conviction this thing's fixed to make a noise like a whoopee cushion."

"Wrong. But don't sit down anyhow, Nimbus likes girls who sway. You got an hour to practice."

"I got an hour to practice breathing. What do I do if I'm offered a drink?"

"You got a choice. You can accept or tell them your ladylike upbringing's against it. I recommend the latter. They're puritanical as hell on Dis and God knows what's likely to be in Cara's liquor."

"Puritanical," I murmured, looking at the dress in the holomirror.

"Right. Oh, and don't forget the glass slippers."

I thought he was kidding. He wasn't. Iridescent plexiglass with four-and-a-half-inch heels. Swaying was going to be no problem at all. My only difficulty was going to be staying upright. I had an idea the revenge wasn't all on one side.

"You still sore, Sword?"

"Me?" he said. Like the cat in the cream jug. "Now what could make you think that?"

The vehicle wasn't exactly a coach made out of a pumpkin but it was sure furnished with rats. And maybe frogs if I could've seen them. Anyhow it was Wings who greeted me.

"Get in."

"You're late. The damned invite was for eight-thirty."

He sneered nastily. "Nobody goes to an Ari party on time. We get there at quarter to ten, and even that's not fashionable. Sword doesn't want to draw attention. He figures Dis is provincial."

"He's too kind. If he'd looked further he might've found someplace they wear real chastity belts and come in the Iron Maiden."

"This was your fucking idea," he growled, and took off at a speed and angle that left my stomach below. Seemed Sword wasn't the only one was sore. Sitting on all that garbage I was in a bit of of pain myself. The jewelry came from Hallway and it was class merchandise. Nothing looks like pure carbon but pure carbon. I don't know who did the artwork but I hadn't thought he was a guy had sadistic friends. I was extending my education.

Countess Cara's house on the edge of the city had its own dome and its own acres of parkland. It looked like a sugar wedding cake complete with pink ice flounces and rose into the empyrean like a Disney castle. There were so many copts buzzing around its towers it looked like the cake had attracted flies. We joined them.

Wings shed his suit on the way, which showed why he was in a bad temper. Either he was in Face himself or he really was a slender dark kid with a ratty mustache that would have liked to be dashing and his implants restricted to places didn't show. The voice had to be a throat program. That boy never talked that way naturally. He had a shiny chauffeur's uniform and a cap with a visor. The only authentically evil thing about him was the look he gave me as he screwed the cap on.

"Cute," I said with appreciation.

"Sword told me not to kill you," he snarled, and took us down even steeper than we'd come up. It's lucky I don't get airsick.

We got interrogated by an automated intercept program a quarter of a mile from the dome. Wings must have had the right answers because they let us in. He dropped onto a lighted pad by the door and got down. I could see he was loving it.

"A scout obeys orders cheerfully at all times," I told him as he gave me his hand.

"Right. I ain't killed you, have I?"

That wasn't his fault. If I hadn't been ready for the jerk that went with it I could have broken my neck. I took care to fall on him, nails and heels flailing. He caught me. It wasn't Face he was wearing because the scratch I left down his cheek oozed real blood. Or a liquid similar.

"Oh, dear," I said sincerely. "At what hour does the action start, Dagobert?"

Back to business. "Garden at midnight. You'll get orders when we're ready."

"Wrong, Dagobert. You get orders, I get information. Do

I tip you now or is it more correct to do it on the way home?''

He got in without answering but he slammed the door so hard it was pure luck it stayed on its hinges.

I'd worried about Jocelyn's dress but I needn't have. I was as good as invisible. I had a nasty moment when I got announced and had to brush cheeks with the Countess Cara, a smooth-faced harpy of twenty-five or so who was probably an ex-school friend of my great-great-grandmother's. She breathed musk and ambergris in my face and pretended to recognize me. I breathed narcissus in hers and pretended to recognize her.

Then I mingled and found Swordfish hadn't overstated Disian conservatism. There were people wearing jewelry in places I hadn't known were invented. And yes, he was right about the guys' pricks.

I wandered Cara's marble halls dutifully refusing drink and other gels and froze out the guys who found the Honorable Jocelyn's fake curves heating. I didn't see Mallore. But Wings was right about fashion. The copts went on arriving and more guests in fewer clothes foamed down the stairs and fell around Cara's neck.

Finally a vision in a throat-to-ankle silver sheath that glimmered like mercury over her insect frame flew in on a skeletal sports copt. She climbed down three steps and struck a pose, waiting for applause.

There wasn't any since everyone was too occupied admiring themselves or getting into other people's pants to notice. But a wiry black guy near me said to the stunning flame-haired girl at his shoulder, "Sweet Nimbus. Doesn't get nicer, does she?''

"Who does, darling?" the girl throated in a growling voice.

"I do?" the black guy suggested. The flame beauty

laughed and ruffled his hair. It was then I noticed she was a boy and wore a ring guess where. Quite a small one by local standards.

"Would you like some introductions?" a voice breathed in my ear. I turned, into the belly-button of seven feet of guy in transparent sandals. Plus a couple of glassy rags gilded around the codpiece. He had a vaguely ambassadorial sash and a row of gilt medals smaller than soup plates. He glanced down. They were level with my hairline even in Jocelyn's heels.

"I'm a war hero by profession. Cara doesn't let me come unless I wear the whole rhythm section. You look lost. How about a drink?"

"Thank you. Our customs . . ."

He winked. He had beautiful eyes, long girl's lashes and thick black hair. A dish. Considering his size, a platter.

"Real champagne? Without additives. I'll take the first swallow."

"Then you fall on me and tear my clothes off."

He raised his brows. "You got some on?"

I grinned palely. He swung, stiff-armed a domestic and took a delicate sip from my glass. Then he kept his hands to himself. It was disappointing.

"McLaren DeLorn, only guy in the world with two names and four capital letters. My father's fault."

"Your mother couldn't stop him?"

"Not in our family. She was in love."

"That's got to be rare."

"Unique."

I looked around the garden of delights. No pigs and giraffes but just about everything else.

"You're a Luney?"

"My sanity's perfect. We just run to height. You've no idea the complications we have with the furniture. Whenever we visit my aunts we have to take our own bed."

"Like Queen Elizabeth. The one who slept here."

"Worse. She could sit at the tea-table without having to look over her knees like a stork." He caught my elbow. "Who would you like to know?"

"Who are the couple?"

"The black guy and his kid? Dancers. Taro and Blaze. Taro's the better, he just dances. Blaze uses a trampoline which is thought unsporting by some. But a very athletic guy. In every sense."

"I bet. Who's the lady in silver?"

"That is Nimbus and no lady. If you'll forgive my saying so."

"She's pretty," I said hypocritically.

"If you like stick-insects. With my shape I've got to, but not when painted." He glanced at a wrist with a discreet light-display under the skin. "Anyhow you're half an hour early."

"What?"

Another lift of the eyebrows. "Aren't you Cinderella? I thought you'd be leaving at midnight. If you give Nimbus half an hour you may not see home."

"That's my slippers."

"You aren't leaving at midnight?"

I recollected myself. "I may. Daddy's very strict."

"There you are, I knew it. Haver," he hailed. An elegant chestnut-haired type who was choosing derms from a little automatic cart.

"Hi. What can I do, before I take off for outer space?"

"Tell the lady about your friend Nimbus. Haver's a film-actor," he explained. "When conscious. Well-known in comedies. He's the graceful charmer turns up in other guys' closets when they come home unexpectedly at two in the morning."

"Then I jump out the window and get photographed falling three hundred feet into a sofa-cushion. You see why

I stay unconscious. Keeps me from thinking what they'll ask for tomorrow. Nimbus? You don't want to know her. Stick with Lorn who's okay, or come upstairs with me and we'll make love first and leave for the stars later. Off screen I'm good.''

''On screen he has to be seen to be believed,'' Lorn said.

''Aphroed to the eyes. It's nice to perform in free fall.'' He covered his mouth. ''I shouldn't have said that. They haven't asked yet but they will.''

I smiled sweetly. Or Jocelyn did.

''How charming of both of you. But I've something particular to ask Nimbus. Like the name of her dress-maker.''

''Don't waste your time, sweetheart, she won't tell you,'' Haver said. ''But she may tell you a couple of other things you'll regret in the morning.''

''All the same. Ciao.'' I wiggled my fingers and headed towards the gleaming silverfish of Mallore.

''Dreadful waste,'' Haver regretted behind. ''She doesn't know what she's missing.''

''Sore loser.''

The last I saw they were bending over the cart. That did seem a waste. Two good-looking guys headed for the high constellations. When you never know if the whole of you's ever going to come down.

Mallore was talking to a bronzed guy with a face like cast metal who seemed to be doing all the listening but not as if he was enjoying it. On consideration he looked the kind wouldn't enjoy anything much, short of a good breaking on the wheel. As I came up he twitched her the faintest rudimentary sketch of a smirk as if his lips really were cast in bronze, murmured something curt and turned definitively away.

She stood in place for a moment and I could have sworn her eyes glittered with tears of fury. Then she caught sight of me and produced a smile clear from the depths of her belly.

"Well, hello."

She was different out of her role. Her face was still elfin but subtly harder and more mature. The little trembly chin looked almost too pointed under the lights, a little too definite. If she clenched her jaws slightly her age might come bursting through like something pupating inside the skin. Her eyes were all pupil again, though so were most other people's by now. Her fluffy hair was teased into a silvered aureole tinged with green at the edges that made her look both ariel and slightly mad. She looked as if it wouldn't take much to make her fly.

It seemed impossible she could stand so close without knowing who I was but Swordfish seemed to have done his job. She smiled at me with wet pink lips, something avid and sticky behind her black void eyes.

"Let me get you something from the trolley, katchen," she belled. The voice had changed too. The silvery tinkle had disappeared and this was a deep husky coo like doves in the woods. I remembered Sword had worked at convincing us she was an actress.

"No, truly. My father's really terribly strict." I wasn't sure what kind of voice my favorite killer had given me but I heard schoolgirl. Shrill and squeaky. "It's dreadfully hot. I was going to walk in the garden."

I batted Jocelyn's briar-bush lashes. She hesitated, caught between attractions. Lorn loomed behind us leading the trolley like a grotesque mechanical lap-dog and stooped to be reproachful.

"I introduced this heartless lady to my nice friend Haver and she's left him to fly to the stars alone. Is that kind? He doesn't even have any vices. Would you like some sweeties, sweet? My hostess expects me to work for a living."

Nimbus glanced avidly over the trolley. "Will you wait a

moment, katchen? Then I'll take you in the garden myself and show you the nicest bits. You'll be ravished, I promise.''

Lorn's eyes met mine and I thought his lid drooped. Then he was bending over drawers and bottles helping Mallore choose her cocktail.

She meant to go wide and far. A couple of derms, a deep whiff from an inhaler and a mainline prickle for instant sparks. I saw her get them. Her flash of silver hair quivered as if with a discharge of electricity. Or maybe it was the rest of her that went rigid like an aluminum post. She took a long, slow, snuffling breath as if she was drawing the whole party in through her lungs.

I wondered what would happen to Sword's plan if she flopped out at our feet. It seemed more than possible. For a moment she stood like a lightning rod doing what it was made for, then she relaxed, tossed her head to free her floaty hair and turned back to me smiling.

"Very well, katchen. Shall we go?"

"To the lime-tree bower?" Lorn murmured, clasping his hands. "Sweet Nimbus. Say I can come too."

"Why don't you go peddle your goodies to all the ladies, male and female, over three miles high?" Nimbus cooed. She put one long silver nail in the middle of his chest and sliced downwards. A line of blood followed it and tinged the transparencies scarlet. Lorn's gray gaze stayed benevolent but his muscles tightened. "Cara's fish footman. Go find a lake. Then jump."

She offered me a slender whalebone arm. As we walked out into the tame forest fruited with colored globes I saw Lorn looking after us with an ambiguous smile. Then he turned back to his ridiculous trolley and disappeared.

Cara's decorator had done a major job on the garden. The trees were wreathed in globes like sugar candies and the little paths and alleys were outlined in fairy-lights. Couples, and other combinations, flittered here and there doing cute and charming things like climbing the statuary, pissing in the flower beds and spraying each other with champagne. A line of gorgeous kids in gilded beast masks were doing a conga in and out of the bushes near the house. They wore smears of gilt paint here and there.

"Taro's third-year ballet class," Mallore said off-handedly. "Quite pretty but all gristle. Dancers are miserably boring when you know them. Nothing in there but expressive motion. Let's go somewhere private."

It didn't look like there was anywhere private but I'd underestimated Cara and her grounds. The sugary lanterns ran out after a few acres and we came to an arrangement of rocks lit by floating glows that drifted lazily. They seemed to be set on some kind of random search pattern and they were finding intertwined corpses in exotic positions. The shadows were rich and velvety. I guess part of the fun was wondering when the glow was going to drift your way and give everyone a gander. Most of them looked too skied to know the difference.

This had the marks of Swordfish country but my invisible brother-figure hadn't bothered to give directions. I was feeling nervous. If he didn't do something soon I could get done over. Nimbus was breathing fast and shallow through her little sharp teeth and I was ready to bet the Honorable Jocelyn's padding wouldn't stand up to her claws for long. Then we'd have a real cat fight. It wasn't exactly what I came for.

She paused and turned her gleaming needles towards me, her lips wet and glistening with saliva. Her eyes looked blind in the faint light, a blank reflection from the sclerotic. It was unpleasant, like being lusted at by some night insect with sucking jaws and more than human senses.

"Where's the lime-tree bower?" I squeaked desperately with one of the Honorable Josh's schoolgirl giggles.

"Would you like it?" she cooed huskily. "Lorn has the most depraved tastes. You wouldn't think it to look at him. If you can see all of him at the same time without a ladder. Come along then, darling child. You shall have it."

Her thin clawed hand caught me again, by the fingers this time, her sharp thumbnail tracing intricate sexual patterns on Josh's palm. We raced through glow-lit darkness over turf starred with night-scented flowers like a pair of debauched nymphs. Maybe all nymphs are debauched. I didn't want to be debauched by Nimbus. There was something about her, entirely physical, made me feel crawly.

Apart from the blood on her hands.

I felt as if I could feel it, warm and sticky on the thin avid fingers interlaced with mine, seeping slowly through the layer of false skin that separated us. And it seemed to me it was like Bluebeard's wife's key. If I ever got it on me it would never come off. Doshky's blood, grown into my hand forever.

There was a bower. I don't know if it was lime trees or not. They were middle-sized with huge pointed leaves and a sharp nighty smell and the branches interlaced to form a kind of cave. Behind it fantastically spired rocks rose up, fringed with ferns and disgusting fairy fungi in garden-gnome shapes.

You had to bend and creep to get in. Mallore bent and crept, dragging me behind. She was unbelievably strong for such a skinny slight creature. Her quicksilver dress caught the light as she ducked into darkness and gave one swift all-over flash. She looked like a snake, fine, graceful and poisonous.

Another of my bad ideas. I either had to follow her or tear loose and rip Josh's marble fingers off. I wasn't sure how strong the plastic skin might be but I'd seen the sharpness of her nails. I ducked in after her and she turned around with that striking-snake motion and wrapped her free hand in my hair. It was part of the get-up and in no danger of coming loose but she'd got me as firmly as if it had been my own.

"Come and get it, baby," she breathed in a soft purring hiss, her face so close I could smell the scent of her mouthwash under her perfume and something more acrid and chemical that must come from what she'd inhaled. I thought her teeth were reaching for my throat. I tried to take a step back and found my damned sandals with their ridiculous heels intertwined with her bony ankles and the hem of her glimmering dress.

Her hand was feeling for my over-decorated lower reaches, playing with the fringes of diamond tears, and I wondered how long it was going to take her to go all the way and rip them out by force. If I'd been Jocelyn I'd have been wetting my legs. The last time we had a catfight she'd been kidding around, playing little girl to my big bully. This time her heart was in it and she was all muscle. I thought she was looking forward to the shriek as she tore the jewels out of my supposedly pierced labia, the gush of sacrificial blood that was to give taste to her pleasures.

In spite of myself I cringed.

And a strong and violent hand separated us and Nimbus vanished. A suddenly as that, like a light put out. A swirl of fast movement and a urinous animal smell circled the inside of the cave of leaves and were gone.

A harsh grunting voice spoke in my ear.

"Rink on Fourth and Ninety-Second, one A.M. Copt'll pick you up quarter to. Go play pretty ladies until. Sword's ready to go."

There was the dungy wind of another passing and he was gone too. It was as if the whole crew had evaporated. I had a sense of a hallucination as if I'd imagined the whole thing and none of them had really been there at all.

I turned back and limped in my murderous sandals over the soft turf back through the rocks and glows to the party.

Lorn was still upright and ambulating. He looked at me with concern and inquired after my health as if he cared. I told him Nimbus had got bored and cleared off with a prettier guy she met on the way and he laughed. It sounded like nothing Nimbus did surprised anyone.

Quarter of an hour later I glanced at Jocelyn's miniature light display, incorporated in one of her carboniferous bangles, and found I was due back at the ranch. Cara was too busy with a quartet of small boys who should have been home in bed to want her cheek not quite kissed again and the only impediment was Lorn, who insisted on seeing me out.

He handed me into the copt and leaned after. "You forgot to lose your slipper."

"What?"

"So I can identify you by it among all the other women in the world later," he said patiently. "I thought it was de rigueur for ladies who quit at midnight."

"Left or right?"

"The nearest. I'm going to take it home and drink toasts out of it."

I peeled it off. As the copt took another vengeful swoop into the air I could see him filling it with care from a crystal flask.

"Clown," Wings snarled.

"Don't be like that. You can have the other one if you like. There's no way I'm going to wear either of them one second longer. I'm lamed for life."

He muttered something under his breath. It sounded like, "I fucking wish."

I shed Face in every direction and pretended not to hear. If I did I was honor bound to claw his eyes out and it was going to make the rest of the route difficult. I carefully strewed pieces of the Honorable Jocelyn all over the seat instead and watched him building up steam to explode. But he couldn't, of course.

It was a night for vengeance.

The rink looked devastated, with peeling walls held together by layers of bills composted by time and weather into papier mâché. The doors were rusted shut and padlocked, covered with obscene scrawls in strata of faded paint. The light-tubes above hung crookedly, dangling by ends of cable. It looked like the Living Dead were liable to start crawling out of the walls.

The whole neighborhood was like that. You could have fought World War Four there without anyone noticing. The way buildings were chipped and fallen in, it looked as if several lots of people already had.

Wings controlled his fury long enough to pick up Moke, I suspected because it also let him dump Josh's remains in the recyc. He did it with the expression of a guy who'd have liked to do the same with the filling.

I'd tried to convince Moke he didn't want to come and had come up against the Moke conscience. He was against it, he hated the whole idea, he thought I was wrong, he expected to be sick and he was coming to bring me home because I was going to need it. Period.

That's my Moke. I figured he was an artistic genius, I knew he was a nice guy, I never did understand why Dosh who could have had anybody wanted to be in love with him. Now I was getting the picture. How can you turn that stuff down?

He sat in the back of the copt with his arm around me, his narrow face set like an ax blade, his teeth clenched under bunched-up jaw muscles. He looked as stubborn as a stone Indian. Wings set out to snarl, found it didn't take and became laconic. His temper also improved when he got back into a suit. The only person I know who can go on disliking Mokey is Swordfish and he's one of a kind.

Wings put the copt down in a lot behind a ruined factory where there was just enough space for the skids among the rubble and got down. I heard his feet crunch among the broken crates and fallen plaster that filled the place.

"Okay," he growled. "Across the road, around the side. Don't make a ticker-tape parade. Just for once."

Moke jumped down after him and offered a hand. It being known I'm too dainty and fragile to climb a step alone. I took it, partly because his hand was friendly and partly because Josh's damned sandals had left me with sprained toe-joints and pulled muscles in both calves. We limped after Wings's invisible steps through a mush of garbage out into the street.

The place was as dead as the end of the world. There wasn't a cat. Sword's presence has that effect, but this was extreme. It looked like it was always that way. Between battles.

In the dirty alleyway that led around the side there was an emergency door which opened smoothly. Behind it was darkness, a ruined corridor with bare laths, doors that had opened onto changing-rooms. A couple still had tarnished gilt stars.

It had been a big draw when it was young, with huge productions when people went to huge productions. When the petted stars of the ice really came here to put on their skates and clumped out over the tiles to make like birds and ballet dancers under the spotlights. The vast drum roof extended over an Olympic-size floor and seats for sixty thousand people. It was dead long before I was born. Like Hallway, I'd thought it was derelict.

Wings pushed another door and we came out into a blinding glare that made me flinch. We'd entered by the performers' gate and the rink lay in front of us.

When Swordfish said it would cost I'd had vague ideas. I hadn't imagined the half. The hall opened on all sides so wide and long the walls receded into shadow. It was a bowl with ourselves in the flat bottom and tiers of blue and red tip-up seats all the way around. The high drum loomed a couple of hundred feet above and arcs blazed out of it with a pitiless light.

And reflected. From a floor of smoothly glittering ice as wide and empty as the surface of the moon. A glacial breath blew up from it over my face and I shivered. Moke shivered beside me and grabbed my shoulders.

"Over there," Wings growled.

The shadow of his hand silhouetted against the arcs gestured to a dais to one side with leather-covered seats that had maybe been the judges' box. We stepped onto a surface that seemed to strike up and bite at my raw feet through my boots.

"And shut it. Sword ain't inclined for conversation when he's working."

"Can it, Tootsie. This is my film. Don't recollect it starred you. There was Moke, me and Mallore. And Dosh. We get to the bit where I tell the ex-heroine where to go and we roll the credits over her bursting like a bullfrog. Go tell your boss so. If he growls I'll bite him."

"Where would you like to start?" Swordfish asked gently at my shoulder. "You want to gnaw my hand, or are you going for the jugular? Sorry, Cass, you're watching. I've seen the lady's habits and I don't feel like exposing you. You can abuse her from a distance."

"And what are you going to do?"

"Hold her still for you. Come on, hup."

I hupped. Moke and me both, having a hand on the scruff apiece.

"Dammit, Sword, I told you she was mine."

"Well, she's mine now," he said coolly.

"Bastard. Swordfish, I do not want shooting. I want this bim liquefied, not liquidated. She's shed enough blood. What I want is for people to laugh at her. Cute Fairy Twinkletoes, losing her glitter-dust and none of the kiddies clapping."

"Fine. And I want you to keep your eyesight long enough to see it. Unless you'd care to tell me now what color you'd like next time?"

I snarled at echoing light. He'd gone.

A step or two got us to seat level where the floor was insulated and we edged between tipped-back chair bottoms towards the box.

The place was almost antiseptically clean. The leather chairs smelled of polish. The tarnished holders where the judges had marked up their awards had been rubbed up, though the matching electronics had disappeared. It was cold, vacant and still as a tomb.

And the arcs glared down waiting for the show to begin. I was trembling, and not entirely with chill. The flaming ice and cold lights had a grimly practical look.

"She murdered Doshky," I said to the bright ice and chill air. The words crackled out of my mouth in crisp white vapor, writing the sentiment in contrails across the surface of the rink.

"Yeah," Moke murmured, subdued. "You sure you want to do this?"

"Yes. I owe Sword. He's fixed it and I got to go through with it. And I owe Dosh too, Mokey. I can't duck out. It was my fault."

"Cass," he said, with unexpected savagery. "You did

not kill Dosh. Will you get that through your head? Don't you know you're punishing yourself?''

''Maybe. Maybe I'm punishing her. I don't think it matters any longer. I started this and I got to finish it. She's as bad as she seems. Worse, maybe. And Sword doesn't have an off-switch.''

''Everyone has an off-switch,'' he said, low. But he settled back and cuddled me. I cuddled back. I felt cold to the bone.

The silence drew out long. The chill rose and froze our hands and feet and started wriggling into our marrow. Moke rubbed my hands and blew warm breath in my ear. We nuzzled. I wished I'd brought furs. I wished I had furs to bring.

A swinging door thudded and a gleaming figure came hushing out like the hologram of one of the silver-sheathed dancers who'd performed to applauding crowds when the place was alive. But this one wasn't on skates.

Nimbus, shimmering in her mercury dress, skidded to the edge of the performers' entrance. She swayed into balance on her precarious high heels and grabbed for the wall to steady herself.

She gasped as the ice bit through her soles and drew herself up. It looked like someone had hold of her. Then she staggered and was on her own. She took a few delicate steps, lifting her sandals as daintily as a pedigree cat. That covered a yard or so of solidified water nearer to the center of the wall. She stood there and looked around. I thought in passing the pedigree of cats doesn't matter a damn. They all go straight for the garbage.

She'd never been short of courage. Her head was high and her manner haughty. Her eyes were full circles of periwinkle so somebody had sobered her up. Swordfish doesn't waste talent on people too stoned to notice.

Her disdainful gaze ran around the hall. Shining ice, shadowed dome, rows of empty seats rising into darkness. The black ceiling above, the flaring arcs. And came around to Moke and me.

"You," she said with contempt. Her voice was somewhere between the hysterical twitter of our Mallore and the cooing purr of the lady who'd been ready to rape me at Cara's. Perhaps it was finally the real Nimbus: clear, authoritative and adult. "What childish game is it this time? Do you think you're going to get away with it?"

She hadn't seen. A ring of pantomime ghosts, their outlines dissipated by reflections, spreading behind her. I know Sword's gang and the sight of them gives me shivers even when I can't see them.

"Nimbus."

Sword's voice was deep and soft and it came from the air eighteen inches over her head. Even I hadn't known he was so near.

It startled her. She half-swung, slipped and caught at the rail. Her eyes searched the glare and caught nothing. Now I knew, I could see his long shadow flung out in a kaleidoscopic star by the beams of the arcs. She'd have had to look down to locate him and her head was so proudly stiff she looked like another inch would break her neck.

"This is our end for your film. The one where Cass wins and you lose. You've triumphed over a lot of co-stars. How would you like to play with me?"

The quiet striptease behind was worth seeing if you like horror flicks. The coolsuits slid silkily to the ice and the Pack was bare. Karloff would have been right at home. Wings in the raw had a feral viciousness I hadn't realized when I laughed at him. Relying on his master's protection. His delicate outline had the warmth and charm of a bronze goblin. And he was the most normal.

Sword had brought all twenty. Their deformities ran the

range from muscle grafts, wolf fur and shark teeth to things
that looked as if they'd no human mother. They had. Only
a few of the mutations are natural and they're the milder,
enhanced a little to give them point. The rest are voluntary.

Dribble was with them, frolicking with his bare bum in
the air, his eager whine sawing our eardrums. He inched
forward on hands and toes to stick his drooling snout under
her skirt. Her foot connected in the usual place and he
retreated yelping.

A whistle brought them to heel. They stood or hunkered,
whichever suited them best, in a ring like a gutterful of
gargoyles.

"Or take your pick. We aren't narrow-minded. Check it's
a guy, they aren't all."

The Pack snickered. I wondered how she was supposed to
know. A couple of the maler males would make a lady
rhinoceros run for cover but there are several I'm damned if
I'd make bets on myself.

Nimbus got marks for guts. She tossed her silvered head,
her throat arrogantly poised. She had her own splendor
under the arcs. Her contemptuous glance ran around and she
stamped a sandal. Her silver skirts flared.

"I'll be interested to see Cassandra win. Are we having
another hair-pulling competition?" Her narrow lip lifted.
"She's good at that, but then she's bigger and the producer
didn't want me to use my nails. I left the scratching to her."

"You wasted your time, bim," I said. My voice was
shakier than I liked. "I don't have claws for it, I'm a
working girl. Plain fingers seemed to get there."

"Of course. You need your hands for safe-breaking,
don't you? I should have thought of that. You work as a
thief."

She bared pointed teeth. Her half-inch talons matched her
dress. They shone like icicles.

"I don't think she'll bother," Swordfish said. "We're

having an ice-ballet and you're invited. Take your partners.''

The sound-system was on hand. A discordant wail by a
full orchestra with a lot of galumph in it. The *Carnival of the
Animals*, maybe. Sword has these moments of humor.

The Pack whooped like the lionhouse at feeding time.
They probably didn't feel the cold. They didn't seem to
need skates either. In a couple of seconds the rink was a
scene would have done big good things for Babar, with
lumpy shapes thudding together, sliding, waltzing and
tobogganing around. From time to time they hit the walls
and something hairy just missed Nimbus on the cannon. She
flinched. They're heavy. You'd have said a Sunday-School
picnic. In the lower depths of Pandemonium.

''Sesame Street?'' she asked, her fiberoptic fluff bristling
with angry electricity. She had to shout. ''I've better things
to do than spend a night at the zoo. You have a choice. You
can call me a traxie or I'll send for the police myself.''

''Not from here,'' Sword said with regret. ''We don't
seem to have paid our bills this month. And we do have
business.''

''Like what?''

Mallore had gone. This woman was grown up, and angry
and dangerous. There was a tilt to her dandelion head and
her eyes reflected the lights like slits of glass. Red patches
burned her cheeks under the makeup. If she felt the cold she
wasn't showing it. Could be she was too mad. Me, my teeth
were rattling like a dicebox.

''This is where you pay for your misdeeds. Are you sure
you won't dance? I'm trying to teach Dribble gentility.''

Her laugh was ugly, like cracking pack-ice. She stood
four-square, arms crossed over her breasts, and you'd have
seen six of her selling fish in the Gooder market behind the
Corn Exchange any Saturday morning. Her chin looked
sharp enough for a snow plow.

"I suppose all the fuss is about that idiot who came running after me bleating when I was trying to reach safety. Away from this madwoman and her private army."

"The guy you murdered," I projected down. "Yeah, that one."

She raised a fair brow. Her voice cut the riot like cheese-wire. "Strong language. But you were jealous from the beginning, Cassandra. You never worked out what was wrong, did you? You're a boy, my dear, and not even a real boy, a fake one. That's why he preferred me. Or even old what's-his-name—Monkey, was it?" She laughed. "At least I'm a girl. Me and What's-His-Name both. Not a ball between us. You think you have balls, don't you? You're mistaken. You're a neutered bitch, nothing more."

"Then I'm a neutered bitch who loved him," I said, my throat closing. "You're right, he didn't love me. But I loved him. That's what counts. I'm not you. I've never killed anyone."

"Be careful, little girl. There's a law of slander."

"For some. Since there doesn't seem to be a law of life, I've had to ask my friend Sword to pay back."

"This one?" She angled her head back. I can't imagine what she saw, but she was faking just fine. "I'll be interested to see it. But pay back what, sweet pet?"

"You shot him," Swordfish said.

"Of course I did. It would be self-defense in any court. The whole bunch were out of their senses and the woman was raving. Again. Everyone's seen her temper."

"He didn't have a gun."

She tossed a luminous head. "How was I to know? I felt the brute's sweaty paws grab me from behind and I tried to defend myself. I was in fear for my life."

Sword laughed. It was a genuine laugh and even shot with admiration. I'd have admired her damned insolence myself if my mouth hadn't been wedged open by a slice of cold stiff air that seemed to have got stuck somewhere halfway down my gullet.

"I don't think you've been in fear for your life since the day you were born. You're the princess who lives in the golden tower and you go on forever. I don't think Cassandra feels like cursing you right now, you've taken her breath away. Shall we tango while she gets it back?"

He cut the music effortlessly too. They were a great duo. The habit of command in both cases, I suppose.

She tipped her head to show the taut line of her throat, aiming her voice at where she judged him to be. She was about two feet too low but she wasn't to know that.

"This is silly. Can we have quiet to talk?"

Sword made a mid-air gesture that stirred the vapor-wreaths we were all breathing out and the orchestra meowed into silence.

"What's she paying you, Tiger? Whatever it is I can double it. Triple it. And give you something in kind to keep you warm tonight. How about it, amigo? I'm bored."

Her voice had gone back to its purring coo. When we raided the house first time she only saw the last bit of the action so she hadn't really made Sword's acquaintance. Maybe she didn't recognize him. I'd thought he scared her.

"Take a look around, princess. Do we look short of money? Everything here's mine. You have paid for it, but that's only fair since it's for you. You're sure you want to proposition me? You wouldn't rather tell the lady you're sorry?"

"There's a lady in the house?" Her tone was jeering. "I've nothing to tell anyone, Tiger. Anything I've done I'd do again. The difference between me and her is I know where I'm going. And where she's going. You don't need to go with her. You can have money if you want it. If there's something else you'd rather have, why, I can probably get it for you. Boys, girls, film parts? Try me."

I swallowed my mouthful of air at last and crunched Mokey's bones in my fists. He grabbed me in protest and pulled one hand into the hollow of his armpit where he was warm. The other he held against his chest with his own on top. He was pretending it wasn't frozen.

"Thanks, but I'm picky. And I have my own ideas about where you're going. I think the colloquial word's down. For murder. We're bound to make at least one stick. With what there is to choose from. We've been making a file."

That got to her. The red patches spread leaving her face mottled.

"You're very brave," she sneered. "Running invisible rings around an unarmed woman in your clever little suit. How'd you think you'd get on if you met me face to face with a gun in my hand?"

"You'd really like to see me?" Sword asked gently.

"Sure I would, nothing man. What's under there, the big bad wolf? You don't scare me a bit. Let's see you. If you're as cuddly as your friends you could be real entertaining. We could all laugh."

"As you like." He was courteous. "I hope you laugh as much as you expect."

Outside the circle of light the hall was empty. The rows of folded seats stretched away in every direction into darkness.

I'd heard that slink of zippers before. It was a hand again, left, pale and abnormally long. It reached over to free the right, an exact match. He began to peel his suit.

Sword had been my brother, teacher and moral conscience for seven years. I knew his warm voice, his cold eyes, a lot of his mind. Maybe too much. I'd never seen him.
Before.

The white arms were slender as the limbs of a ghost crab, almost skeletal. They were streaked from shoulder to wrist with twisting red scars in seamed ridges. Their muscles shifted oddly, standing in relief as taut as wires.

The suit opened over a chest slashed with ragged seams that outlined his ribs and crisscrossed in lumps above his heart. The ribs flared like a greyhound's over his sunken belly. He was torn by marks of violence as if he'd been forged rather than grown, and forged badly. The tendons of his throat stood out like cables joining collarbone to jaw. Above them the gray eyes flamed.

He skinned the suit off all the way to expose a nightmare of scar tissue, hacked, burned, melted and re-soldered. The long narrow hands moved up and ran sharp nails over his hood.

His skull was bare bone, oddly bumpy and seamed by ridges that twisted the skin and even the plates out of shape. The ear nearest me was a kind of sketch as if heat had melted it. I remembered his implants and wondered how many of the scars were surgical, how many battle-wounds and how many decoration. As the Pack understand it.

He turned his face to me and smiled. His forehead ran straight down into eyes without brows or lashes. His nose was a narrow prow, his plaster-white mouth shocking. It was warm, curved and humorous. On one side. A long scar seamed his cheek on the other, just missed his eye and pulled the corner away from yellowed teeth. The ear was a rim around a primitive hole.

He smiled. And smiling, went back to Nimbus.

"I'm Swordfish," his beautiful voice said. "Are you laughing?"

She sucked in breath.

He looked as tall as a lighthouse. The floodlights reflected off his skull and threw the eyes in shadow. Her rictus could have been laughter, but I didn't think so.

"And you said something about a gun in your hand," he

murmured. "I don't have one myself, but if you'd really like it . . . ?"

"Yes, you monstrous bastard," she whispered. Her voice quivered. "I would really like it. But if I take it one of your circus poodles shoots me in the back, of course."

"Back-shooting isn't our style." Sword has this notion of professional honor. "Hilt, give the lady a gun."

The Pack had stopped. They were standing around looking interested. A grinning troll with pale-brown leather skin and a haircut like the Incredible Hulk tossed across a light hand-laser. When she caught it she bent at the knees. Out of his hand that damned hogleg weighed as much as a medium-sized cannon.

"That do, boss?"

"Thanks," Sword said. "You're all formally forbidden to shoot the lady in the back. Or anywhere else." He stood facing her, hands lightly balanced on his hipbones. "Does that even the odds?"

"You bet it does, bonehead," Nimbus said. Her voice was glassy and clear. "Who do you think I am?"

I'd seen that vicious striking motion before. I grabbed Moke's arm, my mouth open to shriek. Nothing came out. The laser spat white. Sword's chest was maybe six feet from the muzzle. A fine mist of blood swirled between them and a coil of smoke that reeked sickeningly of burn.

I wanted to close my eyes. They seemed gummed in place, wide open. Someone said in a squeaky voice, "Sword. No." It could have been me. Moke's fingers were digging grooves in my arms you could have used as irrigation ditches.

The smoke cleared and everyone was standing in the same places. Nimbus's face was blue-white. The big gun sagged in her hand. Sword's churned-up chest showed a rough-edged circular pit where the beam had reflected back, the edges still smoking. The flesh was blackened and crackled around the rim. In the hole a glint of ceramic caught the light, a fan of glimmering ribs that weren't bone, a cylinder, part of a tube that pulsed. His hand moved to take the gun away before she could use it again.

"Interesting materials the Navy uses these days," he said conversationally. "I was betting your aim was good. But I don't think I'll give you another shot, you might hit someplace I'm vulnerable. I haven't had my guts replaced recently and it's a tedious operation. Now, what were we talking about?"

"Lady's taste in guys, boss," the troll rumbled helpfully.

"Yes, that's right."

He stooped with a grace of movement startling in that lumpen monstrosity and caught one of her necklaces with the edge of his nail.

"Pretty. Is it real? I take it the film business pays well."

Nimbus's lips had paled and thinned to a white line.

"Yes," she said tightly. "Yes, it's real, and yes the film industry pays well."

Sword was still smiling. He had to bend over her to undo the clasp and his fingers brushed her neck. She started violently. He straightened with the bright rope strung over his hand, swinging in a flurry of rainbows.

His eyes lazily followed its hypnotic sparkle. Nimbus's tracked after them. Then he extended a palm and gently lowered the necklace in. The fingers closed.

And tightened. I saw the unnatural wires of muscle raising the flesh of his arm and shoulder into cords. The hollow of his armpit deepened to a well of black shadow. The fingers clenched into a knot of bone. Then he let go.

Dull shards pattered on the ice like hailstones. For a moment I didn't register what I saw. When I did my neck hair lifted.

He'd crushed her diamonds to powder.

"I'm sorry you aren't attracted. It's disappointing. Very

few people are interested enough to ask to see. I was sure you'd laugh. Or I wouldn't have taken my clothes off.''

He turned away with a kind of balletic grace, stooping to pick up his coolsuit. The white silk lining was the same color as his fingers. He started to reassemble it.

''Oh—there's one last thing. I know you're proud of your films. So you'll be happy to know this is on camera. It's going out on every holoscreen in the city, live, now. Everybody you know's seeing it. So I really hope you're enjoying yourself because it's one of the biggest dramas you've got to act in. Your own epic for you. Just the way you like it. Make it good. The world's watching.''

''All right,'' Nimbus said viciously. ''Cassandra wants her little revenge. You all make me laugh. You don't understand the first thing about anything. You're interested in the film industry? You want to know the truth about your little friend Doshchenko? I can tell you . . .''

Sword's hand jumped in a flare of lightning.

And Nimbus twirled like a top, her quicksilver dress swirling in a grotesque pirouette, her arms flung high like a dancer at the top of her spin. But the halo of flame that outlined her wasn't a spotlight. Her hair flashed and was gone, her face writhed to ancient blackness, her hands retracted to claws. What hit the pooling water where she'd stood didn't glitter any more. It could have been a twisted log.

I was on my feet yelling.

''Sword, you shit. I asked you not to, I asked you not—''
He turned.

''Sorry, Cass. My fault, I agree. But I didn't kill her. You'll find mine at the top of the ramp. Saw the muzzle-flash just too late. This one's theirs. Tarn?''

A furry specimen broader than it was high with a coarse bristling mane went charging up the steps. The steps creaked. It bent down somewhere in the darkness under the roof. "He's dead, boss. In blackout, mask and all."

The voice sounded female.

"So I saw," Sword said grimly. "Not even good shooting. Comes of aiming at a muzzle-flash. I should have heard him come in. Sorry. If that covers the case. I think the lady was about to be indiscreet."

"I think she was. You promised this wouldn't happen." My voice would have sounded good on a male teen in mid-break. Up and down the scale, wobbling.

"I'm getting hopeless at keeping my word. Cover the body, Hilt. I guess we'd better return it to sender. Both of them. In separate parcels."

He picked up his suit and began to put it back on, over the roped scars and the burned pit of his chest.

"You don't know what I do for you, Cass."

My eyes were scalded by tears and fumed with smoke. I was wrestling an overwhelming urge to vomit. "I can see what you've done. You better call a doctor."

He glanced down carelessly. "Unimportant, or I wouldn't have let her do it. Gutsy piece of work. My type, monster to the bone. It'll mend, which is more than she will. I'd rather it had been legal. What I do for you, you don't know at all."

The suit was on and zippered and the burns, the silver cage of ribs, the smoothly moving pump gone back into nothing. Only the smell still hung like a failed barbecue, the elderly extractors laboring at shifting it. His eyes looked across at me. I couldn't see them for bitter water. Then he pulled the filters down and wasn't there.

I turned to Moke, cold and rigid by my side.

"Take me home, Mokey. I'm sick."

He did. I stumbled out to the copt somehow with him holding me up. Wings was there waiting and he flew us back in silence.

I clung to Moke all the way, trying not to throw up between sobs. He held me in his arms and didn't say a word.

But I knew what Sword had done for me.

I knew it only too well.

I've known it always.

I was too tired to sleep when we got back to the apartment. Even the immense bed made no difference. Moke wrapped his arms and legs around me, he said to warm me up. I think he was even colder than I was. We huddled together under the big quilt and I thought about Sword's promise to cover us with leaves like the Babes in the Wood. At that moment I felt like a Babe.

After a while Mokey fell asleep, his face blank and innocent, his lank dirty-blond hair lying in strands over his forehead. It seemed to me he'd lost weight these last few days. He'd always been skinny but now there were gray hollows in his cheeks and dark circles under his closed eyes he'd never had before, even when he'd insisted on working till he fell over. I thought his ribs were nearly as stark as Sword's and the sharp angles of his pelvis dug into me as I lay against him trying to lose myself.

I'd stopped snuffling but I had a dark veil that smothered the inside of my head and blacked out any picture of tomorrow. Wherever I looked I saw destruction. Dosh was dead. Moke had lost everything; his work, his home, his friends, even his reputation for honesty. And I'd lost myself.

It was the original woman's trap. I could see now the fault had been mine from the beginning. Dosh had wanted his ambitions fulfilled and Moke had wanted to give him his wish. It was me that had known it was wrong. I could have said no, I should have. Without me they couldn't have gone on. And I hadn't. As women don't. Not to disappoint the boys, not to look nasty, not to be old nags. Until they find the boys dead at their feet and nothing to say but, look at you. Woman, coward.

And Moke had done the same. I'd wanted to revenge myself on Nimbus and he'd let me. But he and Swordfish had been right. Seeing her dead had only sickened me. She was wrong, she was evil and I was no better than she was. She destroyed people—I hadn't done such a bad job myself. Dosh, Moke, her. And in the end even Sword.

Oh, I knew what he'd done. He'd broken every principle he had. In the end, to humiliate her he'd humiliated himself. For years he'd controlled people by the threat of what lay under his suit. Now everyone knew, everyone who was looking at a holoscreen last night. Which if I knew anything about Ashton was likely to be three-quarters of the population. I'd seen it myself. Monstrosity without dignity, an inhumanity as pitiable as it was repulsive.

My brother the freak, a cardboard horror with a chestful of mechanics, ultimately mutilated. Could he stay terrifying now everyone knew his deformity? And what comes with the knowledge, disgust, the sick fear of touching in case it might rub off and stick. At the very worst he'd get what he despised most, derisive compassion.

I'd done a great job. I'd seen Swordfish and Mallore as destroyers. I'd destroyed them both. The twisted tree-root dribbling smoke that was all that was left of her stayed in front of me. That and the pulsing pump that served Sword for a heart, the proof he wasn't and never would be a man.

What I'd done to him was worse. I'd learned to hate her, but he'd never done anything to deserve it. Now I had his corpse built into my eyes. The guy who'd given me everything. And was photographed on my brain as a thing, less than human. Swordfish. The monster.

He'd rubbed my neck in the copt, protective and furious. Bought underwear that made me laugh. Simply been there. I'd started wanting to see him.

Well, I'd seen. They say the worst curse is getting what you wish for. And he understood. Like I had a glass forehead. He always had. Sword's a desperately clear thinker. What I'd done to him was worse than what I'd done to Moke and Dosh. And even myself. So much blood, so many deaths. Even the faceless killer Sword had caught too late at the back of the rink, the one I hadn't even seen. I could taste their deaths on my tongue. All of them. Black smoking logs.

In the dawn I slid quietly out from beside Mokey's exhausted sprawl and dragged myself aching and gritty-eyed to the bathroom. I took a minimal shower without colored bottles or sluicing foam. A quick quiet splash and a scrub with a towel. My face in the glass as I shoved my brief crop into the only place it ever goes was the face of a ghost itself, white and bruised with coals under the puffy lids.

Clothes were a problem.

Sword had bought everything I had. Chosen personally, probably handled. With forethought and concern. The idea made me shudder.

I finished by putting on the simplest underwear I could find in the closet and a dark jump that was slinky, since he'd bought me nothing that wasn't, but at least looked as black as I felt. I added boots meant to go with something else, shoved a few toilet things into the dullest bag of my collection and sat down to write Mokey a note.

I was afraid he'd wake up and miss me before I was finished. But he was really flaked out and when I let myself out the apartment was as still as if I'd never been there. That seemed about right.

I'd never used the door or the elevator except for the few steps to the roof. After all, we were on the run and had done all our comings and goings from the helipad at night. This time I didn't have Wings to insult as he drove me around. I stepped out into the corridor, squinching the spongy carpet under my bootsoles, navigated around several planters of tropical vegetation lit by spots that were faking early morning in the jungle, and found the shaft.

Our old elevator in our old warehouse was automatic and solid. Luxury blocks don't waste time on mechanicals. There was a soft-entry in the wall of the passage marked with gilded rectangles printed with arrows for up and down. I pushed through the down-membrane and floated into a grav-tube designed to evacuate stilt-heeled gentlewomen and deposit them at ground-level without disturbing a hair of their coiffures. Since it hadn't any taste it did the same for me.

The lobby was deserted. The inhabitants of this kind of building don't leave for their morning golf or their regulation jog until the sun's got rid of the depressing chemical dew we collect during the night. I was grateful. I wanted to do this job myself. I'd relied enough on other people.

Once in the street with my boots clicking smartly on the raspberry and lemon pavement I remembered there was a man with a gun on my tail. And in this case, not wanting to get roughed up any more than I had to, I hadn't any tools with me.

Moke believed he'd sleep at night and stake out the Dog during the day and I hoped he was right. In his place I'd have been out before daylight waiting for the animals to come to water and I'd have seen two or three days ago the Dog was one of the dead kind. And having missed at one end of town, I'd have tried the other on principle.

Which things being so, I clicked on. At the next intersection I found a hovering traxie and whistled it. I'd meant to walk the whole way, partly to pay myself out as a stupid bitch, partly to get what was likely to be my last look at the street while I could. The raw toes and aching legs I'd inherited from Josh's stilts got together with lack of breakfast and a healthy respect for hired lasers and changed my mind. I got in, filed the illegal gilt card Swordfish had given me and dialed for the Central Square precinct house.

If you've really decided to give yourself up to the cops you may as well do it with a flourish.

The Central Square Precinct's built to terrify and does. It's big, square and gray with blanked-out windows and huge bronze doors with *Police* marked out in the stone above. A set of uncomfortably high and wide steps leads up to them.

I climbed stiffly with boots that pattered in a little mousey way under the looming façade, and walked through into the high wide lobby. I don't know why all public buildings are painted puke-green but they are. This one was. There was a tall desk in fake mahogany to one side slightly lower than Mount Everest where the hopeful and hopeless clients had to yell up to make themselves heard. No doubt it's a symbol of the lofty ideals of Justice. Or something. I moused over and stood at the base.

The cop on duty was either at the tail-end of a long hard night or the nose-end of a long hard day. Whichever, he was blinking, grumpy and half-awake. He looked down at me as if he'd found me in his salad.

"Hi," I said as brightly as I could. "I'm Cassandra Blaine."

So much for fame. He looked as if he'd never heard the name in his life.

"I'm wanted," I told him. "For damage to property,

arson, assault upon the persons of two police officers, taking and driving away a vehicle without permission, like one police copt, and quite possibly accessory to murder. And also, mainly, for having bitched up a Coelacanth Productions mega-film starring everyone's favorite Nimbus that was supposed to kill me and my mate and making the producers lose their money. I'm also a thief. And it was me fixed last night's big holovision spectacle that got Nimbus burned on screen. Is that enough for you or do you want me to tell you about my income tax?''

The guy had suddenly wakened up and he didn't look as if he'd enjoyed the experience.

''Hey,'' he yelled into his interphone. ''Get me some muscle down here. I've captured the Blaine bitch.''

''You better make some of it female,'' I suggested. ''Getting me stripped by guys might turn out to be a bad idea. From several points of view.''

He glared but added in a louder yell in case the whole division had already mobilized, ''And make some of that female.''

Then he reached into his belt holster for a blaster as big as the Transalpine Tunnel and aimed it at the middle of my head. I'd have been happier if his hand hadn't been so obviously shaking.

''Drop that bag on the floor, slow and easy,'' he sandpapered, the way they're taught in the Academy. I always think it must do their throats a lot of no good. ''And then put your hands on your head.''

''Okay,'' I said, conciliatory. ''There's nothing in it but my laundry anyhow.''

I laid the bag down, folded my hands over Meister Damien's masterpiece of punk croppery and waited for the muscle.

The rest of the squad arrived in a stampede, four hefty guys and a bim who maybe qualified as female though I've

seen more appealing figures on heavyweight catch stars, and
proceeded to surround me. You could tell I was one
dangerous guy. If I hadn't been feeling depressed I'd have
been flattered. They shoved me in several different directions, felt me up once each in case the guy before had
missed something—Miss Heavyweight Ashton Central took
so long about it I began to think she had exotic sexual
orientations—and upended my bag on the floor.

Naturally there was nothing in it but laundry. You could
tell they were disappointed. They turned it inside out in case
there was a howitzer hidden in the lining and ripped the
inside about a bit. When they still didn't uncover any
artillery Miss Heavyweight led the competition in sneering
at my underwear. I was glad Sword wasn't there. If he'd
heard their opinions of his tastes in female clothes none of
them would have made lunch.

Booking me took time. We started with a difference of
opinion on what I'd said I was accused of. I stuck to name,
rank and serial number. They claimed I'd confessed to
everything up to and including the assassination of the
President of the Council. I said I'd said the first thing came
into my head to wake the desk-man up because he was
asleep and I wasn't confessing to anything in front of
witnesses. They said I was a female dog, a lady of easy
virtue and my mother wasn't married. My mother would
have been upset about that though she would likely have
agreed with the rest, because you can't get more respectable
than her without being certified.

This went on for a while until they got tired and slung me
in a cell until I'd remembered my manners. That was going
to take some time. Razor taught me not to pay attention to
cells and my mother said I hadn't any manners to remember.

It was getting lateish and I hadn't had anything to eat. I'd
catfooted out of the apartment without breakfast so's not to
make a noise for Mokey. Anyway then I wasn't hungry.

Four or five hours of assorted cops yelling at me in relays reminded my belly it had an interest in the world. Not a big one, but enough. They were going to be pleased about that so I didn't tell them.

I sat on the floor in a cotton sack tied at the back that didn't stretch to covering my behind and followed Razor's instructions on resisting interrogation. They run, basically, there's no way of resisting interrogation so you better relax and forgive yourself before you betray your twelve best friends.

After a while I recollected I didn't have twelve best friends. I then considered this line of thought was contrary to Razor's philosophy, and finally concluded none of it was going to make any difference. Then I remembered my stomach and how it had to be pretty late in the day and they hadn't got around to serving the bread and water yet. This is against the law. But our local cops make theirs up as they go along.

You lose your sense of time in Ashton Central's strip cells, with their permanent artificial lighting and total soundproofing. My personal clock said it was halfway to tomorrow and Mokey had to be losing his mind, and I was sorry. If he did as I'd told him, went to Hallway and took his advice about getting out of the country, he'd be better off in the end. If I knew Moke he wasn't going to think so.

I hadn't considered my personal future at all. There didn't seem any point. I was interested in the date of feeding time. And less forcibly in whether Miss Heavyweight was going to get to indulge her bestial instincts again next time they questioned me or whether they'd send a human being in her place.

So when the lock rattled I looked at it with the expression of one of Pavlov's dogs. Ready to salivate if they rang a bell or bite the keeper if they began sawing my skull open.

The cop was male, stone faced—it was a pity, because he wouldn't have been bad-looking if he'd been a person—and didn't have a gun in his hand. He did have my clean clothes, my boots and what was left of my bag. He handed rather than threw them, which is civil for a cop, and said briefly, "Dress." Then he disappeared.

I took advantage of the offer and climbed out of Nameless Prisoner Number Whatever back into the clothes and life of Cassandra Blaine, who was still waiting to see where she was going. It was painful. I'd got tired of Cassandra recently. I'd no reason to suppose she was going anywhere interesting either. But it was a change.

The stony cop came back after a while, checked to see I was decent and nodded at the door. We walked several miles along puke-green corridors. Finally we climbed about a thousand steps and got to basement level.

In these lofty parts there were steel doors with little metal plates in the middle with people's names on them in white plastic. They obviously needed a good interior decorator. I was beginning to feel sorry for cops. Burglars' working conditions are more stimulating.

My cop knocked on a puke slab, interpreted a vibration and opened it.

"Cassandra Blaine, sir," he said stonily and stood back for me to go in. He got no answer but they let him close the door without being told to.

The desk was steel—green—and had two guys grouped felicitously, one sitting and one bending over his shoulder. They both had patches and glittery bits all over their chests and shoulders which would probably have impressed the hell out of me if I'd known what they stood for. They both also had the kind of gray paternal hair that goes with office. Which made them generals, academicians or torturers, pick one.

I looked at them and they looked back.

"Miss Blaine," the sitting one said finally, in the sort of rich sympathetic voice that goes with the hair and the glitter.

I wasn't sure if he was asking or telling but I admitted it anyway. It cuts things shorter. He nodded as if he was pleased with himself, or maybe me, for being right, and waved his hand at the other. I suppose for admiration. At any rate they did some admiring together.

Then the one who could stand showed me a lot of expensive dental regrowth and said, "If you would come this way, please?"

I felt it was time to stand up for my rights, mouse or not.

"Only if it leads to the cafeteria."

They both looked the ways guys look who don't get spoken to that way.

"I beg your pardon?" said Number One. His voice was less rich but I thought honestly puzzled.

"You got the time?" I asked.

He consulted a flat gold chronometer of the sort people wear when they're so rich they find light-displays vulgar and said, "Nearly eight-thirty. Is it of significance?"

"If that's P.M.," I told him. "Seeing the last thing I ate was a biscuit with an anchovy around eleven last night with half a flute of champagne. Get me a ham sandwich and a mug of coffee and if you blow in my ear I'll follow you anywhere. Don't and I'm going to pass out on the floor, starting now."

I thought they reddened, though it may have been the light.

"My dear Miss Blaine!" said Number One.

"I'll see to it," said Number Two. He waved me towards the door. "Do you prefer ham and coffee or anchovies and champagne?"

"I've vulgar tastes. If you haven't any ham I'll take cheese."

"This way," he repeated.

What the hell. Either there was food at the end or there wasn't. If he was kidding I could pass out on the floor anytime.

On the building was a roof, and on the roof was a pad, and on the pad was a copt. Logical. What wasn't was it wasn't a police copt. It was the wrong color and too flossy. The pilot looked like a version of Henry with black overalls piped with silver and a visored cap. Not police at all. That was worrying. Razor told me worrying wastes energy. It never stopped him. I was ushered up a step and shown a leather seat that smelled real and the guy with the glitter sat across the aisle.

He showed me his costly dentistry some more. I considered morosely that he'd fooled me, but if we were going any distance I could eat the seat. At which point a smart bim in a silk dress leaned out of the back with a little silver tray. It had a pile of sandwiches wrapped in a napkin and a flask with the kind of lid you can drink out of.

"We're extremely sorry," she said with a sweet clean smile. "We'd no idea the police had been crass enough to starve you." The guy with patches definitely went redder. "I hope this will keep you going."

I tried both ends of the tray and found ham, cheese and salad sandwiches and hot strong coffee with a lot of sugar. I thanked her nicely to show I had manners when treated right and spent the rest of the trip working on it.

Consequently I didn't see exactly where we went. We landed on a wide roof in the middle of a lot of very fancy buildings, and when the three of us got down—Henry II stayed with the copt—the roof-door led into the kind of decor I'd left behind in the morning. Carpets where they occasionally have to send out Saint Bernards to recover the guests and planters everywhere you can put a planter, full of the kind of plants oughtn't to be in planters.

They had so much interior decoration they could usefully have done an exchange with the Police Department and ended with somewhere fit to live in. We took a medium-length safari to the other side of the hall and ended up at a pair of black glass doors with silver hand-plates.

The bim in the dress went first and used her hand to open the doors. Which made her someone very important or personal assistant to. Since very important someones rarely hand out sandwiches I guessed the latter.

I was right. On the other side of the door was an office half the size of the Sahara and equally decorated with palm trees in planters. In the distance at the far end, in front of a set of wraparound windows tall and wide enough for a cathedral, was a floating slab of marble with interesting pink patterns in the stone, interesting bronze ornaments around the edges and a man in the same metal reclining in a free-form chair behind.

Before we'd covered the first five miles I'd recognized him. It was the guy Nimbus had been having the unsatisfactory conversation with at Countess Cara's party just before she'd got around to seducing me. Or at least the Honorable Jocelyn.

"Miss Blaine," he boomed. His voice was big, bronze and gongy too. His teeth were pure Oriental pearls. His suit had cost several Rajahs their ransoms and if he'd been wearing their ears on a string around his neck I wouldn't have been surprised. I think the word for him was feral. Something powerful, dangerous, mostly gone back to the wild and sitting here purring because for the moment he chose to. "What a pleasure to meet you. Do sit down."

That gave me the run of a tan suede chair with squashy cushions that were probably newly replaced every morning whether anyone sat on them or not, another in raspberry silk that looked like you ought to wear it rather than spoil its lines with your hind end, and a tobacco-colored couch a hundred yards long in quilted velvet. There were other possibilities among the oases but those were the three you could use without a loud-hailer.

I chose the couch as offering the best chance of ever being able to get back out and put myself a little off-center to the left. Razor detests exact symmetry. He says it draws the eye by looking unnatural.

"A drink?" the bronze man proposed. He deigned to very slightly notice the guy with the patches who was standing a long way down-stage right looking uncomfortable. A curt gesture sent him towards a chair in one of the oases. It wasn't the oasis I'd have chosen personally because it looked to me like the spidery green thing that overhung it probably ate people. "Commissioner?"

"I believe Miss Blaine likes champagne," the silk-dressed bim said warmly, as if she was getting around to pronouncing us man and wife.

"Splendid!" the bronze man enthused.

The patched specimen muttered in an embarrassed tone he'd care for a whisky. I don't know if he got it but it's possible he did because after I'd had my steamed-up flute I did hear a faint tinkle of ice-cubes a long way in the distance.

The bronze man concentrated his warm beaming attention on me. If I hadn't seen him freezing Nimbus's ass off only last night I might have thought he had a future as a furnace.

"Now," he said, as I took a cautious sip. I didn't think it was likely to be concentrated vitriol but you never know. "I hardly suppose you know me. Jason Cordovan."

He waited for applause. Since I'd never heard of him I looked neutral and waited.

He was a quick study. He gave me five seconds to prove I knew him after all and proceeded to enlightenment.

"Head of Coelacanth Studios. Your employer in the past and, I very much hope, the future."

That did catch me with my breath down. I had a job not to choke on my champagne.

"Yark?" I said.

He smiled a warm pearl smile. I wondered if he shot bullets with it when he wasn't using it and wished I had a Kevlar overtunic. "But you mustn't be surprised. That was an astonishing performance. Truly astonishing."

"It was?" I was looking out of my eye corners to see if his keepers were around. Dammit, I'd just finished ruining him.

"Oh, but yes! Our audiences have been stunned by you. You're what we've been looking for. The inevitable successor to Nimbus." His bronze mouth made a faint disgusted pout. "Poor Nimbus. An ignominious end to a fairly distinguished career. But she was getting on. Beginning to be rather coarse and obvious. It was her perfect exit. I couldn't have planned it better myself." He beamed at me as if I was his favorite daughter. Or dessert. Or something.

"Miss Blaine, you're so fresh and genuinely young. You have a wonderful, a truly wonderful career in front of you. Your talents—exactly fitted to the brand of action adventure our audiences find appealing. I'm willing to offer you the most generous contract. You can very nearly pick your own terms. I'm willing to go to the utmost lengths to give you whatever you would like to have."

There was a little pause while he waited for me to fall on his neck.

"Let me get this straight," I said. "Am I under arrest?"

He looked pained. "Of course not. A regrettable experience. But no doubt we can work it into your next film. All experience is useful to the young star. The Commissioner has brought you here himself as proof that you're as free as the air." He gestured expansively. "What would the police want to hold you for?"

"Knocking out two of their officers and stealing their copt."

His scornful hand waved it aside. "A fascinating sequence of our film. We have excellent relationships with the police. The local forces have always been most co-operative."

"Stealing the cash to pay for our private film-show out of your bank account?"

I thought that would get him. It didn't. Another airy wave. "A nothing, my dear Miss Blaine. A mere nothing. I admire your friend's genius in doing so much on so little. I'd have paid willingly myself and it would have cost me twice as much. My dear child, you've saved me money. Do drink your champagne."

I'd lost my taste for it. I put it down on a little doggy table that had edged up out of the foliage and settled down to a major statement of accounts.

"It doesn't worry you I caused the death of your star?"

"Not in the least. Nimbus was aging. Already career-dead, you might say." Open boyish smile like an Eagle Scout in cast bell-metal. "Frankly, she's been past it for a film or two now, but we've never found anyone to replace her successfully. Your taking over as heroine gave this film the new life it needed. Our sample audience has seen the rushes and the response is very positive. The final scene when you revenged yourself received one of the warmest audience reactions we've had in recent years. There's not the smallest doubt the film will be a hit. Even with Nimbus's emotionals as villainess. That works occasionally. Someone so detestable everyone loves to see her over-thrown. But when you yourself are giving the responses— My dear! So much truly splendid ferocity, such unbridled feeling! You'll be the rave of the season. I promise."

"And my lover's death?" I asked coldly.

He made another of those slight scornful pouts.

"But your lover is the man you choose to save. That's obvious. Young Doshchenko was never in love with you, it was clear. We thought at the beginning he had promise but it became plain he was merely the hero's friend, the sympathetic young man who provokes the climax. Didn't you feel so yourself? Young Mr. Faber is a very attractive hero. It's a pity he cares more for sculpture than for drama or we could have used him. An interesting face, and he would have made a charming partner for a follow-up. I don't suppose we can persuade him? No? A pity. Artists are always difficult to work with."

He looked sympathetic and understanding. "Shall we go over the contract now? Or would you prefer to have an agent or lawyer to represent your interests? I assure you, we have no intention of cheating."

I stood up. "Suppose I don't want to sign a contract?"

That really raised his bronze bows. For a moment they looked almost as if they belonged to a man.

"No? But, my dear Miss Blaine, my only intention's to make your fortune. Over and over. I'm offering you fame, wealth, social position, everything you've ever dreamed of . . ."

"What I've ever dreamed of is going home and finding Mokey still alive and neither of us being chased by anyone." My voice sounded thin and far-off even to me, a mosquito zinging in another room. "Can you give us that?"

His brows were still raised. "Of course. It's the least I can give you. I've every reason to believe Mr. Faber's safe and well. There are no charges against you or any of your friends. You're free. And of course you have salary to come."

His smile was pained. "But you aren't trying to tell me you don't want this opportunity? My dear child, consider.

Half the young women of the world would give all they have to stand in your shoes. Don't throw such a chance away.''

I was feeling too ill to be able to answer as I thought he deserved.

"If any of the young women of the world was in my shoes right now, she'd wish she was somewhere else. Thank you for the kind thought. I'm sure your wishes are sincere in their way. Do you think someone could show me the way out? I think I'm going to be sick."

The silk bim flew forward to take my arm. I guess I had them worried for the carpet. The Commissioner followed me looking as embarrassed as if he'd affronted the great man himself.

They helped me to the copt, put me in and gave the pilot instructions about taking me home.

He was nicer than Henry. He asked me twice if I was all right and finally gave me a slug from a hip-flask that shook me to my toenails but did stop my back from coming unhinged in the middle.

He dropped me on the roof of the apartment block just as the sun was setting and saw me to the door. I stood and waved forlornly as he took off and walked into the lobby.

Behind me the blazing sky threw my shadow over the carpet, a stretched-out black silhouette in a wash of blood-colored light.

I looked exactly like Swordfish.

Mokey flung the door open before I got to the end of the hall and jerked me violently inside. He was so pale you could almost see through him. It took me a minute to see it was rage.

"Don't you ever do that again," he said, in a voice I didn't know he had. "Don't you know I've been going insane? Hallway and I've investigated every cop-house in town looking for you. Sword's had the gang on standby, he was ready to start a war. Then we heard you'd gone. What the hell were you doing?"

"Put me down, Moke, please."

I flopped on the couch and folded my hands on my knees. "Mokey, we didn't know these guys. Do you know they don't care who they kill? Their own stars don't count. Just so long as they make a film. I've been turning down a starring role. As Nimbus. Don't you think that's funny?"

"No," he snapped. "Sword says you got to have a period, he says you been like this since you were fourteen. You got what you need?"

"Men." Suddenly I was doing what I'd been wanting to do all day, laughing and crying at the same time into my cupped hands. "Period! They got simple answers for everything."

"Hey, Cass." He dropped beside me, alarmed. "Sword

263

says his sister's the same. Gets black now and then. You all right?''

I shook my head, hiccupping. "He never had a sister. He's putting you on. Sword crawled out of the earth full-grown. Guys don't get black, huh?"

"Yeah, sure." His voice hardened again. "You any idea how black I been all day?"

"I was paying back, Mokey. Trying to. Nobody wanted my money. They tried to pay me. They're going to. 'Scuse me, I got to go to the bathroom."

I guess it was a waste of good sandwiches. Maybe I ate too quick. When I got through throwing up and Mokey got through looking anguished we started again.

"I hoped you'd have some sense and go."

"And I hoped you'd have some sense and stay. Can't I make you believe it's not your fault?"

"No. Because it is. But it's okay, I stopped trying to put it right. It's too late. Everything's too late, Moke. How the hell did you get into Sword? I thought you two guys didn't speak."

"There's one subject we speak about. Don't ask which. You look like hell. You want some milk or something?"

"I hate milk. And now I've got a fucking period. And if you tell me about Sword's imaginary sister I'll kill you."

He looked suddenly happier, as if I'd relieved his mind. There's nothing guys like better than being right.

"It wasn't you, Cass. If it was anyone it was me. You didn't want to get into this goddamned film. I encouraged Dosh." He switched down about a thousand watts. "Poor Dosh. He wanted so badly to be a hero. Well, he got that, I guess."

"No, Moke. Not even that. I bitched the whole thing. You were the hero in the end. You know what the guy said to me? You had to be because it was your life I wanted to save and Dosh didn't count. He never loved me. He thought he was being kind."

"Poor Cassie." He breathed down my neck.

"Poor Moke. Now that's all three of us."

"I don't think we've been through the gamut yet," he said bitterly. "But poor Moke it ain't. Anything but. You don't know all the reasons I been losing my mind."

I tried to grin. "You mean it wasn't all me? Well, that's something. I was feeling bad about you back there. Who else been giving you a hard time?"

"Cass, if you'd got yourself locked up for life today I swear I'd have fucking shot myself. I can only stand so much irony before I curse God and die. You think if you took a pill or something you could consider having something to eat? 'Cause I'm not taking you out until you have. And I want badly to take you out."

"Gimme a pill. And then yes, let's have some food. I just threw up the film company sandwiches, I think I feel better. And I forgot to tell you. We get to go out, they've dropped the charges."

He looked surprised. "I know. That's one of the reasons we quit looking for you. If they hadn't there'd be fighting in the streets."

"You saying you got the charges dropped for me?"

"You saying you got the charges dropped for us?"

We looked at each other.

"Yes."

"Yes."

"Let's eat," he said finally. "Then let's go out. It's going to be worth it. I hate to tell you you're wrong again, Cass, since you got this obsession that shouldn't be encouraged, only you are. Everything isn't wrong and some things ain't too late. Let's eat and go."

We went up to the roof where Moke the confident—I'd never seen him play guy in charge this way—beamed a traxie and handed me into it like Cinderella. I felt a bit like

Cinderella. To the ball gown. He'd insisted on my scarlet catsuit with silver bits, and earrings. I've never known him to care. I mean he likes cute clothes but I could walk down the street in the altogether and he wouldn't lift an eyebrow. It wouldn't have surprised me this time if he'd sent for six white mice and a pumpkin.

He was looking artistic-distinguished himself in clean jeans, a white sweater and God help us, a velvet jacket. Sort of tobacco-colored. Romantic. He even had shoes on. Expensive hand-made loafers that looked like they might dance him to death if he didn't watch it. His hair was washed and combed. He was so nearly pink around the cheekbones I scarcely recognized him. Moke's been off-gray all my life.

Whatever the deal was, it was big.

The traxie, fueled by a gold credit card with a prominent Moke name on it, took us across town and dropped us at the Museum of Modern Art not two blocks from the Central Square Precinct. I thought of mentioning it to Mokey and decided not. He was looking so nearly happy.

"Okay," he said in the new all-male Moke-voice. "Now we go around the front and I show you why we're not on charges."

I trotted behind him thinking maybe I'd got the story wrong and it was really a sex-change version of Mary and her little lamb, and came out in the checkerboard garden with fountains that fronts the Exhibition Gallery. The first thing I saw was a holo, rather larger than life, of one of Moke's more striking pieces of metalware. Right in the middle.

He gave me a tight exultant grin. "Keep going."

I walked cautiously forward waiting for it to bite. The bastard did. The big sap-green letters came whistling out at me on a blast of warm air scented with pines and something that smelled like an intoxicating blast of jet-fuel.

opening today

EXHIBITION
all this month
THE SKY AND THE CITY
sculptures by
MARTIN FABER

entrance C5.00
unemployed C1.00
children under 14 free

The soundtrack had a metallic voice, tubular bells and a lot of virtuoso keyboard with organ riffs built around overtones of Bach. It was all-hell impressive. Classical. I never saw Moke as classic.

He walked confidently up to the big holo while I stood with my mouth open looking like a goldfish in a magnifying-glass, and slapped it the way only the maker gets to do. The damned thing was real. It bonged melodiously under his hand. Not larger than life, just the first time I'd seen it outside the lower deck of a warehouse. It was magnificent.

"But Moke, it died," I said. Squeakily. I'd been getting real moused today one way and another. It was more than time Cassandra got back to form before the cat ate her. I could see it coming.

He turned me a smile of pure simple happiness.

"It's alive," he said. "All of it. The rest's inside. You want to see? I got a pass."

He held it up. It was an Art's professional guild-card. Made out to Martin Faber, with a gray but intelligent holo of holder. He even looked like a guy who was a genius.

"Sure," I said. "In three minutes. I'm just going behind those bushes to have a private attack of vapors. I get this way when I hallucinate."

• • •

''We were wrong,'' Moke said as we walked around the gallery, stopping every few yards to circulate another of his structures and see how good it looked with space around it. ''Eklund wasn't film, he was real.''

''He really wanted your stuff? For this?''

''Not just this. It's the start of an international tour. It goes to Titan next, then Virginity and Argos. They're all places he has galleries. He's buying this one himself.''

That was the big triangular arrangement of girders Moke had most recently got around to spraying in primary colors. It had a card on it saying it belonged to the private collection of H-B Eklund, on display by permission.

''But Mokey, they burned.''

He shook his head. ''Eklund's not the Angel Gabriel. He's an Ari and they all know each other. But I think he's decent. He knows Cordovan, the Coelacanth producer. They belong to the same golf club or something. Cordovan told him he was making this film and there was stuff might interest him in our basement so they sneaked out some shots and he liked what he saw. Then he met me and wanted it. So Cordovan shifted it before they sent the building up. And now it's here.''

''They weren't so delicate with the sculptor,'' I said sourly. ''He didn't mind if you roasted.''

Moke made a face. ''Cordovan's even lower down the list of the heavenly host. He didn't bother to tell Eklund he meant to cook us and as it happened we got out. Eklund was pissed off when he heard but by the time he got around to worrying Cordovan told him it was okay, we were safe. So he was satisfied. He wasn't in on the film. Not his bag. He doesn't watch them.''

''I don't say I like him, but I'd consider doing business.''

''I already have. He called this morning to offer me the show. He had it all fixed. He knew I wouldn't say no. That's when I found you were gone, after I'd got woken by the phone and been handed this and our freedom on a plate. I thought you had to be in the bathroom or something. Then I found your note." The bleakness came back.

"You could remember your friends, Cass. Did you think they'd take that lying down? Hallway scoped every precinct in town before he located you thirteen floors down at Central and the only thing prevented a civil war was, it took time to get reserves of combat gas and by the time it was in place Hall told us you'd left in a private copt. Wings traced it to Coelacanth and we sat down to wait. Sword had sonic canon on hold. Anyone tell you he was a serious guy?"

"He's a serious guy. I guess he and Hall are upset."

"No worse than yesterday." He pulled my arm under his and leaned on it. "Forget it. Hallway sent me home to wait and I waited. And you came. That's all I care about."

We'd got to the end of the gallery where a mound of plaster in the shape of something like a rock, and something like a cave, and something like a guy with a pain in his belly was on a pedestal under a plexiglass dome. The ticket said, "HE LONGS TO BE FILLED. Maquette for work in stone, commissioned by the Royal Opera Ballet of Hampton-in-Argos. Work in progress."

"Yeah," I admitted, reading it. "I guess I see that. But I was right about the heart."

He turned me a serious face. "But I been feeling bad myself. If we'd taken Eklund seriously in the first place instead of looking for scorpions in the lettuce leaves, we needn't have done this motherloving movie at all. We could have told Cordovan where to put it and left."

I turned and spoiled his velvet jacket by grabbing a couple of handfuls in my nasty damp palms. "Drop it, Mokey. I've done my crisis of conscience. Don't make it worse by doing yours. I don't know who's right and who's wrong any more. Maybe all of us. Maybe none of us. What

I do know is you were right to begin with. We can't make any of it unhappen. All I want, and I want it badly, is to leave. There're people on this planet I don't want to share the same air with. And don't tell me they're everywhere, I guess they are, only someplace else maybe I won't have to know them. I'll stay as long as I have to for you, but please don't make it too long. I'm suffocating.''

He took a deep breath. ''So'm I. Eklund's offered me a place to work on Never. He's got space and he fancies being a patron of the arts. Anyhow I think he maybe gets lonely with nobody but Henry and Henry for company. So I said yes for both of us, back before I found out I was by myself. You're my business manager.''

''You got to be kidding. I never managed a business in my life.''

''It's just a matter of planning. Not much different from burglary. I need you, Cassie.''

I took his velvet arm, trying to smooth the crushed bits. The damned stuff was high-class goods, it smoothed. ''Okay, boss. So where are we going to get drunk?''

''Cassandra, it's two o'clock in the morning.''

''What's that got to do with it?''

So we went back to the Gilded Dog, naturally. After all, we owed Eustace money. And we both got very drunk indeed.

We made a call before we left. Hallway'd suggested it and Moke meant to see it out. They were both right.

It was a private clinic out near the eastern dome-edge with private rooms, cedars in the garden and a view of the sunrise. Moke said Hall was paying but I doubted that. I thought if Coelacanth took a good look at their accounts they'd find they were. Hallway's not noticeably rich considering he has the knowhow to rob half the world blind, but he has a strong sense of justice.

A starchy nurse with a stern expression took us through a mile or two of corridor that smelled of disinfectant and regeneration fluid and brought us out on the fortieth floor. She looked us over like we had bombs in our pockets and ordered us not to stay long, the patient was still weak. We tried to look like the shiny boxes held candy and she condescended to leave us alone for half an hour.

We went through a room with vids, tapes and flowers and got to a pale fortyish guy in a chaise-longue on the terrace. He was being languid and trying to fade his regen scars under a sunlamp. For someone twice dead he could have looked a lot worse.

"Hi, Yell," Moke said, sitting on the edge. "Hallway told us they'd got you out of it."

"Sorry we haven't been before," I added, putting the fruit and the geraniums near his left elbow. We hadn't brought liquor because word was they'd just replaced his liver and temptations would be unappreciated, read get you thrown downstairs. "We been busy. We thought about you, honest."

He gave us a wan grin. He wasn't bad-looking with two eyes, and twenty years younger than I'd imagined.

"I heard. You kids been having a shitty time."

"You better believe it."

"Listen, Yell," Mokey said. "We been wondering what you're going to do when they let you go. Hallway said the end of the week. You got anything in mind?"

"Sure." He made a face. "Turn Gooder and start paying my debts, I guess. Can't go back to my old hole under your steps, Hall told me it got burned down. Anyways, they done something desperate to my insides and I can't drink any more. Even the thought makes me queasy. Things've changed, huh?"

"You better believe that, too."

"Yeah, well—" Moke said. He's awkward about being

nice in public. "Cass and me are moving pretty soon. To a real healthy asteroid, good air, sunlight. You might like it. I got a workshop to set up and I could do with help. If you want the job."

"Guy means to be a millionaire," I told him. "He's figuring to employ us all. Don't know I shouldn't've agreed to be a film-star. Then I could have been independent. Criminal but independent. Ain't used to relying on men."

"That's only because you never looked at the people you knew," said my new tough Mokey. "I don't know what's to stop you being independent. I don't want you to be my manager, I want my manager to be you. If you get bored you can burgle Eklund."

"I can imagine it. I burgle him every night and you pay him back every morning." I grinned at Yeller. "You might as well say yes. You've no idea how hard it's getting to say no to him since he got a sniff of fame."

"I always knew he'd make it," Yeller said. He grinned back with a full set of new white teeth, not quite grown. "Count me in. Helping Moke I can do. If you ask me I'll even fly your copts and stuff. I used to be a spacer."

"Thought that was a rumor."

"It was a true rumor. The only bit they left out was I was too drunk to know what I was doing. Guess I got re-formed."

"We all did," I said sadly.

At which point the nurse came and chased us out. But Yell was looking healthier. When we left he was quarreling with her about drinking his vitamins.

So we ended by getting it together.

We went to see The Sky and the City again in the daytime to make sure it existed, and it did. Some of the city fathers were puffing around it looking self-important and we entertained ourselves by watching them sneer at us as the kind of people obviously too low-down to appreciate sculpture. A lot of other guys were there too. Some of them ate their sandwiches under the central construction outside and Mokey liked that.

We got our money from the film company and sent Dosh's share to his father even though he and Dosh never got on, because we didn't like to keep it. It smelled of blood. We sent it anonymously so he couldn't come after us and call us murderers, because he probably would have and it might have been true.

We bought some new clothes and I was right about Moke, he'd started looking distinguished. Just as long as you could keep him away from metal or plaster. I started out to recyc the things Sword had bought me and then couldn't. It seemed like another kind of murder. But I couldn't wear them either so I packed them in my baggage and took them around with me everywhere, which was kind of dumb.

I sent Hallway a lot of colored holocards of Moke's exhibition to say I was sorry, and when he got voted his first award I sent him a colored holocard of that too.

At the end of the week Yeller came out of the hospital kind of tannish and shaky but with all his teeth and we took him to dinner. He drank soda water. So did we to be polite.

Eklund came to see us and he took us to dinner and we all drank a lot of wine, also to be polite, and giggled some. I was beginning to feel like giggling occasionally again when sometimes I forgot who I was.

Then he fixed for us to borrow his yacht to take ourselves to Never so we could settle into our house before the exhibition went on to Titan, where Mokey had to meet the Minister for the Arts. He took Yell with him right away because he figured the Ashton atmosphere didn't agree with him. I think Yell was pleased at the idea of seeing space again, even if it was only from an asteroid.

About three weeks later we finally packed our own gear and set about moving out of the apartment.

Moke had been received by the Mayor and interviewed by a famous vid-show hostess who was old enough to be the Witch of Endor. She spent half an hour batting huge baby-blue eyes at him until he said he began to get vertigo and not know what he was saying, though he sounded all right to me. The neighbors who'd been looking at us like we'd made the smell in the drains started calling him Mr. Faber in the elevator.

Then the fucking damned film came out and was as successful as horrible Cordovan had said it would be, and we refused to look at it. The neighbors started calling me Ms. Blaine in the lobby.

Suffocation was moving in on both of us. We figured if we disappeared they might forget who we were in a day or two and with any luck the apartment could get sold back to the kind of people were meant to live in it. Rich people.

Only it seemed we were rich people. We hoped not to get too used to it and turn nasty.

We sent most of our baggage ahead with Henry, who'd started almost recognizing us now we were Arts and therefore almost human. But we decided to walk at least some of the way and have a last look at Ashton before we lit out for good. We weren't exactly nostalgic but we had guys to wave goodbye to. Like Eustace and Adelaide, and the good-looking kid from the goldfish bowl, who'd moved out of the Dog and was flashing his stuff in an uptown cabaret and growing snobbish. Dosh hadn't been snobbish.

Personally I was feeling a little tearful. It had to be old age. I was never tearful before I got to be twenty-one.

We walked down the main drag of the Strip looking at the neons and the holo-ads and the flashy window displays that all look like stage costumes in daylight, thinner and tackier than you'd imagined they were and in nastier material. We thought about walking down it at night which is the only time it's real and wondered if we'd miss it. And I remembered the places I'd gone with Dosh and the apache games we used to play, and it seemed a long time ago when I was much younger and knew nicer people. Though when I tried to think what was wrong with the guys I knew now, I couldn't.

Moke took hold of my elbow, which was a thing he'd been doing a lot lately, every time I started to get morbid. I think he thought maybe I'd go and try to give myself up to somebody again, though I'd sworn I was through for this incarnation.

"Hey, look at this," he said.

It was a sign I was turning leaky. I took a big sniff and looked. It was a bag shop. I've never got out of the habit of carrying enormous bags even though I'm never tooled these days, and they had splendid ones big enough to carry a cannon. A couple were in silver and gold and one was bronze leather with silver cut-outs and a stylized peacock with a spray of tail in real feathers. It was class gear. I got an immediate attack of healthy lust which shows Moke knows where the switches are.

I was leaning in to look at it when I saw something glitter and it wasn't in the window. It was a reflection on the other side of the road.

And I remembered suddenly there was a laser-artist on my tail who'd taken so damned long to catch up I'd forgotten about him, what with being called Ms. Blaine and all by everybody as if the world had forgiven me. And I turned around and reached at my hip for a darter that wasn't there. And I saw I was dead. All before the muzzle of his gun had stopped glittering in that single second he turned it towards me.

And in the same instant I saw the guy and his grin and his

lifted laser, he and they disappeared in a plasm of shimmering light only comes from a major disruptor charge. The guy flung up his arms and the gun melted and the charge went up with a swoosh like flash-powder, and everything in the street stood still in time and space like the universe had frozen and was hanging on the point of spooling backwards.

Swordfish couldn't have been more than ten paces behind him. I saw him for a moment backlit by that worldfreezing flash, a slender black outline as the circuits of his coolsuit temporarily gave up trying, tall as a wind-devil and graceful as a dancer, and then my eyes were full of red and green after-images. All in the shape of Swordfish. But his suit had cut back in and he'd gone.

I looked and looked among the crowds that came running at the commotion, trying to make out the little blurred ripple of reality would say he was moving right there, and saw nothing. Nothing but strangers, guys with shocked white faces and yodeling voices, milling about as if it was going to make the slightest difference to anything. But I didn't see Sword at all. He'd vanished back into the scenery as if he'd never existed.

Mokey pulled me away in the end and we cleared out before the cops came around asking questions. The guy hadn't hit me, so nobody but us knew he'd meant to, so nobody was looking. We dodged down a couple of side streets, got off the Strip and called the nearest traxie.

Half an hour after that we were sitting in the cushioned seats of Eklund's yacht drinking Eklund's champagne and watching the spiral patterns of our world disappearing beneath us. We were holding each other's hands, not exactly as lovers do but because we were both still cold and shaking.

"It's going to be great," Moke said at last. He didn't sound especially convinced.

"Yeah," I agreed. "It's going to be great. It really is."

And we cuddled each other. Sure, it was going to be great. It's just sometimes, when you really look at it, you wonder what great means and how you'd know it if you saw it.

I'm Cassandra and I foretell the future. I think I'm going to live a long time and do a lot of things and have a great life. I foretell the future and nobody believes me. Sometimes I don't even believe myself.

I'm Cassandra, and I'm signing off.